GAYLORD M

Revenge of the Wrought-Iron Flamingos

This Large Print Book carries the
Seal of Approval of N.A.V.H.

Revenge of the Wrought-Iron Flamingos

Donna Andrews

Thorndike Press • Waterville, Maine

Published in 2002 by arrangement with
St. Martin's Press, LLC.

Thorndike Press Large Print Mystery Series.

The tree indicium is a trademark of Thorndike Press.

The text of this Large Print edition is unabridged.
Other aspects of the book may vary from the original edition.

Set in 16 pt. Plantin by Al Chase.

Printed in the United States on permanent paper.

ISBN 0-7862-3925-5

To all the dedicated reenactors and crafts-people who contributed to my research. Thanks for preventing so many embarrassing mistakes and anachronisms — I hope you can forgive and laugh at the equally embarrassing ones I've made instead.

To the friends who listened oh so patiently to everything I learned about muskets, cannons, eighteenth-century costume, Colonial-era medicine, and countless other subjects that went into the writing of this book, I can only promise that at least I'll have a new and different set of obsessions next time.

And especially to Tracey and Bill, for continuing to let me borrow Spike; Elizabeth, for always pushing me to be a little better (not to mention the usual ending magic); Lauren, Mary, and Sheryle, for sharing words, wisdom, and pizza; Suzanne, possibly the world's best long-distance coach and cheerleader; Dave, who unmasked Cousin Horace, despite the assumed name; and all my on-line friends who were there when I needed them and understood when I wasn't there because I had to write.

To Ruth Cavin, Julie Sullivan, and the crew at St. Martin's, and to Ellen Geiger and Anna Abreu at Curtis Brown, for taking such good care of all the practical publishing stuff so I could concentrate on the fun part.

And to Mom and Dad, for choosing to live in the middle of the Yorktown Battlefields. It's all your fault, you know, and I can't thank you enough.

1

"I'm going to kill Michael's mother," I announced. "Quickly, discreetly, and with a minimum of pain and suffering. Out of consideration for Michael. But I am going to kill her."

"What was that?" Eileen said, looking up and blinking at me.

I glanced over at my best friend and fellow craftswoman. She had already unpacked about an acre of blue-and-white porcelain and arranged it on her side of our booth. I still had several tons of wrought iron to wrestle into place.

I scratched two or three places where my authentic colonial-style linsey-woolsey dress was giving me contact dermatitis. I rolled my ruffled sleeves higher up on my arms, even though I knew they'd flop down again in two minutes; then I hiked my skirts up a foot or so, hoping a stray breeze would cool off my legs.

"I said I'm going to kill Michael's mother for making us do this craft fair in eighteenth-century costume," I said. "It's absolutely crazy in ninety-degree weather."

"Well, it's not entirely Mrs. Waterston's fault," Eileen said. "Who knew we'd be having weather like this in October?"

I couldn't think of a reasonable answer, so I turned back to the case I was unpacking and lifted out a pair of wrought-iron candlesticks. Eileen, like me, was flushed from the heat and exertion, not to mention frizzy from the humidity. But with her blond hair and fair skin, it gave the effect of glowing health. I felt like a disheveled mess.

"This would be so much easier in jeans," I grumbled, tripping over the hem of my skirt as I walked over to the table to set the candlesticks down.

"People are already showing up," Eileen said, with a shrug. "You know what a stickler Mrs. Waterston is for authenticity."

Yes, everyone in Yorktown had long ago figured that out. And Martha Stewart had nothing on Mrs. Waterston for attention to detail. If she'd had her way, we'd have made every single stitch we wore by hand, by candlelight. She'd probably have tried to make us spin the thread and weave the fabric ourselves, not to mention raising and shearing the sheep. And when she finally pushed enough of us over the edge, we'd have to make sure our lynch mob used an authentic colonial-style hemp rope instead of an anachronistic nylon one.

Of course, my fellow craftspeople would probably lynch me, too, while they were at it, since I was her deputy in charge of organizing the craft fair. And in Mrs. Waterston's eyes, keeping all the participants anachronism-free was my responsibility. When I'd volunteered for the job, I'd thought it a wonderful way to make a good impression on the hypercritical mother of the man I loved. I'd spent the past six months trying not to make Michael an orphan. Speaking of Michael . . .

"Where's Michael, anyway?" Eileen asked, echoing my thoughts. "I thought he was going to help you with that."

"He will when he gets here," I said. "He's still getting into costume."

"He's going to look so wonderful in colonial dress," Eileen said.

"Yes," I said. "Lucky we don't have a full-length mirror in the tent, or we wouldn't see him for hours."

"You know you don't mean that," Eileen said, with a frown. "You're crazy about Michael."

I let that pass. Yes, I was crazy about Michael, but I was a grown woman in my thirties, not a starry-eyed teenager in the throes of her first crush. And Michael and I had been together a little over a year. Long enough for me to fully appreciate his many good points, but also long enough to notice a few shortcomings. The thing about costumes and mirrors, for example. And the fact that getting dressed to go anywhere took him two or three times as long as it took me.

Not that I complained, usually; the results were always spectacular. But at the moment, I'd have traded spectacular for available to help. I wrestled an eight-foot trellis into position and sat back, panting.

"Maybe I will wait until he gets here to finish this," I said.

"But Mrs. Waterston wants us all set up by ten!" Eileen said. She rummaged in the wicker basket she was using instead of a purse, then shot a guilty glance back at me before pulling out her wristwatch.

"It's 9:30 already," she said, thrusting the watch back out of sight beneath the red- and white-checked fabric lining the basket. Familiar gestures already: the furtive glance to see if anyone who cared — like me, theoretically — was looking before someone pulled out a necessary but forbidden modern object. And then the hasty concealment.

Eileen should have figured out by now that as long as nobody else spotted her, I didn't give a damn.

Then again, we'd found out this morning that Mrs. Waterston had enlisted a dozen assistants, whom she'd dubbed "the Town Watch." In theory, the watchmen were under my orders, available to help with crowd control and prevent shoplifting. In practice, they were the reason I was running late. I'd spent all morning trying to stop them from harassing various frantic craftspeople about using modern tools to set up, and keeping them from confiscating various items they'd decided were "not in period." The crafters had started calling them "the Anachronism Police."

"I'm nearly finished with my side," Eileen said. "If you like, I could —"

A loud boom interrupted her, seeming to shake the very ground. Both of us jumped; Eileen shrieked; and her pottery rattled alarmingly. We could hear more shrieks and oaths from nearby booths.

"What on Earth!" Eileen exclaimed, racing over to her table to make sure none of her ethereally delicate cups and vases had broken.

"Oh, Lord," I muttered. "I thought she was kidding."

"Kidding about what?" Eileen asked.

"What the hell was that, a sonic boom?" shouted Amanda, the African American weaver in the booth across the aisle.

"The artillery," I shouted back.

"Artillery?" Eileen echoed.

"The what?" Amanda asked, dropping a braided rug and trotting over to our booth.

"Artillery," I repeated. "For the Siege of Yorktown. That's what this whole thing is celebrating, you know —"

"Yeah, I know," Amanda said. "October 19, 1781. The British finally throw in the towel and surrender to George Washington and the Revolutionary War is over. Whoopty-do. Let freedom ring, except for my people, who had to wait another eighty years. So what's with the sound effects?"

"Another of Mrs. Waterston's brainstorms," I said. "She hired a bunch of guys to fire a replica cannon to add to the authenticity of the event."

"You mean, like a starter's gun to open the fair?" Amanda asked.

"Demonstrations for the tourists, maybe," Eileen suggested.

"Actually . . ." I said.

Another thunderous boom shook the encampment. This time we heard fewer shrieks and more angry yells.

12

"Actually," I began again, "she's going to have them firing continuously, to simulate the siege. Washington's troops shelled the British nonstop for a couple of weeks before attacking their entrenchments."

"She's going to have them doing that all day?" Eileen asked.

"Probably all night, too, unless someone can find an obscure county ordinance to stop it." Someone like me, probably. I'd already promised half a dozen townspeople who'd seen the artillery setting up that I'd find a way to silence the cannons at bedtime. Now that the shelling had actually begun, I'd be swamped with complainers any second — and no matter how irate they were, none of them wanted to tackle Mrs. Waterston directly.

"Bunch of loonies," Amanda muttered.

No argument from me.

"Bad enough I have to dress up like Aunt Jemima," she said, as she returned to her own booth. "And now this."

"Oh, but you look . . . wonderful," Eileen called. "So authentic!"

Amanda looked down at her homespun dress and snorted. She was right, unfortunately. I'd always envied Amanda's stylish urban wardrobe, with its vivid colors and offbeat but sophisticated cuts. I'd never before realized how well her chic outfits camouflaged a slightly plump figure. And when you threw in the cultural associations an African American woman raised in Richmond, Virginia, was bound to have with colonial-era clothing . . .

"Oh, dear," Eileen murmured. From the sudden crease in her normally smooth forehead, I could tell that the last point had just dawned on her. "This must be awful for poor Amanda! Do you think we should —"

"Look sharp!" hissed a voice nearby. "Here she comes! Put away your anachronisms!"

2

"Oh, dear, Mrs. Waterston will be furious that you're still unpacking!" Eileen exclaimed.

"I still have fifteen minutes," I said, turning to see who'd given the warning. Just outside our booth I saw a man, a little shorter than my five-feet ten inches and slightly pudgy, with a receding chin. I had the feeling I'd recognize him if he were in, say, blue jeans instead of a blue colonial-style coat, a white powdered wig, and a black felt hat with the brim turned up in thirds to make it into a triangle — the famed colonial tricorn hat.

"Oh, you look very nice, Horace," Eileen said.

Horace? I started, and peered more closely.

"Cousin Horace," I said. "She's right. You look great in costume. I almost didn't recognize you."

Cousin Horace looked down at his coat and sighed. Normally he loved costume par-

15

ties — in fact, he assumed (or pretended) that every party he attended was a costume party, and would invariably turn up in his beloved gorilla suit. Usually even Mother had a hard time convincing him to take the ape head off for group photos at family weddings. I wondered how Mrs. Waterston had managed to browbeat him into putting on the colonial gear.

"It's just one of the standard rental costumes from Be-Stitched," he said, referring to Mrs. Waterston's dressmaking shop. "You'll see dozens just like it before the day is out."

"Well, it looks very nice on you," Eileen said.

"Meg, you have to talk to Mrs. Waterston," he said. "She listens to you."

News to me; I hadn't noticed that Mrs. Waterston listened to anyone — except, possibly, Michael. What Horace really meant was that no one but me had enough nerve to tackle Mrs. Waterston.

"Talk to her about what?" I said, feeling suddenly tired. Cannons? Anachronisms? Or had some new problem arisen?

"Now she's going on about talking authentically," he added. "Avoiding modern slang. Adopting a colonial accent."

"Oh, Lord," exclaimed Amanda from

16

across the aisle. "Who the hell does that witch think she is, anyway?"

Horace glanced at me and skittered off. Eileen looked pained.

"Who died and made her queen?" Amanda continued.

"Great-aunt Agatha," I said. "Who didn't actually die; she just decided that at ninety-three, she didn't have quite enough energy to continue chairing the committee that organizes the annual Yorktown Day celebration. Mrs. Waterston volunteered to take her place."

"Yeah, she's got enough energy," Amanda said. "It's the common sense she's lacking."

"We'll probably be seeing a lot of Mrs. Waterston," Eileen said. "She's Meg's boyfriend's mother."

"Oh," Amanda said. "Sorry."

"Don't apologize on my account," I said. "You can't possibly say anything about her that I haven't said over the past year. Though not necessarily aloud," I added, half to myself.

"Take my advice, honey," Amanda said. "Dump him now. Can you imagine what she'd be like as a mother-in-law?"

Unfortunately, I could. I'd spent a lot of time brooding over that very prospect. But for now, I deliberately pushed the thought away, into the back of my mind, along with all the other things I didn't have time to worry about until after the fair.

"Oh, but you haven't met Michael!" Eileen gushed. "Here, look!"

She walked across the aisle to Amanda's booth, digging into her wicker basket as she went, then pulling out a bulging wallet. She flipped through the wad of plastic photo sleeves and held up one of the photos. Amanda peered at it, her face about three inches from the wallet.

"Not bad," she said.

"He's a drama professor at Caerphilly College," Eileen said. "And a wonderful actor, and we all think he's just perfect for Meg."

"If you could lose the mother," Amanda said. "Is he going to be around today?"

"Of course," Eileen said. "He and Meg are inseparable!"

Well, as inseparable as a couple can be, living in different towns several hours' drive apart and trying to juggle two demanding careers that didn't exactly permit regular nine-to-five hours. Another reminder of problems I was trying to put on hold until the damned craft fair was over and done with.

"Okay, I'll try not to say anything too nasty when 'Blue Eyes' is around," Amanda said. "If I recognize him. My glasses are banned," she said, with a disapproving glance at me. "Not in period. Only wire rims allowed."

"Sorry," I said; shrugging. "Anyway, Michael's pretty hard to miss."

"Everyone's a blur from two feet away," Amanda grumbled.

"He'll be the six-foot-four blur in the white French uniform with violet cuffs and gold lace trim," I said.

"You're right," she said, with a chuckle. "I think I'll probably manage to pick him out of the crowd."

"That's my son Samuel he's holding," Eileen said. "It was taken at the christening. Here's another one we took at the reception afterward."

"Very nice," Amanda said. She glanced nervously at Eileen's wallet, beginning to suspect how much of its bulk came from baby pictures.

"And here's one of Samuel with his daddy," Eileen continued, flipping onward. I could see a trapped look cross Amanda's face.

"Not in period," I sang, clapping my hands for attention as our first-grade teacher used to do. And when Eileen turned with a hurt look, I added, "Come on. Help me out. We're supposed to be setting a good example for the others."

Eileen sighed, stowed her anachronisms, and returned to our booth. I don't know why I bothered. She'd pull the photos out the minute my back was turned. Amanda would have to fend for herself if she wanted to dodge Eileen's hour-by-hour photographic chronicle of the first two months of young Samuel's life.

Don't get me wrong; I've got nothing against kids. I love my sister Pam's brood, all six of them — although I prefer them one at a time. As young Samuel's godmother, I was perfectly willing to agree with his parents' most extravagant boasts about his winsome charm and preternatural intelligence. I could even see that producing an offspring or two might be something I'd be interested in doing eventually, under the right circumstances and with the right collaborator.

But, I'd already seen Eileen's pictures several dozen times. At least she'd left the infant prodigy himself home with a sitter. I was getting very, very tired of having people dump babies into my arms and warble to the immediate world what a natural mother I was. Especially when they did it in front of

Michael. Or his mother.

Speaking of Mrs. Waterston, if Horace was right, I probably would need to straighten her out about the accent problem, before she browbeat all the crafters into mute terror. But at least I could postpone the ordeal until she dropped by my booth. I peered outside to see how close she was, and breathed a sigh of relief. She was still a good way off, standing in front of her tent, in the middle of our temporary, fictional town square.

We'd set up all the tents and booths of the fair like the streets of a small town, its aisles marked with little street signs painted in tasteful, conservative, Williamsburg colors, with names taken from Yorktown and Virginia history, like "Jefferson Lane" and "Rue de Rochambeau." Thirty-four street signs, to be precise — I knew, because I'd had to think up all the names, arrange for Eileen's cabinetmaker husband to make the signboards, and then forge the wrought-iron posts and brackets myself.

In the center we had what Mrs. Waterston called "the town square," complete with a fake well and a working set of stocks that I was afraid she had every intention of using on minor malefactors. Not to mention her headquarters tent, which she'd decorated to match some museum's rather ornate recreation of how General Washington's tent would have looked.

Mrs. Waterston turned to look our way, and I winced. She wasn't dressed, like the rest of us, in workday gowns of wool, cotton, or linsey-woolsey. She wore a colonial ball gown. The white powdered wig added at least a foot to her height.

"What the hell is she wearing on her hips?" Amanda said from her vantage point across the aisle.

"Panniers," I said, referring to the semicircular hoops that held out Mrs. Waterston's dress for at least a foot on either side of her body. "Don't the historical-society folks ever wear panniers up in Richmond?"

"Not anyplace I've ever seen," she answered. "Remember, Richmond didn't do too much worth bragging about in the Revolution. They're all running around in hoop skirts, fixated on the 1860s and St. Robert E. Lee. And I thought Scarlet O'Hara looked foolish," she added, shaking her head. "She must be three feet wide, and no more than a foot deep."

"That was the style back then," I said. "Like Marie Antoinette."

"Looks like a paper doll," Amanda said.

"How's she going to get up if she ever falls down?"

"You could trip her and we could find out," I suggested.

"Don't tempt me," Amanda said, with a chuckle.

Mrs. Waterston still stood in the town square, turning slowly, surveying her domain. A frown creased her forehead.

"Oh, Lord," I muttered. "Now what?"

"What's wrong?" Eileen asked.

"Mrs. Waterston's upset about something."

"Mrs. Waterston's always upset about something," Eileen said. "Don't worry. I'm sure it's not your problem."

Probably not, but that wouldn't stop Mrs. Waterston from making it my problem. I'd worked like a dog to make the craft fair successful. I'd twisted crafters' arms to participate. Begged, browbeaten, or blackmailed friends and relatives to show up and shop. Harassed the local papers for publicity.

And it worked. We'd gotten a solid number of artists, and their quality was far better than we had any right to expect for a fair with no track record, especially considering the requirement for colonial costume. Most of the best crafters were old friends, some of whom had passed up prestigious, juried shows to help out. I hoped Mrs. Waterston understood the craft scene well enough to appreciate that without my efforts, she'd have nothing but amateurs selling dried flower arrangements and crocheted toilet paper covers.

And wonder of wonders, with a little last-minute help from Be-Stitched, they were all wearing some semblance of authentic colonial costume. And by the time the barriers opened and the crowd already milling around outside began pouring in, I'd have all the anachronisms put away, if I had to do it myself.

So why was Mrs. Waterston frowning?

"Miss me?" came a familiar voice in my ear, accompanied by a pair of arms slipping around my waist.

"Always," I said, turning around to greet Michael more properly. I ignored Eileen, who had developed a maddening habit of sighing and murmuring "Aren't they sweet?" whenever she saw us together.

"So, shall I set the rest of this stuff up?" Michael asked, eventually.

"Please," I said, and stood back to give him room. Maybe I'd be set up on time after all, and could take a last run around the grounds to make sure everything was ship-shape.

I caught Amanda sneaking a pair of glasses out from under her apron and shook my finger at her, in imitation of Mrs. Waterston. She stuck out her tongue at me, put the glasses on, and watched with interest while Michael shed his ornate, gold-trimmed coat, rolled up the flowing sleeves of his linen shirt, and began hauling iron. Then she looked over at me and gave me a thumbs-up.

"What on Earth is that!"

Mrs. Waterston's voice. And much closer than I expected. Though not, thank goodness, quite in our booth. Not yet, anyway. Still, I started; Amanda ripped her glasses off so fast that she dropped them; and Eileen began nervously picking at her dress and hair.

Michael alone seemed unaffected. I wondered, not for the first time, if he was really as oblivious to his mother's tirades as he seemed. Maybe it was just good acting. Or should I have his hearing tested?

"Put that thing away immediately!"

Eileen and Amanda both looked around, startled, to see what they should put away. Michael continued calmly trying to match up half a dozen pairs of andirons on the ground at the front of the booth. I peered around the corner to see who or what had incurred Mrs. Waterston's displeasure.

"Oh, no," I groaned.

"What's wrong?" Michael said, putting down an andiron to hurry to my side.

"Wesley Hatcher, that's what," I said.

"Who's that?" he asked.

"The world's sneakiest reporter," I said, "And living proof that neither a brain nor a backbone are prerequisites for a career as a muckraking journalist. Wesley," I called out, as a jeans-clad figure retreated into our booth, hastily stuffing a small tape recorder into his pocket. "If you're trying to hide, find someplace else."

Wesley turned around, wearing what I'm sure he meant as an ingratiating smile.

"Oh, hi, Meg!" he said. "Long time no see."

Actually, he'd seen me less than two hours previously, when he'd tried to get me to say something misquotable for a snide story on how craftspeople overcharged and exploited their customers. With any other reporter, I'd have seized the opportunity to give him the real scoop on the insecure and underpaid lives so many craftspeople led. But I knew better than to talk to Wesley. I'd made the mistake of talking off the record to him years ago, when he was earning his journalistic reputation as the *York Town*

Crier's most incompetent cub reporter in three centuries. Like the rest of the county, I'd been puzzled but relieved when he'd abandoned our small weekly paper, first for a staff job with the *Virginia Commercial Intelligence*, a reputable state-business journal, and then, returning to character, for the sleazy but no doubt highly paid world of the *Super Snooper*, a third-rate tabloid. Why couldn't he have waited until Thanksgiving to come home and visit his parents?

"So, got any juicy stories for me?" Wesley asked.

"Get lost, Wesley," I said.

"Aw, come on," he whined. "Is that any way treat your own cousin?"

"He's your cousin?" Michael asked.

"No," I said.

"Yes," Wesley said, at the same time.

"Only a distant cousin, and about to become a little more distant — right, Wesley?" I said, picking up a set of andirons as I spoke. It wasn't meant to be a physical threat, but if Wesley chose to misinterpret it as one. . . .

"I'll stay out of your way; just ignore me," Wesley said, sidling a little farther off.

Which meant, no doubt, that Wesley thought he could pick up some dirt hanging around my booth. Or possibly that he knew about the orders my mother had given me to "find poor Wesley a nice story that will keep his editor happy." Wesley was a big boy; why was helping him keep his job suddenly my responsibility? I'd taken him on a VIP tour of the festival last night, hoping he'd find something harmless to write about. I'd even shown him the stocks and let him take some pictures of me in them, pictures I knew he'd find a way to misuse sooner or later. What more was I supposed to do? And what had he done to upset Mrs. Waterston?

I peered out again. To my relief, Mrs. Waterston had returned to the town square. Her head was moving slowly, as if she were scanning the lane of booths leading up to ours. And she was frowning. Maybe she saw something unsatisfactory about our entire row of booths — but no, that was unlikely. This row and the adjoining one were the showplaces, closest to the entrance, where I'd put the best craftspeople with the most authentic colonial costumes and merchandise. I'd kept the weirder stuff toward the back of the fair. More likely she was watching someone walking down the row. Someone who was about to pass my booth, or maybe even enter it. . . .

"Hi, Meg! Has anyone asked for me?"

My brother, Rob.

"No, not yet," I said, eyeing him. I couldn't see anything wrong. His blue jacket, waistcoat, and knee breeches fit nicely; his ruffled shirt and long stockings were gleaming white; both his shoes and the buckles on them were freshly polished; his hair was neatly tied back with a black velvet ribbon, and a tricorn hat perched atop his head at a jaunty but far from rakish angle. Not for the first time, I envied the fact that he'd inherited our mother's aristocratic blond beauty.

"Meg?" he asked. "Is there something wrong? Don't I look okay?"

"You look fine," I said. "Help Michael with some of my ironwork."

"I'm supposed to be meeting someone on business, you know," he announced, for about the twentieth time today. "I don't want to get all sweaty."

"Well, work slowly if you like, but try to look busy."

"Why?" he asked, shoving his hands in his pockets.

"Because Mrs. Waterston is coming this way," I said, glancing over my shoulder. "Would you rather help me out or do whatever chore she has in mind for you?"

"Where do you want these?" Rob asked,

snatching up a pair of candlesticks.

"I've got nearly everything out of the crates and boxes," Michael said. "I should probably go check on the rest of my regiment."

"Fine," I said. "Rob can help me finish."

"I'll bring back some lunch," he said, leaning down to kiss me. "You'll be here, right?"

"Actually, I'll probably be running up and down all day, keeping the crafters and 'the Anachronism Police' from killing each other," I said. "And if things get slow, I need to go down to Faulk's booth for a while."

"Can't Faulk mind his own booth?" Michael said, frowning.

"I'm sure he can," I said. "But he's supposed to inspect my dagger."

"Oh, have you finished the dagger?" Eileen exclaimed. "The one with the falcon handle? Let me see it!"

3

So, now, of course, I had to show Eileen the dagger. Not that she had to twist my arm too hard — I admit, I was proud of the dagger. Eight months ago, Faulk, the friend who'd introduced me to ironworking when we were in college together, had come back to Virginia after working for the last several years with a world-renowned swordsmith in California. He'd been burning to share what he'd learned about making weapons, and, I confess, I'd caught the bug.

The last couple of months, I'd been working on a dagger, with an intricate ornamental handle and a highly functional steel blade. I'd finished it — at least I hoped it was ready for prime time. But Faulk was the expert. I'd been looking forward for weeks to showing him the dagger.

Eileen oohed and aahed over the dagger so loudly that Amanda came over to see what was going on. Michael, I noticed, was standing aloof, still frowning. I realized, suddenly, that this wasn't the first time over

31

the last few months that he'd shown a certain coolness, even irritation, whenever I'd mentioned my dagger. What was the matter with him, anyway? He didn't seem to feel threatened by my blacksmithing; what was so different about making swords?

I turned my attention back to the dagger in time to grab Amanda's hand before she touched the blade.

"Careful!" I said. "It's razor sharp; you could slice your finger off."

"You get much call for working daggers?" Amanda asked.

"There's a growing market for period weapons," I said. "Renaissance fairs, Society for Creative Anachronism folks — you'd be surprised."

"They let people run around at Renaissance fairs with sharpened swords?"

"No, but this is a test piece," I said. "Proof that I've learned the first stages of what Faulk's been teaching me about the swordsmithing craft. I had to handforge the steel for the blade, just the way they would have in the 1300s, and sharpen it to perfection."

"Can't you just buy the blades somewhere these days?" Rob asked. "From Japan or something? That'd be a lot easier."

"Yes, and you can get them pretty reasonably from India and Japan, and most people couldn't afford a handforged steel blade. But even if you're usually going to buy your blades and just make the handles, Faulk says it's important to learn how they're made the traditional way, so you really understand the steel. You're much better able to choose a good blade if you know how they're made."

Michael frowned again when I mentioned Faulk's name. Aha! Maybe it wasn't swords that bothered him — maybe it was Faulk. As I realized that, he smiled — was it a genuine smile, or was he just making an effort? — and disappeared into the crowd with a slight wave.

"Mr. Right not keen on the sword-smithing project?" Amanda asked.

I shrugged. Damn, she had sharp eyes. I'd only just picked up on it myself.

"Well, you seem to be in good shape," boomed a voice from outside the booth.

Mrs. Waterston. We all whirled, and Rob, who had been testing the blade of my dagger, yelped as he cut himself slightly.

"I told you to be careful," I said, taking the dagger back as Rob sucked his finger with a martyred air.

Mrs. Waterston fixed her gaze on Rob. And frowned.

"Haven't you got anything useful to do?" she asked. She was, I noticed, speaking with an accent that might be mistaken for British, but only by someone who'd never heard the real thing.

Rob looked uncomfortable, and tugged at the ruffled neck of his shirt.

I found myself resenting Mrs. Waterston's immediate assumption that Rob was loitering about with nothing to do. Irrational, since that's just what he would have been doing if I hadn't scared him into action. But then, he was my brother. I might disapprove of his character in private, but I wasn't about to give Mrs. Waterston the privilege.

"He's been helping me unpack," I said. "Put the stand for the dagger right in the middle of the table, Rob."

"Besides, I'm meeting someone here," Rob said. "A business meeting."

"A representative of one of the software companies that's interested in buying Lawyers from Hell," I added. "You know, the computerized version of the role-playing game he invented."

"Oh. I see," Mrs. Waterston said. "By the way, I've been meaning to speak to you about people's accents."

"Don't worry; I've already given orders

about that," I improvised. "Since the fair's located behind American lines, we're going to represent colonial crafters, not British ones. The Town Watch has orders to arrest anyone speaking in a British accent and put them in the stocks, as suspected Tories."

"I see," Mrs. Waterston said, blinking. "Well, then, carry on," she added, in something closer to her normal accent.

She scrutinized Rob once more, as if she still hadn't quite gotten used to the notion of him as capable of inventing something for which grown-ups would pay good money. Then she turned and sailed off, though not without difficulty. The lane had grown more crowded, and she had to turn sideways every few feet to squeeze her panniers through the crowd. Instead of a galleon in full sail, she looked like a barge being towed through a crowded harbor.

"Wow," Cousin Horace said, peering around the edge of the booth. "That was great."

"So go tell the Town Watch about arresting Tories," I said. Horace disappeared.

"Thanks," Rob murmured, his eyes still on Mrs. Waterston's retreating form.

"No problem," I said. "I thought the guy wasn't supposed to come till noon, though."

"I didn't want to miss him if he came early," Rob said.

Two hours early? Well, it was important to Rob.

"You're welcome to stay as long as you keep out of the customers' way. Or, better yet, make yourself useful. Bring some more stuff out from the back."

"Of course," Rob said, nodding vigorously, and disappeared behind the curtain concealing the storage area in the back of our booth.

"Are you really meeting the software-company guy here?" Eileen asked.

"Yes," Rob said, dragging out one of my metal storage boxes. "It solves the problem of what to wear."

Eileen looked puzzled.

"The first time Rob met with a software company, he got all dressed up in a three-piece suit," I elaborated. "They all showed up in jeans and T-shirts."

"And sandals," Rob said. "I felt like an idiot. So the next time, I showed up in jeans and a T-shirt."

"And I bet they were in three-piece suits," Eileen said.

"Bingo," I said. "So when we heard the latest guy was coming today, while the fair was on, I told Rob to meet him at my booth.

He can scope out what the guy's wearing, suggest that they meet at someplace less crowded in half an hour, and change into the uniform of the day, whatever that turns out to be."

"What if he shows up in costume, too?" Rob asked.

"Then drive him up to Colonial Williamsburg and eat at one of the taverns," I said.

"That might work," Rob said. "Thanks. Where should I put these?"

I turned to see him holding up a pink wrought-iron flamingo.

"Back in the box, quick," I said.

"Why?" he said. He was holding the flamingo out at arms length, inspecting it.

"Put it away, now," I said, dropping a set of fireplace tongs to race over to the box. "Mrs. Waterston will explode if she sees it."

"I don't see why," he said, as I snatched the flamingo from his hands. "It's kind of cool in a weird way. I like it."

"You would," I said, opening the case to shove the flamingo inside. "It's a complete anachronism and —"

"And you've got a lot of them," Rob said, peering into the case. "Any chance you'd give me —"

"Meg!"

Mrs. Waterston was back. I slammed the lid of the case closed and sat on it, hard, for good measure, ignoring the yelp of pain from Rob, who didn't quite move his hand fast enough to avoid getting nipped by the closing lid. And the small crash to my left, where a customer had dropped one of Eileen's vases and was now cowering against the curtain at the back of our booth.

"Yes?" I said, ignoring Rob, who was grimacing and shaking his injured hand. "What's wrong, Mrs. Waterston?" I couldn't quite manage a smile, but I think I achieved a polite, interested expression.

"These people you brought are impossible!" she exclaimed.

"Which one in particular?" I asked. Eileen had gone to the customer's side and was making reassuring noises, I noted. I stood up from the chest, warning Rob, with a glance, not to open it again.

"That female glassblower," she said. "She's wearing men's clothes."

"Merry's giving glassblowing demonstrations at noon, two, and four," I said. "She can't wear skirts for that."

"Why on Earth not?"

"Because it would be a serious fire hazard," I said. "Burning was one of the leading causes of death for women in the colonial or any other historical era when cooking and heating methods involved open flames. One good spark and these skirts could go up like so much kindling," I said, shaking my own skirts with resentment. "So, unless you really like the possibility of Merry reenacting the death of Joan of Arc in front of all the tourists, I suggest you overlook her gender for the time being."

"She could at least wear proper clothes when she's not demonstrating."

"I'll see if that's possible," I said.

"Why wouldn't it be possible?"

"She may not have brought another costume, and it might be hard for her to make any sales at all if she's spending all her time either demonstrating or changing in and out of costume."

"That's no excuse," Mrs. Waterston fumed. "Don't these people realize we're trying for authenticity here? Don't they understand —"

Doesn't she realize that these people are trying to make a living, I thought; and I was opening my mouth to say so, and no doubt precipitate the argument I'd been avoiding for so long, when I realized that Mrs. Waterston was staring, openmouthed, at something behind my back.

What now, I wondered.

4

I turned to see what had stopped Mrs. Waterston in midtirade: a slender, twenty-something black man, wearing a turquoise velvet coat, a peach brocade waistcoat, tight black-velvet pants, and enough lace cascading at the throat and sleeves to decorate a bridal gown. From the ornate silver buckles on his shoes to the powdered wig on his head, he was a walking fashion plate from the late eighteenth century. He leaned with one hand on an elegant silver-trimmed black cane, inspecting a pair of my candlesticks through a quizzing glass, with a supercilious look on his face.

"Oh my," Mrs. Waterston murmured.

"Tad!" I shouted, and rushed over to hug the new arrival.

"Meg, dear," Tad said, with more than the usual hint of a British accent. "You look divine!"

"You don't have to sound so surprised," I said. "I do clean up well when I try. You're looking rather presentable yourself."

Tad replied with a graceful bow, and twirled so I could see his outfit from all sides.

"That color's great on you," I said. "And the wig's such a good touch."

A rather necessary touch. Mrs. Waterston would never approve of the dreadlocks hidden underneath.

"Mrs. Waterston," I said, turning to her. "May I present my friend Thaddeus Jackson?"

"How do you do," Tad said, with another bow.

"What a lovely costume," Mrs. Waterston said. "But are you sure it's quite . . . authentic?"

"Oh, completely," Tad said, and began pointing out some of the finer details of his clothes, while I struggled to keep a straight face. I didn't think Mrs. Waterston would dare come right out and say what she really meant — that however accurate Tad's outfit was for the period, you'd have a hard time finding many African American men in colonial times wearing that much silk, velvet, and lace.

I caught Tad's eye, pointed to Mrs. Waterston, and made a little shooing gesture. Without missing a beat, he offered her his arm and, still talking, gently eased her out of my booth and sent her on her way with another sweeping bow.

"I should have worn the other costume," he said, reentering the booth.

"Other costume?" Eileen asked.

"Tad was originally going to come as a runaway slave, in homespun rags and leg irons," I said. "I talked him out of it."

"Oh, you should have done it, Tad," Eileen said. "It would have done so much to raise people's consciousness about the oppression and injustice of the times."

"Don't start that again," I said. I had noticed that Tad wasn't his usual buoyant self. Was the subject upsetting him, or was it something else? "Tad, what's wrong?"

He shrugged.

"I brought you something," he said.

He glanced around, then reached inside his coat and took a small, square, paper envelope from an inside pocket. A CD, I realized; I could see the luminous silver disk through the round cellophane window in the front of the envelope.

"Better put this away before the Anachronism Police see it," he said.

"Right," I said. I stuck the CD in my purse — not my modern purse, of course, which I'd hidden behind the curtain at the back of the booth, with all the other anachronisms, but the white linen haversack slung over my shoulder. "What is it, anyway?"

"A patch for CraftWorks," Tad said. "Nothing major. Don't try to install it during the fair. Wait till you get home. It should work fine, but you want to do a full backup first. It's all in the read-me file."

"What's CraftWorks?" Rob asked.

"The program I use to run my business, remember?" I said.

"Run your business?" Rob said. "I thought the whole point was that you made everything the old-fashioned way, with hammers and stuff."

"Not the ironworking, all the financial and organizing stuff," I said. "Keeping my books, ordering supplies, managing inventory, tracking stuff that's in shops on consignment, paying bills, sending bills, applying to shows, and keeping my schedule — everything."

Normally Tad would have beamed to hear me give what amounted to a glowing testimonial for CraftWorks. Today he didn't even smile.

"Tad, that reminds me — I had this idea for something to expand CraftWorks," I said. "Maybe you could put up a Web page where people could go to download updates and check out show schedules and — Tad? Earth to Tad?"

"Sorry, I was zoning out," he said, with a forced smile. "Look, maybe I should level with you about something."

"Okay," I said. But before he could continue, Michael showed up, along with three other pseudo-French soldiers from his unit.

"Ma chérie!" Michael exclaimed, and proceeded to introduce me to his comrades in a mixture of French and French-accented English.

Michael's fellow officers all kissed my hand, and said polite things in French. At least I assumed they were polite things. I'd taken French in school but somehow it never quite took, and I was notorious for having spent two weeks in Paris without once eating anything that even faintly resembled what I thought I'd ordered.

Michael, on the other hand, spoke French fluently, with an accent so perfect it caused native speakers to swoon with national pride and ecstasy. That was supposedly the reason he'd joined a French regiment, although before he decided the French had cooler uniforms, he'd been well on his way to developing an intense sympathy for the losing British side.

At any rate, he didn't seem to object to

the polite Gallic nothings his friends were murmuring to my knuckles, so I assumed they weren't actually propositioning me. I replied *"enchanté"* or *"merci"* to whatever they said and smiled a lot. I wished Tad would rescue me, but he smiled, waved, and disappeared into the crowd.

Well, with any luck the French forces would drift off sooner or later. They were glancing at the portion of our booth they could see — Eileen's side, actually — with polite uninterest.

"Ah, they are yours, these potteries? *Très jolies,*" one said, in the offhand tone of someone who actually thought pottery was *très* boring but wanted to be polite to the *demoiselle* sharing a tent with his brother-in-arms.

"No, my friend Eileen does the potteries," I said. "I do the hardwares."

I stepped aside so the French could see my side of the booth.

"You're a blacksmith?" he exclaimed. His eyes widened, and he dropped both the blasé air and his French accent. "Cool! Can you mend things?"

"Metal things, yeah," I said. "Do it all the time."

"Like bayonets?"

"Sure," I said.

"You made this?" another of the soldiers asked, indicating my dagger.

"Yes," I said. "The blade, too; not just the hilt."

"Do you take commissions?"

And so, for the next half hour, the faux French soldiers milled about my booth, examining my ironwork — especially the dagger — and apparently finding it to their satisfaction, as they grew more and more enthusiastic about commissioning me to mend or make various bits of weaponry and equipment.

I confess, I was less than enthusiastic at first. Call me mercenary, and I won't argue with you; I work iron for a living, not a hobby. And while I wasn't exactly starving, I had long ago learned that I couldn't pay the rent if I gave attractive discounts to everyone who was related to me, lived in my neighborhood, had gone to kindergarten with me, or, in this case, happened to share a hobby with my boyfriend. So when they asked me what I'd charge to make things, I gave them accurate estimates, possibly a bit on the high side, since in some cases I'd have to do quite a bit of research on top of the actual blacksmithing.

I found myself warming to them when I realized they didn't even blink at the prices

I'd quoted. In fact, they all took my cards (including a stack to distribute to the rest of the regiment), kissed my hand several times each, clapped Michael on the back, and marched off in obvious high spirits, singing *"Au près de ma blonde."*

"You've made quite a hit with the guys," Michael said, beaming. "You'll have to come to all the events after this."

"Events after this?" Michael had only joined the group so he could participate in the reenactment of the Battle of Yorktown and help make his mother's event a success. Or so he'd said. Was he really planning to keep on doing reenactment stuff? Since when had he and the guys become such buddies? Perhaps this was only a temporary burst of enthusiasm, sparked by how much he enjoyed running around in his French uniform. Maybe he'd lose interest again when he remembered that the National Park Service wouldn't let reenactors pretend to be wounded or killed, even without the stage blood he'd offered to bring.

"I think there's a skirmish next month," Michael said, taking a piece of parchment-colored paper out of an inside pocket. "Yes. Around Thanksgiving."

"I think both our families are expecting us for Thanksgiving," I said.

47

"Great; that's perfect — I'm sure your dad would love to come, too. He's been having a great time; all the guys love his booth. I'll go ask him, shall I?"

He ran off, clutching his parchment, without waiting for an answer.

"Oh, Lord," I muttered.

5

"What's wrong, honey?" Amanda asked, dodging a stroller as she crossed the aisle to my booth. "You seem upset about something."

"Michael's having much too good a time doing this reenactment stuff," I said.

"Isn't it sweet?" Eileen said. "They never really grow up, do they?"

"No, they don't," Amanda grumbled.

"He's talking about keeping on with it after this weekend," I said.

"Well, that's nice," Eileen said. "It's something you can do together, isn't it?"

"It involves camping out in ruggedly authentic colonial conditions," I said. "I'm not very keen on camping out under any conditions."

"I'm a city girl; I know just how you feel," Amanda said, looking around as if the nearby trees scared her more than muggers. "And my idea of camping out is staying at a hotel without a four-star restaurant."

"You wouldn't like these outings," I said.

"The one I went to, they served salt beef and hardtack."

"Is that stuff even edible?" Amanda asked, wrinkling her nose.

"Theoretically, I suppose; although if you ask me, they almost make starving to death sound like a sensible lifestyle option," I said. "I couldn't wait to get to a McDonald's afterwards. For that matter, neither could Michael."

"Maybe he's not serious about keeping on with it, then," Amanda said.

"Sounded serious to me," I said. "He's gone off to Dad's booth to enlist him, too."

"I didn't know your dad had a booth," Eileen said. "What on Earth is he selling?"

"Band-Aids and cheap thrills," I said, rolling my eyes.

"What?" Amanda asked.

"He volunteered to organize the first-aid station," I explained. "Somehow he convinced Michael's mother that it would be a good idea to have it serve as an educational tool, too."

"What a wonderful idea," Eileen said.

"So he's done up a replica of what an army medical tent would look like in 1781, authentic down to the last gory detail."

"Oh, gross," Amanda said.

"Don't let Dad hear you say that," I said.

"It's one of his hobbies, collecting antique medical equipment. He's absolutely tickled at having a chance to show it all off. Although all of the surgical instruments are reproductions that he had me make. You don't find that many genuine eighteenth-century scalpels and surgical saws floating around, and if you do, you don't take them out in humidity like this."

"He's not actually getting any patients, is he?"

"He had a few people earlier who thought they had heat exhaustion, but the authentic colonial operating table seems to have marvelous healing powers. None of them felt the need to lie down on one of the camp beds after seeing that exhibit."

"Imagine that," Amanda said, chuckling. "Oops — got a customer back at the booth; catch you later."

Eileen and I had customers of our own, and for the next hour or so, my mood improved considerably as great numbers of sightseers and a smaller but satisfactory number of buyers wandered through the booth. The day stopped feeling like a ghastly mistake and more like a pretty normal first day at the craft fair.

Well, maybe not completely normal. In addition to a reasonable number of tourists and shoppers in modern dress, the aisles thronged with soldiers — redcoats sweating under bearskin hats; the occasional French soldier, scanning the ground for mud that might sully his spotless white uniform and hordes of blue-coated Continental soldiers, most with the red cuffs and lapels that indicated a Virginia regiment, but some with the white, buff, or pale blue trim representing other parts of the country. And occasionally unusual uniforms — a kilted Highlander; men in green whose waxed mustaches seemed to suggest Hessians; or a brace of frontiersmen, ambling along in buckskins with long rifles over their shoulders.

And women in long skirts, most wearing corsets. Although they corrected anyone who actually said "corset." The proper term was either "stays" or "jumps," and apparently there was a distinct difference between the two, though not one I could understand. They all looked the same to me, their upper bodies rising from their full skirts rather like ice cream cones and spilling out over the top to a greater or lesser extent, depending on personal preference or body type.

I assumed they'd look down their noses at my less-authentic natural figure, but apparently, running around uncorseted merely labeled me as "slatternly." They saved their most scornful glances for the women — usually very young — wearing neither sleeves nor caps.

"Hmph!" one exclaimed when a bare-armed teenager ran by, looking more like a character from a Pre-Raphaelite painting than a proper eighteenth-century lady. "Ought to run that strumpet out of camp!"

I deduced, from looking at the speaker's outfit, that a respectable colonial lady could display almost any amount of bosom as long as she kept her arms covered and wore a mob cap or a wide, flat straw hat to preserve her dignity.

At any rate, the colonial era was a great time to be a blacksmith. I'd brought a much larger than usual stock of small bits of hardware — hooks, tripods, trivets, and other old-fashioned oddments that people might find useful for cooking over an open fire, camping in an old-fashioned tent, and living generally under the eyes of the Authenticity Police. I was doing a decent business already, and I had a feeling things would improve after some of the shoppers went back to the colonial encampment and figured out what tools they'd forgotten to pack and how much more useful some of my hardware would be than whatever they had brought. Not to mention the large number of colonial dames and gentlemen I saw returning for a second or third time to study larger pieces with the sort of acquisitive look that crossed centuries. If even a tenth of them gave in to temptation before the end of the weekend . . .

Rob hung around underfoot, pretending to help out, while lying in wait for opportunities to pull out one of the flamingos and wave it around. I'd turn around to find a flamingo head peeking out through the opening in the back curtains or peering around the side of the booth. Once, when I left to run an errand, I came back to find Rob working on a ventriloquism routine, using the flamingo as the dummy.

"You need to switch roles," I snapped at him. "And you get to pay the fine if the Anachronism Police show up and catch you doing that."

And they did show up, with alarming frequency. The fair had only been open an hour or so, and I'd already had to settle a dozen arguments between the Town Watch and the crafters about so-called anachronisms. After I'd officially pronounced a host of items historically acceptable — including glass bottles, leather shoelaces, iron skillets, corkscrews, potpourri, and an antique-looking abacus — the Town Watch had grown considerably more tolerant. Or at least more wary of bothering me. Although I wished I could shake the suspicion that they were down at the history section of the local library, looking for grounds to overturn some of my rulings.

And sooner or later, I was going to have to tackle Mrs. Waterston on the subject of the fines the Town Watch levied on anyone caught with an anachronism that even I couldn't explain away. I'd managed a temporary truce by decreeing that no one had to pay any fines until the end of the fair, which gave me until 2:00 P.M. Sunday to talk Mrs. Waterston into rescinding the fines.

But I'd worry about that later. For now, it was a beautiful day. I actually stopped feeling self-conscious about saying "Good morrow, mistress." I no longer gaped when I saw whole families in period costume, down to the toddlers and infants. I rejoiced when someone pulled out a book, pointed to some bit of antique hardware, and asked, eagerly, if I could possibly make something like it.

I was writing up the details of one such commission when I felt someone hovering at my elbow.

"I'll be with you in a moment, sir," I said over my shoulder.

"Promises, promises," came Michael's

voice. "I was looking for Rob, actually."

"Rob?" I said, turning around. "I caught him trying to do a puppet show with a couple of my flamingos and chased him out to run errands."

"Flamingos?" Michael said, and his puzzled look reminded me that I'd so far avoided telling him about the ghastly birds. "What flamingos?"

"I'll fill you in later," I said, wincing. "What did you need Rob for, anyway?"

"This is Roger Benson," Michael said, introducing a middle-aged man, about my height, wearing modern clothes and a bemused look. "The software-company guy. He's been wandering around seeing the sights. I ran into him over in the encampment, asking directions to your booth."

"Quite a shindig you have here," Benson said, glancing around. "Very profitable, I suppose."

"Well, I hope the crafters are going to do well," I said. "I don't think the organizing committee is looking for a profit — they're not charging admission, of course, and any proceeds from the concessions are going to the local historical society."

"Still, it promotes tourism, doesn't it," he said. "Big industry around here."

Yes, it was, but he'd struck a sour note

somehow. Of course I was hoping to make a tidy profit for the weekend. But still, how could someone walk from an encampment straight out of a history book, and through the picturesque streets of the craft fair, passing so many incredibly believable costumed reenactors, and only think about how profitable it must be?

Cool it, I told myself, forcing a smile. You don't have to like him. If he buys Rob's game and makes it a hit, who cares how mercenary he is? In fact, maybe mercenary is a good thing under the circumstances.

Still, as I introduced him to Rob, who was just returning with two authentic pewter mugs — discreetly filled, thank goodness, with the dual anachronisms of ice and Diet Coke — I cast a glance over at Michael. A British grenadier and a buckskin-clad frontiersman were in the lane just outside, giving an impromptu lesson on the differences between a musket and a rifle to half a dozen boys. Michael was watching, too. Then he noticed a freckled little girl clinging to her mother's hand, but trailing behind, taking in the sights with wide eyes. He bowed deeply to her, the white ribbon cockade on his hat nearly touching the ground, and she broke into a wide smile. Then she and her mother disappeared into the crowd and Michael returned to watching the gunnery demonstration.

Okay, I thought, as I turned back to Rob and Roger Benson. If he likes all this, we'll go to more reenactments. It's not that bad.

"Quite an outfit," Benson was saying, looking at Rob's costume.

"Well, I wanted to fit in," Rob said, looking sheepish.

"Oh, I understand," Benson said. "When in Rome. Wish you'd warned me it was going to be like this; I could have gotten a costume myself."

"Oh, you can rent one, very inexpensively," Eileen put in. "Mrs. Waterston, the festival organizer, had her dress shop run up dozens, so people who get here and want to join in the fun can do just that."

"Really," Benson said. Why did I suspect he wasn't all that thrilled at the idea of renting a costume?

"Yes, what a good idea," I said. "Rob, why don't you take him along to the costume rental shop?"

"Uh . . . yes, thanks," Benson said, looking resigned. "I'll do that. Before we do, Rob, I just wanted to ask —"

"How is it going, anyway?" Michael said, drawing me aside.

"Not bad," I said. "Getting a lot of commissions, assuming they don't all fall through."

"I doubt that," he said. "My unit alone wants enough ironwork to keep you busy for a couple of months. Bayonets, swords, buckles, things I don't even know the names of."

"I could get to like your unit," I said. "If someone in it would learn to cook edible period food, I could love it."

"I had no idea you knew how to make all that reproduction hardware — I mean you do, don't you?"

"Most of it, yes; or I can figure it out," I said. "I've already done a lot of period medical instruments for dad, you know. And if I need help, I can always ask Faulk. If he doesn't know how, he'll know who does."

"Faulk again," Michael said, his good mood evaporating. "I'm sorry, but I'm really getting tired of hearing about Faulk all the time."

6

"Michael," I said, with exasperation. "You can't possibly be jealous of Faulk."

"Why not?" he said. "Ever since he got back from California, it's Faulk this and Faulk that —"

"Language, young man!" chirped a gray-haired colonial dame, rapping Michael smartly on the head with a folded-up fan.

"I hear more about Faulk than I do about your family," Michael went on, but in a slightly lower voice.

He was exaggerating, of course; but I didn't think it would help things to say so.

"Well, I have been working very hard on my swordsmithing for the last six months," I said instead. "And he's the one who's helping me."

"And did you have this burning ambition to become a swordsmith before he turned up doing it?" Michael demanded.

"Michael, Faulk is no threat to you. Not only has he been in a serious relationship for several years, he's —"

"Do you mind?" Michael snapped, suddenly. For a second, I thought he'd snapped at me, and I froze in astonishment. Then I realized he was looking over my shoulder. I turned to see Wesley Hatcher lurking just within earshot, notebook in hand. Wesley must have sidled gradually closer, until he could overhear what we were arguing about.

"Trouble in paradise, kids?" he said, with a snicker. "Don't mind me; just pretend I don't exist."

"I usually do," I said, pointedly turning my back. "Look, Michael, let's talk about this later. Just come with me to see Faulk; I'll fill you in on the way."

Michael sighed, and was opening his mouth to reply when —

"Thief! Miserable, low-down thief!"

I whirled and strode back toward our booth. I could see several other crafters heading our way. Crafters take theft alarms very seriously. For many of us, running on tight budgets, with a big part of our capital tied up in stock, it didn't take much shoplifting to turn a weekend craft fair from a profitable venture into a financial disaster. I was relieved to see that the people like Amanda who were running their booths solo weren't leaving them, in case the real thief was lurking to strike while a confederate cried "Wolf!" nearby.

I even saw one of the watchmen. Good. Let the Anachronism Police do something useful for a change.

But when I reached the booth, I was surprised to find Tad giving the alarm. He'd knocked his own wig askew and was shaking his fist at Benson.

"What are you missing?" the watchman was asking Eileen.

"I'm not missing anything," she said. "He just got here."

"Don't be silly," I said, pointing to Benson's slender briefcase. "Do you really think that thing would hold very much pottery or wrought iron?"

Although I confess, I did glance at the table to make sure my dagger was still there.

"Tad," I asked. "Where did you spot him stealing?"

"He stole CraftWorks!" Tad said.

"CraftWorks?" I repeated, glancing toward the curtain behind which my laptop was hidden. "How did he manage that?"

"He's with the company that's putting out a pirated version of CraftWorks."

"Nonsense," Benson said. "I admit, we've put out our own craft-administration software product. Nothing wrong with a little honest competition."

"Honest competition?" Tad shouted. "You took a copy of my software, changed the graphics slightly, and now you're selling it as if you programmed it. Maybe that's what you call honest competition; I call it software piracy!"

"The two programs perform similar functions," Benson said, apparently unruffled. "Naturally there is a certain similarity between the two. A case of parallel development."

"You stole it, outright; and I'll prove it in court," Tad said.

Benson shrugged.

"You can try, of course," he said. "But you'll be wasting your time . . . and a great deal of money," he added, with an unpleasant and patently phony smile. "Particularly if you persist in publicly defaming our corporate name."

"Go ahead," Tad hissed. "Smirk all you like. But you'll see; I'm not going to take this lying down. And you," he said, turning to Rob. "Don't you let him have your software. Oh, he'll make a lot of promises about how much he's going to pay you, but you won't see a dime. The minute you let him have a copy, you might as well kiss it goodbye. I'm not the only one he's done this to; ask around."

With that, he strode off in a cloud of flapping lace and dreadlocks. Benson shrugged.

"So, Rob," he said. "As we were saying . . ."

Rob looked stunned. I had a bad feeling about this. I elbowed the watchman.

"Go make sure he isn't pilfering, too," I ordered.

He lumbered over to interrogate Benson, and I pulled Rob aside.

"What's going on, anyway?" I asked.

"I have no idea," Rob said, looking wild-eyed. "Mr. Benson and I were just talking when Tad ran in, shouting. Do you think there's anything to it?"

I hesitated. Tad was not only a brilliant programmer and systems engineer, he was also a very canny businessman. Companies lined up to pay the seemingly exorbitant fees he charged to build or fix systems. If he thought the man was a software pirate. . . .

On the other hand, in the six months I'd known him, I'd seen Tad get hot under the collar more than once about things that later turned out to be honest misunderstandings or even rumors. He always apologized so charmingly that most people forgave him. What if this was one of those times, and what if Benson was the unforgiving type? We couldn't let Tad spoil Rob's chance of making a good sale.

"Just be nice to Benson until I can find out more," I said. "You don't want to alienate him, but if there's any chance Tad is right, we need to know."

"But Meg," Rob said. "He's expecting me to turn over the software for them to study. I was going to give him a copy today."

He opened his coat and pulled something from the inside pocket — yet another small, square, paper envelope with an iridescent CD-ROM gleaming through its round, cellophane window.

"Give it to me," I said, grabbing the envelope.

"Meg, I know it's an anachronism; I didn't have it out."

"I'll take care of it," I said, shoving it into my haversack. "When Benson asks for it, just tell him you don't have it with you, but you know where it is. That's true, right? I'll give it back when I'm sure he's okay — or let you know when I'm sure he's a crook."

"He won't like that," Rob said.

"Blame me if you like," I told him. "I don't give a damn."

"Okay." He looked relieved.

"But stall as long as possible before you tell him," I said.

"Right."

I rejoined Michael, and Rob ambled back to Benson, who seemed to be telling something remarkably funny to the watchman. Both were laughing and slapping their knees.

"What's so funny?" I asked Michael.

"Nothing that I can see," he said, with a shrug. "The versatile Mr. Benson appears to be rapidly acquiring a slight southern drawl."

"Hmph," I said. "I never trust people who do accents that easily."

"Gee, thanks."

"Oh, it's all right for you," I said. "You're an actor."

"And therefore allowed to be linguistically promiscuous?"

"Well, I wouldn't put it that way," I said, smiling in spite of myself. "But yes; it's what you're supposed to do, but I don't trust people who do that kind of chameleon act in real life. They're either very impressionable or very calculating. Guess what I'm putting my money on."

We watched as Benson shook hands with the watchman, then flung his arm around Rob's shoulder, and led him off.

"Come on," I said. "We have to see Faulk now. He needs to know about this."

"For heaven's sake, why?" Michael said,

his exasperated tone returning as he followed me down the lane toward Faulk's booth.

"Faulk and Tad have been living together for the last year or so," I said. "That's why he came back from California. I like Tad well enough, but he can be a bit of a hothead, so if he's running around shouting threats, Faulk should know. And for that matter, Faulk doesn't lose his temper easily, but when he does — well, I want to make sure he hears about the whole mess from someone calm enough to not make it sound like more than it is. He tends to be a little overprotective of Tad. We don't want either of them messing up your mother's big event do we? And — Michael?"

He had stopped in the middle of the lane.

"Living together?" he said. "As in living together? I mean — Faulk's gay?"

"Is that a problem?" I asked, putting my hands on my hips.

"Of course not," he said, "It's just that . . . well, I didn't realize. . . ."

"That you've been having fits of jealousy over Faulk for absolutely no good reason?"

He shrugged, rather sheepishly.

"Come on," I said. "We need to talk to Faulk."

"So, I guess he's in the closet?" Michael

said, as we turned into the lane where Faulk's booth stood.

"Not really," I said. "But he tries to keep a low profile; his family's very prominent — First Families of Virginia and all that — and a bit conservative. You can't imagine how upset they were when he first brought Tad home to meet them."

"Because Tad's black, or because he's gay?" Michael asked.

"Yes," I said. "Hard to say which upset them most. His father, anyway; his mother's so glad to have him back in Virginia that she doesn't really care, from what I heard."

"Hard to believe there's still that much prejudice around," Michael said, shaking his head.

"They've had a tough time," I said, hoping sympathy for Faulk and Tad would crowd out any remaining resentment. "Ah, here's the booth."

7

Faulk had a flashier booth than mine, more like an art nouveau wrought-iron gazebo, really, and cleverly designed to show off his ironwork as much as possible. You could assemble and disassemble it quickly with a few basic tools; it packed down into a surprisingly small space; and though it looked airy and delicate, I'd seen it weather high winds that had overturned far more solid and sturdy-looking booths. And, to my amazement, he'd managed to make both the booth and the small iron fence that defined the front of his space completely free of rough edges and points on which clumsy shoppers or rampaging children could cut or impale themselves.

"What's wrong?" Michael asked. I realized I was staring at Faulk's booth.

"I confess: I covet that booth," I said. "Not that particular booth, exactly, but I want one like it."

"I'm sure you could do something just as good," Michael said. "Even better."

"I'm sure I could, too," I said. "I helped make parts of his, ten years ago. I just haven't gotten a good idea. I don't want a clone of Faulk's booth; I want one that's as cool as his, but completely me."

"That's a great idea," Michael said. Did he really think it was a great idea, or was he just happy to see me showing some signs of professional rivalry with Faulk? Hard to tell.

Several tourists had stopped and were pointing up at Faulk's sign, which said, in old-fashioned lettering, WILLIAM FAULKNER CATES: BLACKSMITH. They glanced into the booth, then stepped inside.

"Got 'em!" I said.

"What?" Michael said.

"It's half the battle, you know, getting them to enter the booth. Watch the way people walk down the aisles, staring into booths, and trying to keep from putting even one toe across the invisible line between the aisle and the booth."

"Because if they step in, there's more pressure to buy?"

"Exactly. Same thing if they catch the booth-owner's eye. They try to look at what you're showing without looking at your face or stepping one inch inside your booth. So one of the tricks is to have something that makes them want to come inside."

"Like Faulk's booth."

"Exactly."

Or Faulk himself, for that matter. I caught sight of my blacksmithing teacher, standing in the back of his booth, talking to two customers. Female customers, of course; Faulk drew more female traffic than any other ironworker I knew. Three other customers, ostensibly inspecting various bits of the booth and its contents, were actually staring through the wrought-iron grillwork at Faulk when they thought no one was looking.

And he was worth staring at. He was well over six feet tall with the patrician, blond, blue-eyed good looks people seem to expect from old southern families and the muscular body they more logically expect to see on a blacksmith. He was dressed very simply, in plain blue breeches and a homespun shirt with the sleeves carelessly rolled up; but then Faulk looked good in almost anything.

"Meg!" he cried, when he saw me, excusing himself from the customers with a smile and coming over to give me a hug. I could almost feel the hostile stares of the customers, and Michael didn't look all that thrilled, either.

"I can't stay long," I said.

"We'll catch up tonight at the party, then."

"I just wanted to show you the dagger. I thought it would be risky bringing that to the party."

"At one of your family's parties, butter knives and plastic forks would be risky," Faulk said. "Will there be croquet, or has some alert public-safety agency finally intervened?"

"We're not entirely sure croquet's in period," I said. "But there may be lawn bowling, if we can find anyone who knows the rules."

"I can't wait," Faulk said, sounding insincere. "So let's see the thing."

I unwrapped my dagger and handed it over, hilt first. Faulk took it in his left hand and extended a finger toward the blade.

"Careful, it's sharp," I warned out of habit.

"You'd better hope it's sharp, girl, or I'm sending you back to the whetstone." He tested the grip, then shifted the knife to his other hand and tested again.

"Nicely balanced," he said, nodding. "And I'm impressed that you managed to make it fit so well in either hand. Not easy with an asymmetrical design."

No, it wasn't. I kept my face neutral, as he

stepped out into the sunlight in the front area of his booth, held the hilt up close to his face, and scrutinized the body of the falcon that formed it, occasionally touching a questioning finger to a detail. And while he examined every inch of the blade, whose finish shone in the sunlight with a cool lunar glow, I had to keep reminding myself to breathe. Then he gripped the hilt again and tossed the knife lightly from hand to hand.

"Not bad," he said, walking back toward us.

Suddenly, in one of those lightning motions that always seemed so improbable in a man his size, Faulk slashed downward with the knife, embedding the point deep in the display table and sending one middle-aged woman out of the booth shrieking in terror. The other women watched with openmouthed fascination, and I suspected Faulk and my dagger would inhabit their erotic fantasies for months to come.

"Not bad at all," he said, stepping back from the table and grinning at me.

"Subtle, Faulk," I said, and began struggling to pry the knife out of the wood. I had to wiggle it back and forth half a dozen times. But I wasn't exactly displeased. If I'd done a bad job on the knife — used the wrong grade of steel, gotten the fire too hot or not hot enough, spent too much or too little time hammering it out, or made any one of a hundred other mistakes during the months I'd been working on it — the blade would have been flawed, too weak to take the beating Faulk had just given it.

"You'll make a swordsmith yet," he said.

"Thanks," I said, trying not to look too flattered.

"Well, I suppose we'd both better get back to business," Faulk said. "I'll see you both at the party, then."

"Right — oh, Faulk," I said. "I wanted to warn you — I'm afraid something's happened that upset Tad a bit."

I described Tad's encounter with Benson. Luckily, while Faulk was obviously concerned, he didn't seem to be losing his temper.

"The man's a total weasel," he said. "Your brother can't really be thinking of selling him the game, can he?"

"If Benson tried to steal CraftWorks, I can't imagine Rob will," I said. "No possibility that Tad's overreacting? Or that Benson's just the fall guy and someone else did the dirty work?"

Faulk shook his head.

"I'll tell Rob, then," I said.

"I wish Tad hadn't flown off the handle,"

Faulk said. "Added more fuel to the legal fire."

"What legal fire?"

"Tad's been pretty outspoken about what Benson's done to him, and he's trying to get people to boycott their products. Benson's slapped him with a huge lawsuit. Slander, libel, defamation of character, restraint of trade — you name it."

"It won't hold up in court, though, will it?" I asked. "I mean, if the guy really has done all this."

"It won't hold up in court if it ever gets to court, but I'm not sure we can afford to go on with it," Faulk said. "Benson seems to have all the money in the world to file countersuits and motions, and frankly we're already in debt up to our eyeballs. Don't cross the guy, whatever you do."

He returned to waiting on customers, and Michael and I headed back to my booth.

"Well," he said, after a while. "Your knife's a success."

"Yeah," I said. "And don't you feel better, now that you don't have to feel jealous of Faulk?"

He considered that a moment.

"Not a whole lot," he said. "Faulk's not the problem."

"Could have fooled me."

"He's not; not a big part anyway. It's the whole situation."

I closed my eyes and sighed.

"I mean, here we are, supposedly spending the weekend together, only you're spending every waking minute in your booth."

"While you're off drilling with your regiment," I countered. "I didn't realize you were thinking of this as a way to spend time together. I thought we were helping make your mother's project a success."

"Well, yes," he said. "But — I thought we'd have more time together."

"You're welcome to spend all day in the booth with me," I said.

"Gee, thanks."

"You don't even have to work; just look decorative and amuse me. I don't think they'd let me into your regiment, even if I had a uniform. I'd flunk the physical."

"The problem's not this weekend," Michael said. "The problem's every weekend. If you'd just try moving to Caerphilly. We don't have to live together if that bothers you, but if you could just try living someplace nearby. I'd move up to northern Virginia if I could, except I have to be near the college; you can do your ironworking anywhere."

"Not anywhere," I protested. "I couldn't do it in your apartment, for heaven's sake; I'd burn the place down."

"We could find a place," he said. "Someplace this side of Caerphilly; we could find a place for half the rent you pay in northern Virginia, and you'd be closer to your family."

"Closer to my family?" I echoed. "I thought you were trying to talk me into moving, not scare me off."

"Okay," he said, smiling. "The other side of Caerphilly if you'd rather. What's wrong with that idea?"

"Nothing, really," I began. "Except I want to —"

"Say no to corruption!" a voice screeched into my ear.

I started, and nearly dropped my knife.

8

"Get tough on crime!" the voice went on. "Fenniman for Sheriff!"

"Hello, Mrs. Fenniman," I said, turning to greet Mother's best friend. "How's the campaign going?"

"Oh, it's you two," Mrs. Fenniman said. "Can't recognize anyone in these fool costumes."

She was dressed all in black, as usual, and looked more at home in her colonial clothes than most of the veteran reenactors. She was in her early sixties, like Mother, but while Mother could easily pass for ten or fifteen years younger, Mrs. Fenniman, with her pointy chin and sharp, beady eyes, had looked like an old crone as long as I'd known her. She was wearing some kind of oversized black bonnet, which she pushed back so she could peer up at our faces — the top of her head only came to my shoulder.

"You're running for sheriff?" Michael asked.

"You're not registered voters," Mrs.

Fenniman said, frowning."

"I am in Caerphilly," Michael pointed out.

"Fat lot of good that does me here," Mrs. Fenniman said. "And you, young lady — why the devil do you insist on living up there in the middle of that horrible drug-infested city?"

"Good question," Michael murmured.

"Actually, I'm pretty far out in the suburbs, you know," I said. "We have more trouble with possums than pushers."

"We could use more enlightened voters in this county," Mrs. Fenniman said. "Well, if you can't vote here, at least make yourselves useful. Pass these out."

She thrust a wad of campaign pamphlets at each of us.

"Oh, and Meg," she added. "You did bring the flamingos, didn't you?"

"Yes, of course I brought them," I said, wincing.

"Flamingos?" Michael echoed. "You never did tell me what that was all about."

"Campaign's keeping me so busy I almost forgot to ask about them," Mrs. Fenniman said. "And when I went by your booth a little while ago, you weren't there, and neither were the birds."

"I don't have them out in the booth," I said. "They're not period. But I've got them, don't worry. I was planning on bringing them by your house while I was here."

"That won't work," Mrs. Fenniman said. "I'm so busy campaigning this weekend I'm hardly ever home."

"After the festival's over, then," I suggested.

"Don't be silly," she said. "I'll pick them up at your booth later."

"What's the deal with the flamingos, anyway?" Michael asked.

"Mrs. Fenniman commissioned me to make a dozen wrought-iron lawn flamingos," I said.

"Okay," he said, in a tone that suggested he was hoping for a slightly more detailed explanation. With my family, there usually was a more detailed explanation, although he hadn't yet realized that sometimes he was better off not hearing it.

"It's to get back at the damned yard Nazis," Mrs. Fenniman said.

"She means the landscaping subcommittee of the Visual Enhancement and Aesthetics Committee of the neighborhood association."

"Whatever they call themselves," Mrs. Fenniman fumed. "Bunch of meddling busybodies if you ask me. What business is it of theirs what I have on my lawn? I own the place, don't I?"

"They passed a rule outlawing plastic lawn ornaments," I explained. "Mrs. Fenniman feels they were targeting her plastic flamingo herd."

"I know they were," she said. "I've filed suit to have the rule overturned, but meanwhile they've gotten an injunction against my flamingos. And that damned idiot of a sheriff is backing them."

"So you're escalating to wrought-iron flamingos?" Michael asked.

"The rule specifically permits both iron and stone ornaments," she said. "So it doesn't matter how much they hate 'em; they won't have a leg to stand on. Speaking of legs: you figured out a way to anchor them? I wouldn't put it past the yard police to steal them."

"Each one has a base," I said. "If you want to set them on the ground, they'll stand up just fine. If you want them anchored, all you have to do is set the base in concrete, and they'd need a backhoe to steal them."

"But are they pink enough? They have to be bright, bright pink."

"The enamel matches the last sample I showed you," I said. "I'm not sure it's possible to make them any brighter than that. As it is, they glow in the dark."

"Really?" Mrs. Fenniman said, brightening. "That's outstanding! The plastic ones never did that."

"You don't mean that literally," Michael said.

"Just wait and see," I said.

"I'll come by your booth tomorrow to pick them up, then," Mrs. Fenniman said.

"Just bring your checkbook," I said.

"Pink, glow-in-the-dark flamingos," Michael mused, as Mrs. Fenniman stumped off, raising a cloud of dust in her wake as her long skirts trailed on the ground.

"I just hope she comes by early, before there's much of a crowd," I said. "I do not want a whole lot of people to see the damned things."

"Are they that bad?"

"Wait till you see them, gently glowing in the twilight," I said. "Or maybe not so gently. They rather remind me of the special effects they use in bad sci-fi movies to indicate lethal levels of radiation."

"They sound perfectly charming to me," Michael said. "I bet you could sell a lot of those."

"Quite apart from being glaring anachronisms, they're perfectly hideous, and I have no intention of selling a single one after Mrs. Fenniman claims her collection," I said. "It's hard enough for a woman to get people to take her seriously as a blacksmith; the last thing I want is for people to start thinking of me as that lady blacksmith who makes those cute pink flamingos."

In the distance, we could see Mrs. Fenniman, haranguing people and shoving campaign flyers into their hands.

"Odd," I said. "On her, that outfit makes me think more of Salem than Yorktown."

"Or the Wicked Witch of the West," Michael said, as we resumed walking. "I keep looking over my shoulder for falling farmhouses. So is that why she's running for sheriff? Because they outlawed her flamingos?"

"Yes," I said. "That and the fact that she thinks the incumbent sheriff is an incompetent fool and it's time for a change."

"Well, she may have a point there," Michael said. "But does Mrs. Fenniman have any relevant experience?"

"According to her, after raising two children and keeping her no-good rascal of a husband in line for forty-five years, policing the county should be a piece of cake."

"And what do the county voters think about that?"

"The sheriff's running scared," I said. "His campaign platform seems to be that he's hired a new deputy with big-city police experience and we don't need a new sheriff."

"So who's your mother's family supporting?" Michael said, showing his keen grasp of the realities of small town politics.

"Undecided, so far, since they're both relatives," I said. "Which is why they're both campaigning so hard. See, there's the sheriff now."

We were passing the town square, where the sheriff was just easing himself into the stocks and Cousin Horace was placing a board across two ramshackle sawhorses to make a crude table. As the sheriff settled in, shifting his arms and head in the holes to find a comfortable spot, Horace made a big show out of locking him in with an enormous reproduction padlock Mrs. Waterston had commissioned Faulk to make. Only a show, of course, since the padlock was the old-fashioned kind that needed a key to lock or unlock it, as Wesley had found out to his surprise the night before, when, during his tour of the fair, he'd tried to lock me in the stocks as a joke and I'd easily shaken the padlock open and then off the hasp. For that matter, I could probably have shaken the stocks themselves to pieces in time. They were never designed to be moved fourteen times to suit Mrs. Waterson's evolving notions of how the fair should be arranged, and I hoped Horace had remembered to bring a wrench to tighten the bolts periodically. Still, it looked impressive, and a crowd had already started to gather by the time Horace put out a sign saying, TEN PENCE A THROW and began carefully unloading a bushel basket of rotten tomatoes onto the table.

"Interesting method of campaigning," Michael remarked.

"Meg?"

I looked down to see my nephew Eric tugging at my dress.

"Can I have a dime? Huh?"

"I can probably find a few dimes to fund Eric's participation in the electoral process," Michael said. "We can finish this later."

Preferably after the craft fair is over, I thought, but I smiled and waved as Eric tugged Michael down the lane.

"Damn that man!"

Mrs. Fenniman stood beside me, frowning at the crowd that was starting to gather around the sheriff.

"Who the hell do you think gave him that

idea?" she muttered. "Know damn well he didn't think of it himself."

She fixed me with her sternest glance.

"I need something to top that," she said. "Think of something, will you? And don't just stand there; pass the damned flyers out."

With that, she turned on her heels and strode off, passing out flyers with such force that she nearly knocked one poor woman down.

"Mrs. Fenniman a good friend of yours?" came a voice at my elbow.

Wesley.

"She's a good friend of Mother's," I said, handing him a flyer as I headed back toward my booth. "And a relative, of course."

"Yeah," he said, trotting to keep up with me. "Kind of tough, having two of our relatives running against each other for sheriff, isn't it?"

"Very tough," I said. "I was so hoping someone sane would join the race, but no such luck."

Wesley laughed as if he thought I was joking. Obviously he'd been out of touch with the rest of the family for quite some time. I walked on, shoving flyers into the hands of startled tourists along the way.

As I reached my booth, I heard a cheer go

up from the town square. Wesley snickered.

"I could swing that election," he boasted.

"Yes, isn't the power of the press a wonderful thing?"

"I could," he said. "I've got the dirt right here."

He was holding up something. Déjà vu all over again — yet another shiny CD in a paper envelope, although characteristically Wesley had managed to mar his envelope with a number of grease stains and what looked like a smear of ketchup.

"Put it away before the Town Watch see it," I said, wishing he'd leave. Two women were examining a candelabrum on the outer edge of my booth. I was trying to overhear their conversation without looking too obvious.

"Don't you want to see it?" Wesley said.

"Why should I care?" I asked. "I don't live here anymore. Why should I care which of our crazy relatives gets elected sheriff?"

"You'll never guess what's on it," Wesley said.

"No, I won't even try," I said.

"But if you knew what was on here —"

"Then you wouldn't have a secret to tantalize me with, now would you? You're welcome to come back later and wave your anachronism around to torture me some more, Wesley; right now I'm a little busy. Here, go and pass these out," I said, shoving the rest of the flyers into his hands.

"Your mother said you were going to help me with my story," he complained as he slouched out.

"Later," I muttered, and strolled a little nearer to the customers who were examining a fireplace set — a new design that I was particularly proud of, with a delicate metal vine motif that had been fiendishly difficult to do. I'd been working on getting it just right for over a year, and only in the last couple of months had I produced pieces I thought were good enough to sell. I drifted a little closer, in the hope of overhearing what they said about it.

"Yes," I heard one say. "It's very nice. But much too expensive."

I gritted my teeth and ignored them, pretending to straighten something on the table. I hoped they wouldn't come and tell me to my face that my fireplace set was too expensive. I'd have a hard time saying something polite and noncommittal. And if they tried to bargain the price down — well, did they know how much work it took to make it? How few blacksmiths could have done something that delicate looking and yet that sturdy?

"The other blacksmith had something just like it, and the price was much more reasonable," her friend said. "Let's go back there."

Other blacksmith?

"Eileen," I said, as the two left the booth. "Can you hold things down here? I'll be back in a few minutes."

"Of course," she said.

"Meg, do you have any change?" Michael said, reappearing in my booth. "Your cousin Horace is — what's the matter?"

"A sneak thief," I said, slipping into the lane to follow the two women.

Michael ran after me.

"Who?" he asked. "Those two women?"

"Keep your voice down," I said. "They're not thieves, but I think they're leading me to one."

"Right," Michael said. "Here, take my arm. We'll try to look inconspicuous, as if we're just out for a stroll."

Of course, in his white-and-gold uniform, Michael had never looked less inconspicuous in his life, but we fit in. Every few steps Michael would salute a squad of soldiers or we'd exchange good morrows with some costumed civilians, but luckily we didn't run into anyone who wanted us to stop and talk. And, as I suspected, the two women headed straight for the far end of the fair, where I'd assigned the less-accomplished craftspeople.

"Bingo," I muttered, as they entered a blacksmith's booth in the last aisle.

"What is it?" Michael said.

"Tony Grimes," I said. "Fancies himself a blacksmith, the louse."

"He's not very good?" Michael asked.

"He's not half bad at running a hardware store, which is his day job," I said. "As a blacksmith — well, he should stick to selling nails, not making them."

"That bad, huh."

"Take a look at his stuff sometime," I said. "In fact, take a look right now; I think we'll pay old Tony a visit."

"Meg," Michael said. "You're pretty upset. Why don't we —"

But I was already striding toward Tony's booth.

"It's amazing, Tony," I said, sweeping my glance around booth. "Absolutely amazing."

Tony flinched at my voice, dropped the book he was reading, and hunched his shoulders defensively. He'd have been about my height, if not for that familiar protective stoop, as if he were constantly expecting someone he'd cheated or defrauded to strike him. Apart from that, he was a singularly unremarkable figure, with features so bland even his mother probably had a hard time recalling them when he wasn't around.

The two women I'd followed looked up from the fireplace set they'd been examining. As I suspected, it was a cheap knockoff of the one they'd passed over in my booth.

"Very nice," I said, picking up the tongs from a similar set and eyeing them critically. "You've almost got the shape right — a little lopsided, but most people wouldn't notice. Of course, if I were you, I'd paint it; hide all those nasty weld spatters. I doubt if those welds will hold up in the long run, but then, most people aren't looking to use a fancy set like that, are they? It's just for decoration."

I could see the women looking more closely at the poker and tongs they were holding, and frowning.

"In fact, the only thing I can see really wrong with it is that it's an exact copy of a design I introduced this spring," I said.

"You'd better watch it," Tony snapped. "You could get into trouble, making accusations like that."

"No, you watch it," I said. "What you're doing is a flagrant violation of the copyright laws. I've been talking to a lawyer about what you're doing, and I know a couple of other people have, too."

Tony swallowed nervously at this remark. And it wasn't exactly a lie. After the last time I'd seen Tony at a craft fair, hawking his badly made imitations, I'd spent a long time bending my brother Rob's ear about the problem. Not that Rob knew anything useful about copyrights — after squeaking through the Virginia bar exam last year, he'd spent most of his waking hours working on his role-playing game and supporting himself by what he called "legal scut work" for various lawyer uncles.

"There's only so many ways of shaping iron," Tony said, defensively. "You get all upset whenever I do anything that's the least bit like what you do, and I keep telling you, it's an example of parallel development."

Parallel development? Odd turn of phrase for Tony — where had I heard that before?

"Yeah, right," I said, aloud. "Come on, Michael, let's get back to my booth." And we strode out of Tony's booth — now, for some odd reason, much emptier. Not, alas, completely empty. As we reached the end of the lane, I glanced back and saw that Wesley Hatcher had insinuated himself into the booth.

"Damn," I said. "Now I'll have to talk to that little weasel to make sure Tony doesn't sell him a phony version of the story."

"Tony doesn't look too happy," Michael remarked. "And look, Wesley's taking pictures. I should think the pictures would speak for themselves."

"Yes, definitely," I said. "Good for Wesley; he's finally found something useful to do with himself. I want to warn Faulk. From the looks of it, Tony has ripped off some of his designs, too. I hope he doesn't explode when he hears."

"Maybe someone's already told him," Michael said, as we neared Faulk's booth. "Sounds like an explosion to me."

9

A crowd surrounded Faulk's booth, and we heard arguing voices. We pushed through to find Faulk and Roger Benson squared off, looking as if they were about to come to blows, to the delight of a growing audience. Including Spike, Mrs. Waterston's dog, who was barking with great enthusiasm at both combatants and straining at the leash in his eagerness to jump into the fray. Since he weighed about eight and a half pounds and looked like a black-and-white dust mop, people in the crowd were pointing at him and saying how cute he was. I hoped they'd have the sense to keep their distance.

At the other end of the leash, trying to hide behind a small holly bush, was my brother Rob.

"You had to bring him by here," I said, frowning.

"Mrs. Waterston dumped him on me."

"I meant Benson. Did you have to bring him by Faulk's booth after what happened earlier with Tad?"

"I was sort of distracted," Rob said, nodding his head at Spike.

"Well, go and distract Mr. Benson," I said. "Michael, come help me talk to Faulk."

"Right," Michael said, squaring his shoulders. Rob rolled his eyes but knew better than to disobey his older sister. We marched into the booth together.

"Mr. Benson," Rob began, although it was hard to hear him over the barking.

"Faulk, I need to talk to you a minute," I said. I was trying to pull Faulk away, without much effect, when suddenly I heard a yelp of pain — was that Spike? — followed by an eruption of yells, shrieks, and even louder barking.

"What on Earth?" I muttered.

"You kicked that poor little dog!" a stout woman was shrieking, right in Benson's face. "I saw it! How dare you!"

"He was going for my ankle," Benson said. "And I didn't actually kick him. I just kicked at him. See, he's fine."

"Time was they'd put a dog down if it bit someone like that," someone in the crowd said.

"Nonsense! The man started it, kicking the poor little thing," someone else said.

While the crowd debated whether or not

any actual kicking or biting had occurred, Rob was having trouble holding Spike, who had turned into a snarling, growling fury, trembling with the intensity of his desire to dismember Benson. Suddenly, Spike began making choking noises and fell over on his side. Gasps and shrieks went through the crowd. Rob froze and stared down at the small limp figure at his feet.

"Is he dead?" Rob said. "Mrs. Waterston will kill me if he's dead."

"Nonsense," I said, in a low voice. "He'll be fine. He just pulled too hard against the choke chain and cut off his own wind." As if to prove me right, Spike stirred slightly, lifted his head, and growled.

"He's coming around; he'll be just fine," I said, more loudly. "Happens all the time. I'll take him to the vet to make sure he's okay. You get him" — I indicated Benson with a jerk of my head — "away from here, and keep him away."

"Right," Rob said. He handed me the end of the leash and went over to Benson. The stout woman had backed off to rejoin the ring of hostile faces standing in a semicircle around the entrance to Faulk's booth. Benson was face-to-face with Faulk again.

"You can count on that," Faulk was saying, in the cold tone I knew meant that

Faulk was very, very angry. His hands were clenched into fists, and he was holding one at shoulder level. His shoulder level meant eye level for Benson, and if I were Benson, I'd have thought twice about crossing Faulk.

"Come on, Roger," Rob said, taking Benson by the shoulder and trying to lead him away. "Let's get out of here."

"The hell I will," Benson said, but he let Rob lead him a few steps toward the entrance of the booth, Faulk following behind, as if to make sure they really left.

But just as Benson reached the entrance, Spike, seeing his prey on the move, suddenly leaped up to bark again. He knocked over an andiron right into Faulk's path, and Faulk stumbled forward. Unfortunately, just as this was happening, Benson apparently decided he needed to say a few parting words. He began to turn around, open his mouth, and step back into the booth.

"Another thing —" he began, then he squawked as Faulk's fist met his nose. Then they both lost their balance and fell in a heap, banging various bits of iron on the way down.

Amazing, how much blood a simple nosebleed can produce. And how much panic. A few onlookers fled — I like to think they were going in search of help. A few people waded in to separate the combatants, which wasn't really necessary, as Faulk had the wind knocked out of him and couldn't move, and Benson was less interested in fighting than in flailing about dramatically, yelling that he couldn't breathe, and alternately demanding a doctor and a lawyer.

Wesley appeared, like a vulture scenting carrion, and hovered around in everyone's way, taking notes and snapping photos with his little camera. Mrs. Fenniman and the sheriff both showed up and tried to give Benson conflicting forms of first aid, simultaneously. When it looked as if they were about to come to blows over whether to apply cold or heat to his nose, I ordered them to take Benson over to Dad's first-aid tent, and sent Rob after them to try calming Benson down.

Faulk recovered his breath, stood up, dismissed the departing patient with a look, then went out through the back of his booth and began walking very fast, away from the center of the fair.

"Should someone go after him?" Michael asked.

I shook my head.

"He needs to walk his temper off. He'll be fine if we just leave him alone. Although that does leave the problem of what to do about his booth."

"I can watch it until either he or Tad gets back," Michael offered. "I've helped out with yours occasionally, and he's got all the prices marked and everything."

"That'd be great," I said.

"What about the dog?" the stout woman said. Now that things had calmed down, the crowd was breaking up, but she still stood just outside the booth, watching Spike, who had tottered over to the railing that marked the outside of the booth and was growling half-heartedly at her. I sighed. I had forgotten that in sending Rob off to deal with Benson I'd saddled myself with Spike.

"You were going to take him to the vet," the woman reminded me.

"I'll do better than that," I said, giving Spike's leash a tug to get him moving. "I'll take him to a doctor."

"Oh, I'm sure your Dad will love that," Michael commented, taking a proprietary pose at the back of Faulk's booth.

I helped Michael pick up the booth before I took off — I wasn't anxious to arrive before Dad had finished with Benson. Then I made my way across the town square and over to Dad's booth — actually a large tent at the opposite edge of the green, with a sign over the entrance that said, PHYSICIAN AND SURGEON.

Things looked a little different from when I'd last seen his tent on my way into the fair that morning. Dad had recruited two bedraggled-looking reenactors to lie outside, pretending to be patients and adding atmosphere. The patient to the left of the tent's entrance had a bloody bandage over both eyes. The one on the right appeared to be an amputee until one noticed that there were bits of straw poking out of his truncated leg and that the real leg disappeared into a hole in the ground.

"Very impressive," I said, as I approached the tent.

"If that miserable beast tries to pee on my leg again, I'll use this," the faux amputee said, waving an authentically crude wooden crutch.

"Oh, lord," said the other man, peeking out from under his bandage. "Hang on to the leash this time, will you?"

So they'd already met Spike.

"Don't worry," I said, shortening the leash to keep Spike away from them.

"Meg!" Dad said, appearing in the opening of the tent. "What's up? Another nosebleed?"

I sighed. In just a few hours, he'd managed to give his new colonial costume the same well-worn, rumpled look as all the rest of his clothes. And while he'd carefully grown his hair long enough to tie back in colonial fashion, he had so little hair left that the black velvet ribbon almost hid it. From a distance, it looked as if he'd glued the bow to the back of his largely bald head. Ah, well.

"Could you take a look at Spike?" I asked. "I'm not sure whether Benson actually kicked him or just tried."

"Certainly!" Dad said, taking Spike's leash and leading him into the tent. I followed, ignoring the muted cheers for Benson from the two reclining patients.

I looked around. Dad had been improving on the décor inside, too. I'd already seen the ramshackle operating table, the side tables piled with reproductions of period jars and bottles and flasks, and the artistic arrangement of scary-looking metal instruments. The skeleton dangling from the top of the tent was new. And he'd brought in several jars of leeches. His booth was probably the only one in the fair that the Anachronism Police hadn't complained to me about. I wondered if they were impressed by its authenticity or just too horrified to come in.

"Isn't it grand!" he exclaimed, seeing me look around.

"Lovely," I said, glancing down at the sawdust coating the ground around the operating table. "Please tell me those aren't real bloodstains."

"Of course they are," he said. "Real chicken blood."

"I should have guessed," I said, dragging Spike back from some blood-soaked sawdust that he'd decided looked tasty.

"Let's get the patient on the examination table, shall we?" Dad said, moving several glittering surgical knives aside to make room.

"We?" I said. "You mean you're going to help me pick him up?"

"Well, maybe you should do it," he said. "I don't want to alarm him."

Didn't want to get bitten, more likely. Because I'd once saved Spike's life, he'd developed an inexplicable and unrequited fondness for me, which meant that my odds of getting bitten were much lower than most people's. Although trying to hold him while Dad performed his examination would normally have leveled out the odds again.

Fortunately, Spike was too busy trying to spit out the blood-soaked sawdust to bite, though keeping him still was a lost cause.

"I can't check his heartbeat unless you can get him to stop growling," Dad said.

"Fat chance," I said. "Besides, it's his ribs I'm worried about, not his evil little heart."

"Doesn't seem to be anything wrong with his ribs," Dad said. "I don't think he's injured at all — just mad as hell."

Which was normal for Spike. If he'd begun acting angelic, I'd have told Dad to check for a concussion. After a little more poking and prodding, Dad gave Spike a clean bill of health and I took him back to my booth where, to my astonishment, Rob eventually showed up to claim him.

10

"What a horrible day," Rob said, "and more to come. I'd better take Spike back to Mrs. Waterston's house and feed him."

"Fine," I said. "You didn't leave Mr. Benson alone, did you?"

"He went back to his motel," Rob said, sounding tired.

"Are you sure?"

"I watched him drive off."

"Good riddance," I said. "I hope that's the last we see of him."

"Well, actually, I think he's coming to Mrs. Waterston's party," Rob said.

"Are you sure?"

"He rented a costume," Rob said, with a shrug.

"Oh, great," I said, as Rob ambled off with Spike. "That should be a laugh a minute."

I sighed, plopped my haversack on the ground, and sat down, feeling suddenly tired.

Two members of the Anachronism Police

came in, carrying a birdbath, accompanied by a potter, presumably its maker. I wasn't in the mood, but I closed my eyes, counted to ten, then opened them again, and smiled as sweetly as I could manage.

"Can I help you?" I asked.

"Oh, no," one watchman said, starting to back away.

"It's not really important," the other said. He tripped over an andiron in his haste to leave, sending the dish of the birdbath sailing. The potter leaped up and caught it as if it were an oversized ceramic Frisbee, then followed them out of my booth. I could hear the three of them bickering as they scurried down the lane. Apparently I'd just blown the Miss Congeniality award. I closed my eyes again and massaged my temples.

"Long day," Amanda said, coming up and leaning against my table.

"The longest," I agreed. "And not over yet. We still have the party."

"You make that sound like as much fun as a firing squad," Amanda said. "What's wrong with the party?"

"I just want to put on my jeans and relax, not keep wearing these damned skirts," I said, shaking the hem of my dress and raising a small cloud of dust. "And Michael's mother will be having conniption fits at every real or imaginary thing that goes wrong."

"Well, tell her not to get her panniers in a twist," Amanda said, smiling. "The tall, dark, and handsome Michael will be there, of course."

And Michael, of course, which would make up for everything — normally. But if Michael showed up at the party hell-bent on having a serious discussion on the progress of our relationship . . .

"What's wrong?" Amanda asked. "Have an argument?"

"More like a continuation of an ongoing discussion," I said. "Which isn't much better, actually."

"So I gathered. What's the problem anyway? I mean, the mother's an ogre, of course, but you of all people should be used to dealing with impossible relatives."

"He wants me to move in with him," I said. "Or at least move closer, so we can see more of each other."

"And your problem is?"

"I don't know," I said. "Makes me nervous, though."

"Honey, every unmarried woman I know complains all the time about how she can't find a guy who isn't scared of commitment.

Sounds like you found one who's interested in commitment."

"And I'm the one who's scared."

"If that mother of his comes as part of the package, maybe you should be scared."

"And maybe I should just be committed. Michael's great, and like you say, I'm used to dealing with crazy relatives. What's one more? It's not him or his mother. It's me."

"Well, stick to your guns," she said, patting me on the shoulder. "You'll know when the time is right."

She scurried back to her booth to accost a customer, and I sighed. Would I know when the time was right? Maybe the time was as right now as it ever would be, and I was blowing it, big time.

"Well, Faulk finally showed up," Michael said, strolling in. "Just in time, too. I have no idea how to shut up his booth."

"Thanks for filling in for him," I said. "Hope you didn't have to miss any regimental events."

"I thought you resented me going to regimental events," he said.

"No, I don't," I began, and then changed my mind. "Look, let's not get into that again now, when we only have maybe fifteen or twenty minutes before we're late for your mother's party."

His face relaxed into a smile.

"Good point," he said. "Only we actually have about thirty seconds before we're late," he added, glancing at a pocket watch that he'd pulled out of his waistcoat.

"Damn!" I said. "Hang on a minute while I shut things up."

"Don't worry. She's not calling the roll and taking off points for attendance."

"That's what you think," I muttered.

I hastily grabbed my cash box and my laptop and ducked behind the curtain into the storage area, where I nestled them safely in one of my metal storage cases, and padlocked the case.

"Oops," Michael said. Apparently he'd tripped over my haversack and was now shoveling the contents back in.

"Thanks," I said as he handed it over. "Although I don't think I had quite that much hay and straw in it to begin with."

"Well, you never know when they might come in handy," he said, with a grin. "Come on. The party awaits."

We left the craft-fair grounds, nodding good evening to the members of the Town Watch who were going to patrol it for the night, and headed for the party.

The craft fair occupied a large field that belonged to the Park Service, just south of the small neighborhood where my parents lived, and separated from it by a two-lane blacktop road. If you followed the road west a few hundred yards, you'd arrive at the edge of the Yorktown Battlefields, where we were all encamped with our picturesque but uncomfortable period tents. Most of the reenactors had gone back there to attend one or more regimental meetings, rehearsals, or parties. By this time, we were almost the only ones heading in the other direction, toward Mrs. Waterston's party.

We did run into someone we knew, though. When we glanced down the highway before crossing, I saw a sleek Jaguar, pulled off to the side of the road, its silver paint glowing in the fading light. The driver's side window was open, and someone in one of the generic rental coats was leaning down, talking to a sleekly coifed blond woman inside.

"That'd make a great photo," Michael said, nodding toward the car. "Study in contrasts, then and now, and all that."

Then the pedestrian straightened up and we recognized him.

"Benson," I said, though not loudly enough that the man himself could hear me. He glanced round, as if looking to see if anyone had seen him. We pretended not to notice him, and he hurried off ahead of us. The car drove away in the other direction, past us, and back toward the battlefields and town. The driver didn't seem to notice us.

"Wonder what he's up to," Michael mused.

"Something sinister," I said. "I think Tad is right; I don't trust that man."

"I don't know," Michael said. "You'd think a really hardened villain would have figured out how to skulk around without the telltale furtive body language."

"Yeah, he might as well just jump up on the table and shout, 'Look at me! I'm up to something!' " I said. "But just because he's a bad actor doesn't mean he isn't a villain."

"Recognize the woman he was talking to?" Michael asked.

"No," I said. "Don't think she's from around here."

"Well, let's not worry about it," he said. "You can tell Rob you think the guy is crooked, and that'll be the end of it."

"Good idea," I said, and felt a lot more cheerful. The very idea of Rob telling Benson to take a hike made me more cheerful. In fact, if Rob balked, I might even volunteer to do the job myself.

11

Buoyed by the thought of telling off Benson, I led Michael along the path toward the Moore House, the white-frame farmhouse where, in 1781, the British and Americans had signed the surrender documents to end the siege of Yorktown and, for all practical purposes, the Revolutionary War. Mrs. Waterston wanted to hold her party inside, but the Park Service hadn't approved. They'd let her use the grounds, though. As we drew near, I could see that the house was softly lit from within, as if by candlelight — although knowing how picky they were about fire hazards in historical buildings, I doubted they used real candles.

Strings of lanterns hung from the trees, illuminating the lawn with pools of light and pockets of shadow. Electric lanterns, of course, which probably irritated Mrs. Waterston, but they had the kind of flickering bulb that could almost fool you into thinking of real candles. A string quartet played soft classical music, and I could hear the faint hum of conversation.

Mrs. Waterston swept through one lighted area. Either I'd forgotten how extreme her costume was, or she'd gone home to put on an even taller wig. I glanced down at my sensible linsey-woolsey gown, feeling underdressed.

"Don't worry," Michael said, catching my glance. "Mrs. Tranh has a ball gown for you."

I sighed. Mrs. Tranh was Mrs. Waterston's partner in the dress shop. Like everyone else in town, I'd originally assumed Mrs. Tranh worked for Mrs. Waterston. Over Memorial Day weekend, after watching the strike scenes in a TV rerun of *Norma Jean* and imbibing a few too many glasses of Merlot, I'd become quite agitated about Mrs. Waterston's apparent exploitation of Mrs. Tranh and her other Asian employees. I had threatened to go down to Yorktown and organize the downtrodden sewing ladies. I had visions of us singing "We Shall Overcome" in Vietnamese, while waving beautifully embroidered protest banners.

Michael had spoiled all my fun by revealing how things really worked. His mother and Mrs. Tranh each owned half of the business. Mrs. Tranh hired and managed the seamstresses, kept the books, paid bills and taxes, ordered fabric and other supplies, and generally ran the place.

"So what does your mother do, anyway?" I'd asked.

"Well, she got together the initial capital, and she handles sales and marketing," Michael said. "And she deals with the customers. Mrs. Tranh would hate doing that."

True, but still, if you asked me, Mrs. Tranh was doing the lion's share of the work, yet having to split the profits fifty-fifty. Perhaps that accounted for Mrs. Tranh's dogged insistence on not speaking English with Mrs. Waterston.

I knew perfectly well that Mrs. Tranh could speak reasonably fluent, if somewhat eccentric, English and that she understood the language almost perfectly. The only time she ever pulled the *"je ne comprends pas"* line on me was when I tried to disobey her orders.

With Mrs. Waterston, however, she insisted on speaking only French. Mrs. Waterston's French was considerably worse than mine.

"Anyway, she's done a wonderful costume for you," Michael said, interrupting my wandering thoughts.

"Oh, dear," I said. "As hot and sweaty as I

am, I'd rather crawl into a bath, not a brand-new costume."

"You'll hurt her feelings," he said, "and mine. I helped her figure out what to make."

"It doesn't have panniers, does it?" I asked. "I am not wearing panniers."

"I have no intention of disfiguring you with panniers," Michael said. "That has got to be one of the most ludicrous, unflattering fashions ever invented."

"Amen," I said. "But let's not tell your mother."

"Of course not," Michael said. "But having seen Mom's idea of colonial fashion, I'm thinking next year we should forget about the Revolution and reenact the War of 1812. I'm rather partial to Empire fashions — all those low cut, clinging, diaphanous gowns —"

"Oh, is that what you have in mind for my ball gown?" I said. "Much better than the panniers."

"I wish," he said. "Ah, there's Mrs. Tranh."

Mrs. Tranh's stern features broke into a smile when she saw us. She was standing by the costume racks with two of "the ladies," as she called her seamstresses. We had managed to convince Mrs. Waterston that requiring costumes of mere spectators would decimate attendance, but for certain key events that were open mostly to staff — such as her welcoming party for the crafters — Mrs. Waterston had made costumes mandatory. Just in case anyone showed up without a costume, Mrs. Tranh had brought a large rack of the rental costumes — colonial dresses in demure Williamsburg colors and a range of sizes for the women, and for the men, a collection of shirts, knee breeches, and coats. Mrs. Tranh and the ladies were there to collect the modest rental fee and help stuff the guests into costumes.

At the moment, Mrs. Tranh seemed to have her hands full. Two men had arrived wearing Hawaiian shirts so garish that even Dad would have turned up his nose at them, over cutoffs so ragged they contained more hole than cloth. I recognized both of the men wearing these glaring anachronisms as fellow crafters — a soapmaker and a leatherworker — and would have waved if I thought I could get their attention. They were both intent on escaping to the bar. They didn't stand a chance. Mrs. Tranh's ladies routinely dealt with brides having prewedding hysterics and bridesmaids whose mood veered toward homicidal when they saw their dresses and realized the acute embarrassment and physical torture their supposed good friends were inflicting on them. Dealing with a few reluctant men would be child's play.

The clothing rack was already two-thirds full of confiscated modern garments. Normally, only a minority of my fellow crafters favored gaudy Hawaiian shirts, shorts in fluorescent colors or horse-blanket plaids, and other luridly colored garments — we were a diverse crowd, but jeans and natural fibers tended to dominate most gatherings. I suspected a plot to sabotage the period purity of the party, but Mrs. Tranh and the ladies would take care of that.

"Hello, dear," came my mother's voice from behind me.

"Hello, Mother," I said, turning. "How are —"

I stopped short, my jaw hanging open, when I saw Mother's costume. She had outdone herself, as usual. More to the point, she had outdone Mrs. Waterston, and I had no doubt it was deliberate. I glanced over at Mrs. Waterston who, luckily, was playing gracious hostess to a group of newly arrived guests. She hadn't seen Mother's costume yet, and if I ran for cover now, I might make it far enough from ground zero before she did.

Still, I couldn't help lingering long enough to compare the two. Mother's outfit went just a little bit further than Mrs. Waterston's did, in every way I could think of. Her white powdered wig was a few inches taller, and sported a noticeably more varied collection of bows, flowers, baubles, and artificial birds. At least I hoped they were all artificial. Her waist was laced smaller, and her panniers were a few inches broader. Her overskirt seemed to have at least one more set of ruffles than Mrs. Waterston's, and her petticoat definitely had a slightly wider lace edging. About the only thing not bigger and better was the beauty mark. Although, come to think of it, I didn't remember Mrs. Waterston sporting a second beauty mark. Mother had one, perched precariously at the edge of her décolletage, which was, of course, alarmingly more extreme than Mrs. Waterston's.

Mother swept away, fanning herself with a fan ever so slightly more ornate than Mrs. Waterston's.

"Your mother looks nice," Michael said, in a suspiciously noncommittal tone.

"Yes, I can't wait to see your mother's reaction," I said.

He rolled his eyes.

"It's very odd, don't you think?" I went

on. "It's almost as if she knew exactly what your mother was wearing and deliberately set out to show her up."

"But how could she possibly know that?" Michael said.

I pointed to Mrs. Tranh, who, while ostensibly supervising her seamstresses, had turned her attention to the party and was glancing intently from Mother to Mrs. Waterston and back again.

"Oh, God," he said. "They must be feuding again. I hate it when they do that."

Maybe the party wouldn't be so boring after all, I thought, as Michael and I approached Mrs. Tranh.

"We got your costume," she said. "You go in dressing room and change now."

"I wish you hadn't gone to so much trouble," I said.

"I rather make ten dress for you than one of those," she said, indicating the blandly pretty colonial dresses on the rack.

"Yes, but this whole weekend is already such a lot of work for you."

She shrugged.

"No problem," she said. "Lot of work; lot of money for the ladies. Lot of work for her, too," she added, jerking her head at Mrs. Waterston, who was over by the bar, apparently giving the bartender the third degree about something.

"Yes, isn't it lovely how it's kept her out of your hair for so long," I said.

Mrs. Tranh rolled her eyes.

"Don't worry," I said. "I'm sure she'll find another project before too long."

"She better," Mrs. Tranh muttered. "You and Michael gonna get married, maybe? Let her plan the wedding?"

Michael chuckled. Had he put her up to this, the rat? Or had she come up with the idea on her own? Either way, I wished she'd drop the subject.

"I should change," I said.

"Make it a big wedding, biggest one we ever had in town," Mrs. Tranh said. "Keep her busy for a whole year, planning a wedding like that."

"I'll keep it in mind," I said, retreating toward the dressing room.

"And grandchildren!" Mrs. Tranh called after me. "Plenty of grandchildren! Keep her real busy!"

I ducked into the dressing room. Outside, I could hear Michael laughing and talking with Mrs. Tranh in a mishmash of French and Vietnamese. I pressed a hand to my cheek, which felt hot. Was it the weather, or my embarrassment? Dammit, I thought, I wish everyone would stop trying to push us toward the altar. Maybe my problem wasn't fear of commitment; maybe it was just plain, old-fashioned stubbornness. Maybe if everyone started trying to pry Michael and me apart. . . .

Later, I told myself, and I shed my workday gown and turned to see what Mrs. Tranh and her ladies had made.

They'd designed it to go with Michael's white-and-gold uniform that was clear. Off-white dupioni silk shot with gold threads, and trimmed with lots of lace, most white but some gold.

The improvised dressing room contained a full-length mirror. I held the dress up in front of me and sighed. I couldn't just let Mrs. Tranh do this for me for nothing. Even though Michael had probably already paid her, I had to do something to thank her.

First, of course, I had to get into the dress. And for that I was going to need help; it hooked up the back. And was it my imagination . . . no, I spread the material at the waist to see how it fit. Definitely too small. I wasn't fat, but I wasn't anorexic either; I could see no chance of squeezing into that dress.

I heard the curtain rustle. Mrs. Tranh, I assumed, or one of her ladies, come to help me into the dress. I'd have to break the news that they'd miscalculated, I thought as I turned.

And found myself looking up at Michael.

12

"Mother would have a fit if she saw the glaring anachronisms you're wearing instead of plain, sensible, colonial undergarments," he said, putting his arms around my waist. "Although I rather like them."

"Not surprising," I said, reaching up to put my arms around his neck. "You picked them out. Do you own stock in Victoria's Secret or something?"

"No, but maybe I should buy some," he said, reaching down to kiss my neck.

"You should," I said. "Might as well get something out of all the money you spend there."

"Oh, I do," he said, with the sort of soft laugh that distracted me completely from the business of getting into the costume.

I was about to suggest that we skip the party and adjourn to our tent when I heard Mrs. Waterston's voice outside, berating someone.

"Damn," Michael said. I had reason to believe his thoughts had been running along the same lines as mine, but his mother's voice brought both of us back to Earth. "We don't dare leave her alone for long; she's so keyed up there's no telling who she'll upset. I'd better behave, and lace you into your costume."

"Hook me up, actually, but I don't think it's going to work," I said. "This thing is definitely too small."

"Not when you put the corset on," Michael said.

"Corset?" I said. "You've got to be kidding!"

But no, when I looked back at the hook on which the dress had been hanging, there was, indeed, a white-and-gold corset. The real thing, with boning and laces up the back.

"You're right," I said. "Although they'd have called it 'stays' in this time period."

"I stand corrected."

"Look at all the work she put into this," I said. "All that lace and decorative stitching that no one will ever see."

"I think it was intended for a small but select audience," Michael said. "She told me you'd need help getting into it."

"Badly thought out," I said. "It should be designed so I need help getting out of it."

"Oh, I'm sure you will," he said.

Although it took longer than expected, for one reason or another, Michael eventually managed to lace me into the stays — not all that tightly, thank goodness. I'm not into bondage. But it did take enough off my waist that the white-and-gold gown fit like a second skin.

"I suppose we'd better go out and let Mrs. Tranh admire her creation," Michael said.

"And see what your mother has gotten up to," I added.

"That, too," he said.

"I like this dress already," I said. "It's probably an anachronism of the first order, but she's given me pockets."

I put a few essentials in the pockets and stepped outside, where we allowed Mrs. Tranh and the ladies to ooh and ahh over their handiwork for a few minutes. Then we braced ourselves and stepped out into the party.

We must have stayed longer in the dressing room than I realized — the party had gotten crowded, and almost all of the rental costumes were in use. The effect was rather impressive, as if we'd really been transported back into colonial Yorktown.

At least from a slight distance. Closer up, women didn't look too bad — "One size fits most" is easier to achieve with period dresses. Although most weren't wearing stays, of course, so they hadn't quite achieved what I was now learning to recognize as the authentic period silhouette.

The men, alas, looked pretty motley. Apparently, Mrs. Tranh had estimated on the small side in making the men's costumes, and a fair number hadn't been able to get into the tight knee breeches. Looking around, I could spot half a dozen men whose costumes looked perfectly fine until you noticed that beneath their blue coats you could spot denim or fluorescent polyester or garish plaid.

Luckily, Mrs. Tranh and the ladies had also made a lot of what the reenactors called "overalls" — though to me, they looked more like long white gaiters. The overalls began at midthigh and reached down to cover the tops of the shoes, which meant that you only caught occasional glimpses of the modern pants when their wearers walked. Or modern shoes, for that matter. Evidently Mrs. Waterston hadn't even tried to provide period shoes, simply instructing people to show up in dark shoes if they didn't have proper footgear. She'd had me make a quantity of large buckles that could be clipped onto a shoe to give at least a suggestion of authenticity. I saw my handiwork gracing a remarkably wide range of shoes. They made penny loafers and black leather Reeboks look rather plausible, at least from a distance, but I wasn't sure they did anything to improve the authenticity of Air Jordans.

Fortunately, the majority of the guests came in some kind of costume. Except for the deliberate rebels, most crafters just wore whatever they'd been wearing all day. What they'd probably be wearing for the next two days, for that matter. Well, that would add to the air of authenticity. Michael had invited half a dozen of his fellow French soldiers, and a few people had burst forth with truly wonderful costumes. Tad was still resplendent in his silk and velvet, while Faulk had decided to pay homage to the Scottish side of his ancestry by wearing a kilt and was attracting a great many admiring glances.

So was I, though for rather different reasons.

"Meg, you look fabulous," Amanda told me. She was still in her homespun outfit, but from the look on her face I could tell she was kicking herself for not researching period party clothes. "And you've lost weight," she added. "I didn't notice it in that baggier dress you were wearing all day."

"That's because I didn't lose any," I said. "I'm wearing a set of stays under this dress; the damned things really do take inches off your waist."

"Where does it put them?" she asked.

"It pushes everything up and out," Michael said, with an appreciative glance.

"Well, yes, actually it does," I said, adjusting the lace at the edge of my bodice in a vain attempt to disguise exactly how very much of me there was to push up and out.

"Isn't that a mite uncomfortable?" Amanda asked me.

"Actually, it isn't," I admitted. "Sounds weird, but it gives your back a lot of support which, after standing around all day, isn't exactly a bad idea. And it doesn't feel constricting — but more regal, if that doesn't sound too weird. I mean, there's no way you can slouch in this thing."

"Yes, it makes you look taller," Michael said. Which didn't bother him, of course, since at six feet four inches he still towered over me, no matter how much taller the stays made me.

"Taller, yeah; and that's not all," Amanda said, chuckling. "Honey, you'd better keep your eye on her in that thing. You don't want some fast-talking redcoat to cut you out."

"Don't worry," Michael said, putting a proprietary arm around my waist. "I intend to."

We strolled around the party, taking in the sights. The string quartet was a little shaky. Obviously, they hadn't been here all day, like the rest of us. They still jumped every time the cannon fired, while most of us had learned to ignore the artillery. I wondered if the residents of Yorktown in 1781 had gotten so oblivious to cannon fire. Probably not, if each boom signaled that somewhere in town a cannonball was about to fall. A couple of houses in town still had cannonballs in their sides. Although I knew at least one of the most picturesquely embedded cannonballs, the one in the Nelson house, had fallen out in the twentieth century and was cemented back in by a Hollingworth cousin who worked for the Park Service, during preparations for the 1931 Sesquicentennial — one of the things they don't tell the tourists.

Someone had told Mrs. Waterston that lawn bowling was a popular social activity in colonial Virginia, so she'd roped off part of the lawn and provided several sets of balls, hoping some of the guests would strike up a game and add to the picturesque period atmosphere.

Unfortunately, she'd neglected to provide a set of rules, and anyone who actually knew how the game was supposed to be played had long since deserted the bowling lawn.

By the time Michael and I arrived, we found a standoff between a group who wanted to play something resembling horseshoes without any stakes and a flock of my aunts, advocating a mutant form of wicketless, malletless croquet. The argument was purely theoretical, since the balls had long since been appropriated by my nine-year-old nephew, Eric, and his friends. They hid in the bushes, rolling balls out among the guests' feet, trying to see how close they could come to selected relatives' ankles without actually hitting them. From time to time, you could hear startled squawks from various parts of the crowd, as someone stepped on a ball. If you happened to be watching, you'd see the victim's head suddenly disappear into the crowd, usually accompanied by a small eruption of food and drink.

"Oh, dear," said the sheriff, who was standing nearby, sipping punch and absent-mindedly combing the occasional stray tomato seed out of his beard. "I suppose I should do something about those boys."

"Definitely," I said. "Tell them to lay off

my craft-fair friends and our family and go after someone who deserves to break his neck. Like him," I added, pointing to the buffet, where Tony-the-louse was loading up a plate.

The sheriff laughed, nervously.

"Or better yet, them," Michael said, pointing to the other end of the buffet, where Wesley Hatcher and Benson stood talking.

The sheriff followed Michael's finger, then, when he saw Wesley and Benson, his eyes widened, and he choked on his punch.

"What's wrong?" I asked, as Michael slapped him on the back.

"I'd better go talk to those fool boys," he said, when he'd coughed most of the punch out of his windpipe.

"What do you suppose got into him?" Michael asked.

"Good question," I said. "Something certainly shook him up, and I suspect it was Benson. I just wonder why."

"Could have been Wesley Hatcher," Michael pointed out. "They were standing together. Why don't I go help him out with the kids, and maybe I'll get the chance to ask him."

"Good idea," I said.

I sipped my wine and watched from the

edge of the yard while Michael and the sheriff tracked down the rogue bowlers. I was enjoying being quiet and alone. Having spent the whole day talking to customers, craftspeople, tourists, reenactors, and stray relatives, I just wanted to sip my wine in peace and talk to nobody.

With his usual flair for turning up when least wanted, Wesley Hatcher sidled over toward me. He was staring rather fixedly at my décolletage, and I wondered if I should keep an inch or so of wine in my glass to throw at him in case he said something disgusting.

Apparently, Wesley hadn't completely forgotten what I was like. When he realized I had seen the direction of his stare, he smiled nervously and developed a keen interest in the other guests.

"So, is this a party or a wake?" he asked.

13

"Oh, come on, Wesley," I said. "It's a very nice party."

"Bo-ring," he chanted. "How can you stand it around here?"

"Welcome to small-town America, Wesley," I said. "Last time I looked, they hadn't blockaded Route 64; you could leave any time."

"Yeah, but what's the point?" he said. He sounded a little tipsy. "I had vacation coming to me, so I'm taking it while I can. You can be sure they won't pay me for it if the rag folds."

"Is your paper going to fold?" I asked. Not that I cared one way or another about the *Super Snooper*. Apart from scanning the headlines if the grocery line was running slow, I never paid the slightest attention to it. But this did rather cast Wesley's triumphant return to his hometown in a very different light.

"Who knows?" he said, shrugging. "Whole industry's going down the tubes.

Maybe I should do the whole roots thing, come back and work at the *Town Crier*."

Or maybe not, I thought, since he'd left town one step ahead of several juicy libel suits. "I should think going back to the business magazine would be more interesting," I suggested.

"Don't rub it in," he growled.

"Don't rub what in?"

"The magazine's dead," he said. "Bigger company bought it out and sacked the whole staff. I got out just in time, moving to the *Snooper*."

"Sorry," I said.

"Yeah," he muttered, and took a gulp from his drink. "So am I. I did some good work there."

"Charlottesville Businessman Kidnapped by Aliens?" I suggested. "Elvis Sighted in Norfolk Shopping Mall?"

"Real work," he said. "Legitimate journalism. Not the crap I'm doing now. It ruined my career when the *Intelligence* folded, if you want to know the truth. If I could just break a story, a really juicy story, something I could use to land a job on a legitimate publication. . . ."

He chugged the rest of his drink.

"Hell, even a better tabloid," he added. "Then I'd still be a scum-sucking bottom feeder, but at least I'd be a wellpaid one."

To my surprise, I found I was starting to feel just a little sorry for Wesley. It was a novel sensation, and I pondered it in silence, while Wesley crunched an ice cube from his glass.

"So help me out, will you?" he said, through a mouth full of ice. "You know everything that goes on in this burg; you always did. Your mother said you could find me a story, something juicy I can run with."

"Get lost, Wesley," I said. "The only story I know is that we're having a fabulous celebration of Yorktown Day, with the biggest crowds the town has seen since the Bicentennial, and everyone's having a wonderful time."

"That's not news, it's PR," Wesley grumbled. "Why don't you — hey, what's that?"

"That" was Tad and Roger Benson, raising their voices in another argument. Wesley scurried over to get closer to the action, reaching into his pocket for his notebook as he went. I decided I could hear just as well from where I was. Neither was trying to keep his voice down.

"I never touched your damned booth," Benson was saying. He was holding a bloody handkerchief handy, as if he expected his nose to begin bleeding again at any moment.

"The hell you didn't," Tad shouted back. "I know damn well you went through everything in the booth; you didn't put things back carefully enough to hide that. But it won't do you any good. I've put the evidence where you'll never find it."

"Evidence," Benson snorted. "You haven't got a shred of real evidence and you know it."

"I've got enough to prove everything."

"Should we do something?" Michael said, appearing at my side.

"No," I said. "Not yet anyway."

"I suppose this would be a bad time to bring up the fact that if anyone rifled the booth it was me, looking for another pad of receipts when I was filling in for Faulk."

"A very bad time, I should think. Later, when Tad has calmed down. I wish Tad would stop going on about how he's got the evidence put away in such an incredibly safe place."

"Why?" Michael asked. "Don't you think he has evidence?"

"I bet he has," I said. "But I'm not all that sure my purse is such a safe hiding place. I have this sneaking feeling the evidence is on a CD-ROM Tad handed me earlier."

135

"Good grief," Michael muttered.

The shouting match reached a crescendo, and Tad stormed off. He hit a stray lawn-bowling ball on his way and for a few seconds, he pedaled and flailed his arms furiously like someone trying not to fall off a unicycle. Then he recovered his balance, if not his dignity, and strode out into the darkness beyond the glow of the lanterns.

When Tad disappeared, I glanced back to see what Benson was doing. And saw, though I couldn't hear, that Faulk, too, had a few things to say to the software pirate. He stopped talking as I watched, and they stared at each other for a few minutes. It was scarier than watching Tad square off with Benson, partly because of what had happened earlier. I think everyone at the party was watching, fearing — or hoping for — a rematch. And partly because Tad and Benson were about the same size, while Faulk towered over either one of them. And maybe partly because, despite the *sturm und drang,* I'd never heard of Tad hitting anyone, but I'd seen Faulk lose his temper and finish an argument with his fists, especially in college, when I first knew him. He'd worked a lot on controlling his temper over the last fifteen years, but I still kept my fingers crossed every time I saw him get angry. And, apparently, accidentally bloodying Benson's nose hadn't done a thing to improve his temper.

I breathed a sigh of relief when he turned and stalked out of the party. Following Tad, I suspected, since he headed in the same general direction. I wondered if that was a good thing or a bad thing.

So did Michael, apparently.

"Should someone go after him? Them?" he asked.

"I don't think so," I said. "Tad seems to be pretty good at calming Faulk down," I said.

"And pretty good at involving Faulk in his problems," Michael said. "Would Faulk need calming down if it wasn't for Tad?"

I shrugged.

"I just wish Rob would at least try to keep Benson out of trouble," I said. "Where is he, anyway?"

"Rob? I haven't seen him all afternoon."

"If he's in my booth playing with the flamingos again —" I muttered.

Michael chuckled.

"Yes, he does love the flamingos," Michael said. "You should make him a brace."

"Never," I said. "Those are the only flamingos I will ever make and I'm beginning to wonder if it might not be easier to scrap the damned things and give Mrs. Fenniman her money back."

"You mean you wouldn't even make me a flock?"

"Not unless you were planning on putting them somewhere I'd never ever have to look at them."

"What a pity. I was thinking they'd make such a nice present for Mom. We could install them in a couple of weeks, when she goes down to Florida to visit her sister. It's still warm enough to pour concrete, right? She'd be so surprised."

"Okay," I said, smiling in spite of myself. "I might make an exception for your mother, since I know how overwhelmed she'd be."

Michael and I burst out laughing. I glanced around to see where Mrs. Waterston was before making another joke and saw her, rather nearby. She heard our laughter, turned, saw me, and frowned.

I sighed, wondering what I'd done now. I could never get over the feeling that she saw me as a highly unsatisfactory incumbent in the position of Michael's girlfriend, and as a completely unsuitable candidate for the vital position of daughter-in-law. Maybe she was a big part of my problem with commitment after all. Maybe I'd feel differently about moving in with Michael, much less

138

(maybe? eventually? if things worked out?) marrying him, if I sensed something even vaguely resembling approval from her.

Suddenly she headed our way.

"Hello, Mother," Michael said when she reached us. "You look very nice."

"Hello," she said. "So do you."

She glanced over at me as she said it, leaving me to guess whether I was supposed to be included in the "you" or not. I resisted the impulse to tug at my dress. Not only did the neckline seem much lower all of a sudden, but every time I looked down, my breasts looked much closer than I was used to seeing them. I had to fight the irrational fear that if I stumbled they would fly up and smack me in the face.

"Meg," Mrs. Waterston said, "did you find that recipe yet?"

"Recipe?" Michael echoed. He knew perfectly well how implausible it was for anyone to ask me for a recipe.

"I'm sorry. I've been so swamped getting ready for the fair that I really haven't had time to look. I will as soon as I get home, though."

"I'd appreciate it," she said, and sailed off.

"What was that about a recipe?" Michael asked.

"I owe your mother a recipe," I said.

"What recipe?"

"The beef with peppercorn sauce she had when she came to dinner at my place in June."

"You made the beef with peppercorn sauce?" Michael asked.

"You don't have to sound so incredulous," I said. "I'm not such a lousy cook."

"No, just an infrequent one," Michael said. "I had no idea you made that. I thought you got it from Le Rivage after you burned the roast."

"Well, of course I did," I said.

"Then why is she badgering you for the recipe?"

"Well, I didn't want to admit that I'd served her carryout food."

"Didier's *filet au poivre* isn't exactly carryout food."

"Yes, but I didn't want to admit I hadn't made it myself. So, when she asked for the recipe, I pretended I'd mislaid the card, and I looked up a recipe that sounded like the same thing and sent it to her. Apparently I didn't guess that well."

"I still don't understand. . . ." he began.

"You never will," I said, with a sigh. "It's a chick thing."

"Next time, just tell her it's an old family recipe, and your mother forbids

140

you to give it out."

"Now that might work," I said. "Better yet, I'll confess."

"That you didn't cook the sauce?"

"No, I'll confess that I lost the copy of the recipe Mother gave me, and was trying to write it down from memory, and that she'll have to get it from Mother. Mother can do the old family recipe bit much better than I ever could."

"Yes, and Mom would certainly understand your mother not wanting to give her the recipe," Michael said.

His mother had taken up a post near the center of the party, about ten feet from my mother. The two had their backs to each other, and they were both laughing, talking, and gesturing with practiced gaiety.

Suddenly they both turned and, as if on cue, reacted with visible (though implausible) delight and surprise at seeing each other and managed, despite their enormous panniers, to maneuver themselves close enough to kiss each other carefully on or near the cheek.

I wondered if real colonial grande dames lost quite so much hair powder over the course of an evening. Mrs. Waterston's shoulders had been speckled with it, like artificial dandruff, and now, when her towering wig and Mother's happened to touch during their choreographed embrace, a small cloud of powder rose, reminding me of the haze of musket smoke that began to cover the reenactors' battlefields after the first volley or two of musket fire.

"I have a bad feeling about this," I said.

"Maybe I should go round up your dad, so he and I can distract them if necessary," Michael said.

He kissed me on the cheek and launched himself through the crowd.

"Start looking near the food," I called after him. I wasn't sure he heard me, but then he knew Dad well enough by now to figure that out on his own.

I wasn't sure what had happened to set them off, but Mother and Mrs. Waterston definitely looked as if they were squaring off for battle, which in their case didn't get beyond polite sarcasm and veiled insults, but I would still rather not see them get into it.

I was about to work my way closer to them, to see if I could do anything to distract them, when I sensed someone coming up behind me. I caught a glimpse, out of the corner of my eye, of one of Mrs. Waterston's ubiquitous blue rental coats.

Not again, I thought.

14

"So what's the scoop with this Faulkner character?" Wesley Hatcher said stepping a little closer. "Where have I seen him before?"

"At craft fairs, I suppose," I said, wincing inwardly. "He's a nationally known blacksmith."

"No, that's not it," he said. "I don't normally waste a lot of time at these things, but I know I've seen him somewhere."

Unfortunately, he probably had, in a way. Faulk and his prominent patrician father did have a strong family resemblance, and I could imagine how old Mr. Cates would react if he found his family's private life plastered across the front page of the *Snooper*.

"I know there's a story there somewhere," Wesley mused.

"Wesley, could you interrogate me later?" I said. "I have a bit of a headache."

Which was, I realized, not entirely a lie.

"Probably oxygen deprivation," Wesley

said. "I don't know how you can breathe in that outfit."

"Wesley —"

"Although, come to think of it, I can see it every time you do breathe."

"Very funny."

"Hey, you don't feel a sneeze coming on, do you? I'd love to see that."

He had, I realized, inched close enough so that he was now staring down the front of my bodice. He must have had enough alcohol to overcome his previous caution.

"Wesley, if you drool on me, you'll be the one with the headache," I said, taking a giant step away. "In fact, if you don't go away this minute, I will claim you tried to paw me, and even the people who don't know you will believe it when they see this dress."

"Spoilsport," Wesley said, but he knew better than to argue with me. He melted into the crowd, heading toward the bar. I closed my eyes and rubbed my forehead. Maybe I shouldn't have chased Wesley away. At least when he was leering at my cleavage, he wasn't pumping anyone else for information on Tad and Faulk. Maybe I should go after him.

But no, someone else had already distracted him. Tony-the-louse, who had been standing by the bar, drinking steadily, greeted Wesley's arrival with a bellow of rage.

"You lousy snoop!" he shouted, and threw his pewter mug at Wesley.

"Hey!" Wesley said, as the mug bounced off his head. "What do you think you're doing?"

"If you publish that damned article, I'll rip you in two," Tony said, lurching forward to grab Wesley by the arm.

"Leave me alone," Wesley said, shaking Tony's grip off while backing away.

"Cheap, shoddy workmanship!" Tony roared. "Wait till I test one of my pokers on your head! See how shoddy that is!"

Wesley turned and ran. Tony gave chase, and they careened through the party like billiard balls. Conversation stopped until they broke free of the crowd, and then resumed, as Tony, loping slowly but persistently, disappeared in the direction he thought Wesley had taken.

I wondered, briefly, if someone should go after them. Probably unnecessary, I decided. Drunk as he was, I didn't think Tony could catch Wesley, much less do him any harm. And judging by the frown on Mrs. Waterston's face, I had every hope she'd declare each of them persona non grata for the rest of the festival. I closed my eyes again and smiled slightly, contemplating the prospect of Wesley getting kicked out of Yorktown, or at least banned from the craft fair.

"Good job, lady."

I opened my eyes to see another of Mrs. Waterston's blue rental coats, this one containing Roger Benson. Someone had made the mistake of letting him get his hands on a pewter mug that probably held at least a pint and a half of liquid, and the bartenders had compounded the mistake by filling it with something alcoholic — probably more than once, from the boiled lobster color of his face, which nearly matched the bloodstains on his shirt.

"It's your doing, I know that," he said, slurring his words slightly. "Told that brother of yours to hold out on me. Think you can hold me over the barrel for more money."

"That's not the idea at all," I said.

"Crap!" he said, lurching forward and thrusting his face toward mine. Since we were almost the same height, I found myself standing practically nose-to-nose with him — close enough to identify the fumes from his mug as gin and tonic rather than beer. "You don't mean you really believe I stole some lousy program from that miserable little —"

"It's nothing personal, Mr. Benson," I said, interrupting him before he could say anything about Tad that would make me really lose my temper. "But I'm sure you can see that, under the circumstances, it's better for all concerned if we clear up these accusations before proceeding."

"I can't believe you'd actually listen to that crap from Jackson," Benson went on. "You know what they're like — pathological liars, every one of them."

"I've found most of the programmers I've met are unusually honest," I said. "Maybe a little overly literal, but I suppose they can't help that. Or were you talking about MIT graduates? I admit, I do find them a little vague on the difference between reality and cyberspace, but you know, it's not really Tad's fault. They offered him a better scholarship than Caltech and Carnegie-Mellon."

"I don't care where he went to school. He's lying."

"Mr. Benson, I've known Tad for some months, and I've never had any reason to suspect him of lying," I said. "I barely met you five hours ago, and already, if I knew where you were staying, I'd call them up and tell them to lock up the silverware. Don't push it."

"Go ahead, Missy," he said, taking another step forward and spilling some of his gin and tonic on my skirt. "If you want to screw up your brother's chances of ever getting his miserable little game published, just keep on the way you're going. If I were you —"

"If I were you, I'd drop it," I said.

"But —"

"Get the hell out of here," I hissed.

Benson opened his mouth, then realized, even through the alcohol, how serious I was. He lurched away. I saw him stop by the bar for a refill, then he left the party. Good riddance.

Yes, I was definitely getting a headache. If I were a better person, I would go in search of Faulk and/or Tad; hunt down Mother and keep her away from Mrs. Waterston; mingle with the crowd to show off Mrs. Tranh's handiwork; or do any one of a thousand things to make the party a success. Instead, I snagged another glass of wine from a passing waiter and moved a little farther back into the shadows, hoping no one would notice me.

I could see Michael standing in a small group that included Dad, Mrs. Fenniman,

Aunt Phoebe, and Uncle Stanley, within easy reach of the food tables and only a few paces away from the bar. They were all talking animatedly about something. A kamikaze installation of wrought-iron flamingos throughout the neighborhood, perhaps? Probably not. There were bound to be laws against that, and Uncle Stanley was a judge — a federal judge, though. Maybe federal judges didn't care about mere local infractions.

As I watched, Michael stepped toward the bar — a little away from the group, but still close enough to talk to them over his shoulder. I watched as he ferried fresh drinks back to my relatives. I thought of joining them, then decided I was better off where I was. I'd rather be back in the tent, preferably with Michael. I'd have suggested leaving, but I knew that a few more glasses of wine would greatly increase the odds that, when we got there, Michael would be too busy helping me out of my stays to get into a discussion about the state of our relationship.

Someone cleared his throat behind me, and a hand touched my upper arm. I could see that the hand emerged from a sleeve of the now-familiar blue that both Wesley and Benson were wearing.

Okay, I should have stopped to take a deep breath and counted to ten, but I'd had it with these jerks.

"Dammit!" I said, whirling around. "Just leave me the hell alone, will you? I don't want to —"

I suddenly realized that I was yelling at cousin Horace who, of course, was wearing one of Mrs. Waterston's standard-issue blue coats, like Wesley and Benson and half the men at the party.

"Sorry, sorry," he was muttering, backing away as if from a rattlesnake.

"I'm sorry, Horace," I said. "I thought you were someone else."

"I usually am," he said, continuing to back away with a fixed smile on his face.

"Horace! Wait. I — oh, never mind," I said, as Horace collided with a waiter carrying a food tray and melted into the crowd under cover of the falling hors d'oeuvres. People were staring at me, including several disapproving relatives.

Well, I couldn't blame them. Shouting at poor, harmless Horace had to be a new low, even for me. I don't think I'd have felt any worse if I'd kicked Spike. Actually, Spike sometimes deserved kicking, while poor Horace . . .

Clearly I was unfit for human company

right now. People were turning back to their conversations, and from my place at the edge of the lighted area, I found it easy to slip into the shadows under the trees. No one seemed to notice my absence — not even Michael, still absorbed in his animated discussion with Dad.

Which was okay. I needed some time alone. My mother was fond of remarking how wonderful it was that Meg had grown up from a cantankerous child into such an even-tempered young lady. The first time I heard her say it, I burst out laughing. I felt as if I'd spent half my life searching for ways to control my temper. I'd discovered a lot of great stuff along the way — yoga, for example, and even my ironworking career. Pounding on things with a hammer does wonders to work off anger. But I still thought of myself as a volcano waiting to blow. Although these days I usually managed not to blow until I was by myself, and to get my anger out of my system before going back into the human race again. Which isn't my definition of even-tempered, but I suppose it's better than nothing. Lurking in the shadows wasn't going to do the trick tonight, though. I needed someplace more private where I could pace, mutter, curse, and maybe even kick a few things for good measure.

There was precious little privacy to be found in the tent city where Michael and I were camping. Mother and Dad were hosting the usual motley assortment of relatives, some of whom were sure to be lurking around the house.

The booth. No one would be at the fair grounds this time of night. I could not only get the privacy I needed, but I could even work off some of my temper rearranging my ironwork. And, come to think of it, I would feel better if I collected my cash box and laptop and took them to the tent. Even though I had locked them in the storage cases, I'd actually rather have them with me.

I fished in my pocket and checked the wristwatch I'd hidden there. It was nearly ten; the party was supposed to go on until eleven. I'd have at least an hour to cool down and meet Michael back here at the party.

I slipped away, stopping by the dressing room to collect my haversack from Mrs. Tranh's ladies. The string quartet faded in the distance as I strode down the lane toward the craft-fair grounds. I fumbled in my haversack until I found the laminated badge that identified me as one of the exhibitors and hung it around my neck, just in case I ran into any nitpicking members of the Town Watch, although that seemed unlikely. The last time I'd looked they were all at the party, diligently guarding the buffet tables and the cash bar.

Maybe this wasn't such a good idea, I thought, as I slipped through the silent lanes, starting at shadows. The party noise seemed far behind now. Even the intermittent boom of the artillery sounded subdued, and the crackle of my footsteps on the straw-covered lane seemed deafening. And then, as I neared the town square —

"Help!" came a cry. "Can anyone hear me? Help!"

I quickened my steps and got a good grip on my haversack, so I could use it as a weapon if need be, all the while telling myself I was an idiot for not going in search of help. The bag wasn't much of a weapon, and if I actually had to cosh someone with it, I'd probably break my cell phone.

When I reached the square, I stepped on something. A hand. I peered down, and saw Tony-the-louse lying facedown on the gravel.

"Tony!" I exclaimed. I bent down and touched the hand. Still warm. I was about to check for a pulse when a loud snore reassured me that Tony wasn't dead. Only dead drunk.

"Meg? Is that you?"

Wesley's voice. I recognized it now.

"Wesley?" I called. "What's wrong? Where are you?"

"Over here."

"Over where? In case you hadn't noticed, it's a little dark out here."

"Over here in the stocks."

I ventured further into the square, until I could see the stocks. I could also see Wesley's back, rump, and legs. He was wiggling, trying either to escape from the stocks or to turn and look at me, but his head and arms were pinioned too tightly for either.

I strolled around to the front of the stocks. Wesley, still trying to break free, rattled the padlock that secured the stocks.

"There you are!" he said.

I checked the padlock. It wasn't just for show. Someone had locked it. And the spare key wasn't hanging on the hook beneath the platform where we left it in case of accidents.

"Don't just stand there, get me out," Wesley said.

"I'd be happy to if I knew where the key was."

"That idiot Tony has it, of course."

"You might have mentioned that before I walked all the way over here," I said, turning back to where Tony lay snoring.

But Tony didn't have the key — not in his hand or any of his pockets, and I didn't find it lying on the ground around him.

"He must have dropped it while he was capering around," Wesley said, when I reported my failure.

"Capering around?"

"After he locked me up, he was running up and down the square, taunting me until he passed out," Wesley said. "You'll need to search around some more."

"Fat chance," I said. "See you."

"You can't abandon me here!" Wesley shrieked.

"I'm not abandoning you. I'm going in search of help," I said. "I'm sure one of the other watchmen has the key, and if I can't find one, I'll use Horace's wrench and unbolt the hinge on the other side."

"Hurry up," Wesley grumbled.

I felt a little less nervous as I left the square for the lane leading to my booth. And, I had to admit, also a lot less out-of-sorts. Seeing Wesley in the stocks had improved my mood, and taking refuge on the familiar ground of my booth — not to mention taking possession of my laptop and my cash box — would complete the recovery, I was sure. Illogical, of course, since the ground my booth stood on was no more familiar than a hundred other small squares of land on which Eileen and I had set it up over the last few years. Still, the booth was, however temporarily, my turf. But instead of feeling safe, I felt my anxiety soar when I stepped into the booth and looked around.

It was a shambles. Half the ironwork on the table had been tipped over, and the rest had been knocked off to join the jumbled heap on the ground.

A strong wind? No, Eileen's pottery was completely undisturbed. Even the spray of dried heather gracing one delicate vase barely stirred in the still, humid air. Someone had vandalized my side of the booth.

"Tony, you snake," I muttered, as I reached down to set a candelabrum upright.

Which probably wasn't fair; I could think of a few other people who might have it in for me. But for some reason I was sure Tony had done this.

Even if I hadn't known about the time he'd done the same thing to Faulk's booth, I'd have guessed; it was just his style.

Crude. Mindless. And ultimately ineffective, since he'd at least had the decency to leave Eileen's stuff alone, and he'd have had to work a lot harder — and use better tools — to cause any permanent damage to my stuff.

Unless he'd gone after my laptop, I thought, suddenly. Or unless someone had cleverly faked the kind of damage Tony would do as a cover-up for a raid on my cash box.

I put down the andirons I'd been picking up, rushed to the back of the booth, and swept the curtain open. I was expecting to find a similar scene of shambles — the storage case jimmied open, fragments of my laptop strewn around, my cash box overturned and empty, save for a few small coins.

I wasn't expecting to find a body.

15

"Well, at least he's in period," I muttered, as I looked down at the body. Whoever he was — his face was hidden by an inexpensive tricorn hat — he was wearing one of Mrs. Waterston's ubiquitous blue colonial coats. With my falcon dagger buried to the hilt in the middle of the back.

I backed away, fumbled in my haversack, and managed to locate my cell phone. Thank heaven for anachronisms. It took me two tries to hit the ON button, and I was so rattled that I got directory assistance instead of 911 the first time I dialed.

"I do hope you're somebody I used to like," I said to the body as I stood looking down at it and waiting for the police to arrive. "Not a lot, of course; but if you're someone I didn't like, the sheriff will probably arrest me on the spot." At least that was the way it always happened in the mystery books my dad constantly read and recommended to me — the cops loved to suspect whoever found the body. Owning the murder weapon and the scene of the crime probably weren't too cool either. I found myself resenting the deceased, whoever he was, for managing to involve me so thoroughly in his murder.

And of course, by that time, I couldn't stand not knowing who he was. I picked up a pair of iron firewood tongs, stepped a little closer to the body again, and used the tongs to lift up the edge of the tricorn hat, just enough to see his face.

Roger Benson.

"Damn," I said, letting the tricorn hat fall back into place. I could feel my headache kick in again, just at the sight of him, even before I started to consider all the complications his murder could cause.

"So, what's the problem here?" came a familiar voice from behind me.

"Someone's been murdered, Sheriff," I said

"Murdered!" the sheriff exclaimed. "Oh, dear."

He stepped forward, rather hesitantly, and peered at the body.

"He's in costume," he said.

"Most of us are," I said. Including, of course, the sheriff himself, who had changed out of his tomato-spattered blue colonial coat into another one in an astonishingly vile shade of greenish mustard.

"Yes, but is there any chance this could be one of those living-history reenactment things?"

"I doubt it," I said.

"Sir?" the sheriff called. "Sir? Excuse me, but if you're doing a reenactment, could you kind of give us a clue? So we don't have to get all the squad cars and ambulances and such out here and spoil the period ambiance? Sir?"

No response from the corpse — and unlike the sheriff, I wasn't holding my breath, waiting for one.

"Who is he?" the sheriff asked. "Do you know?"

I held out the fireplace tongs. The sheriff looked at them as if he had no idea what I was suggesting, so I reached out again myself and lifted the tricorn hat enough for us to get another glimpse of Roger Benson's face.

"Oh dear," the sheriff said again. "I hope Monty gets here soon."

"Monty?"

I let the hat fall down again.

"My new deputy," the sheriff said. "He's got big-city police experience."

"Really? What city?"

"Cleveland?" the sheriff said. "Or is it

Columbus? Someplace in Ohio."

"Cincinnati, maybe?" I asked.

"Could be. Someplace like that. You can ask him when he gets here."

I nodded. Not that it mattered, but it gave us something to babble about while we both stood staring fixedly at the late Mr. Benson.

"He does all our homicides," the sheriff went on.

"You've had a lot since he got here?" I asked. Yorktown wasn't exactly a hotbed of crime.

"Oh, no," the sheriff said. "Actually, I can't remember that we've had one since he got here, come to think of it. But if we had, he'd have been the one to handle it. He had a lot of experience back there in Cincinnati."

"Or Cleveland."

"Wherever," the sheriff agreed.

"So what do we have here?" boomed a flat midwestern voice.

I turned to see a tall beanpole of a man in a deputy's uniform, standing at the entrance to my booth with his hands on his hips.

"Murder," I said, as the sheriff and I walked over to meet the newcomer. A little brass nametag on his chest said "R.B. MONT-GOMERY," so I assumed he was the homicidally experienced Monty.

161

"I see," Monty said. He took a small notebook out of his pocket, checked his watch, scribbled something in the notebook, then looked back up at me. "Want to tell us about it?"

"Nothing much to tell," I said, rubbing my forehead. The headache was getting worse.

"What happened, he try to stiff you for your fee?" Monty said. "Or are you going to claim you changed your mind at the last minute and had to defend yourself?"

My mouth fell open in astonishment, and I stifled the impulse to giggle. I was willing to bet he'd started to inspect me from head to toe and gotten stalled just below shoulder level.

"Monty!" the sheriff exclaimed. "This is my cousin, Meg Langslow. She was attending a costume party when she found this body."

"Costume party?" Monty said, looking around the deserted booth.

"The party's at the Moore House," I said. "I was leaving the party to go back to my tent, and I stopped by my booth on the way to pick up my cash box. I found the booth ransacked" — I indicated the fallen ironwork — "and a body in my storage area, behind those curtains."

"I see," Monty said. He was still studying my costume with overmuch interest.

"Look, Monty," I said. "I don't know how the hell they do these things in Columbus —"

"Cincinnati," the sheriff corrected.

"Actually, I came here from Canton," Monty said, frowning.

"But here in Yorktown, we expect our law-enforcement officials to do something when they arrive at a crime scene. Something more than leer at the witnesses."

"Witnesses, sure," Monty said, with an insulting chuckle.

"Aren't you going to check the body, Monty?" the sheriff asked.

"I don't want to contaminate the scene any more than it's already been contaminated by you two," Monty said. "I'm waiting for the crime-scene technician; I've sent a patrol officer out to find him."

"We have a crime-scene technician?" the sheriff asked. "When did that happen?"

"You remember, that file clerk who turned out to have a chemistry degree," Monty said, with exasperation. "You signed off last month on sending him up to Richmond for the training courses."

"Oh, Horace," the sheriff said. "That's right. How's he doing, anyway?"

"Well, we'll find out when he gets here, won't we?" Monty said, looking at his watch.

Just then Cousin Horace, looking more mouselike than ever, stuck his head around the corner of my booth.

"Jimmy said you wanted me here," he said. "What's the — Oh, hi, Meg."

"You know this man?" Monty demanded.

"It's a small town, Monty," the sheriff said. "Everybody knows everybody; I keep telling you that."

"I'm Meg's cousin," Horace said, rather timidly, as if he still wasn't sure of his welcome.

"I thought he was your cousin," Monty said to the sheriff.

"Yes, he's my cousin, too," the sheriff said.

"We're all cousins," Horace said.

"Nearly everybody in town is cousins," I said. "You've got to make allowances for inbreeding, Monty. We're actually not that bad. You should see some of the cousins we hide in the attics."

I suppose it would have been different if I'd said that in front of someone who'd find it funny. But Cousin Horace and the sheriff had grown used to just nodding and smiling whenever I said anything they didn't understand, and their reactions probably gave Monty the idea I was serious. I sighed.

"Why don't you let Horace do his crime-scene thing?" I said. "If you don't want to listen to my story now, I'd like to go someplace where I can lie down. I'm getting a headache."

"Oh, I want to hear your story all right," Monty said. "And you're not going anywhere until you take off that dress."

"Excuse me?"

"I need it for evidence," Monty said.

"Evidence?" the sheriff echoed.

"She says she found the body, but how do we know that?" Monty explained. "We need to test the dress for blood spatters."

Horace, the sheriff, and I looked down at my dress — which, except for the faint damp spot where Benson had spilled his gin and tonic, looked perfectly spotless.

"Minute blood spatters, okay?" Monty said.

Just then, I saw Michael and Dad coming down the lane.

"Meg! What's going on?" Michael called. "They came and got your cousin Horace and —"

"Stand back!" Monty snapped. "This is a crime scene!"

"Michael, could you go to the tent and get

165

some clothes for me to change into?" I asked. "Jeans, please. I think the masquerade's over for the evening."

Michael looked around, decided that I was safe enough with Dad, Horace, and the sheriff at my side, then nodded and took off.

"Meg, what's happened?" Dad asked.

"Someone killed Mr. Benson in my booth," I said.

"Killed?" Dad said. "Do you think it's murder, then? How exciting!"

"Who's this?" Monty asked. "Another cousin?"

"Well, yes," the sheriff said. "By marriage, anyway. This is Meg's dad."

"Would you like me to examine the body?" Dad asked.

Monty looked alarmed and stepped protectively between Dad and the body.

"He's a doctor," I explained. "A medical doctor. He's . . . uh, he's had some experience with crime scenes." I didn't mention that his experience consisted largely of horning in on any homicide investigation that happened in his vicinity; I didn't think that would do much to allay Deputy Monty's obvious distrust. Dad beamed at me.

"I think we'd rather have the coroner for that," Monty said.

"He might still be at the party," Dad said, looking at his watch. "Want me to go and see? This'll go a lot faster if we catch him before he starts for home."

The fact that it might also give Dad a chance to talk the coroner into letting Dad help him was, of course, irrelevant.

"I'd appreciate it, James," the sheriff said. "And maybe one of the female officers, if you see any? To supervise when Meg . . . um . . ."

"Right," Dad said.

Oh, great, I thought. I had to wait for a suitable audience to change out of my dress. I hoped Dad would hurry. The air was getting cool, which wouldn't have bothered me if I'd been fully dressed.

"And I'll look for someone to rescue Wesley while I'm at it," Dad said.

"Oh, my God," I said. "I forgot all about Wesley!"

"That nosy reporter? What's wrong with him?" Monty asked, his hand hovering over his gun.

I explained Wesley's plight, and they all had to troop out to the town square to take a look, leaving me and Horace at the crime scene.

I watched, interested in spite of myself, as Horace donned a pair of latex gloves and began collecting evidence. This was a new side of Horace, I realized. He examined things, photographed things, put things in plastic bags, and dusted everything in sight for fingerprints. I wouldn't go so far as to say that he exuded confidence or anything hokey like that, but he didn't drop or break anything the whole time, which had to be a first for Horace.

The others returned, and we all stood around watching and listening to the occasional distant whine of complaint from Wesley. Eventually Dad arrived with the coroner. Who, to no one's surprise, pronounced Roger Benson dead, and scuttled away to let Horace do his forensic chores on and around the body. I watched with fascination as the previously squeamish and mild-mannered Horace fingerprinted the deceased as if he'd been hobnobbing with corpses all his life. Okay, if Monty had even accidentally helped bring about this transformation in Horace, maybe he wasn't all bad.

Dad, prevented from joining in the forensic fun, went off to continue searching for someone with a key to the padlock on the stocks. And the coroner was characteristically cagey about the time of death.

"I can't give you a range of less than three

of four hours until I do the postmortem," he said. "And maybe not then."

"We can estimate closer than that even without the postmortem," I said. "I left the party at about ten, and I was talking to Benson about fifteen or twenty minutes before I left. Allowing about five minutes for the walk, he couldn't have gotten here much earlier than nine forty-five. And I'm sure you know what time I called 911."

"Ten thirty-five," the sheriff said. "Ricky paged me as soon as he got the call."

"See? That narrows it down to about forty-five minutes, from nine forty-five to ten thirty."

"And your own notebook will back that up," the sheriff said. "What time was it when you started interrogating Meg here?"

"Ten forty-five," Monty said, frowning.

"Are you sure?" the sheriff said. "It's a good fifteen minutes from the station down here."

"I wasn't at the station when I got the call," Monty said. "I was already heading this way to investigate a noise complaint about those damned cannons."

"We have our time range, then," the sheriff nodded, looking pleased with himself.

"Of course, we only have Ms. Langslow's

word that Mr. Benson was still at the party at nine forty-five."

"Ask around," I said. "If no one noticed my quarrel with him —"

"Quarrel? You had a quarrel with the deceased?"

"Yes, I had a quarrel with the deceased; so did several other people," I said. "The man was not well liked."

"Another cousin, I suppose," Monty said.

"Mr. Benson?" the sheriff said. "No, he's no relation. In fact, he's not from around here."

"Which means he's probably only been here about ten years or so, right?" Monty said, sounding a little resentful.

"More like ten hours," I said. "He came to town for a business meeting with my brother, Rob."

"Now that's interesting," Monty said.

I was afraid he'd think that.

16

Horace continued patiently scraping and sampling around my booth, like an ant in strange territory, examining every leaf, twig, and dirt clod on the off chance it might be edible. Meanwhile, Monty badgered me into describing every encounter I'd had with Roger Benson during the day. I already didn't like the way this was going. Although I was obviously still Monty's favorite suspect, he showed far too much interest in Rob, Faulk, and Tad. And also far too much interest in leering at my costume, to judge by the increasingly black looks he got from Michael.

The ambulance crew came and left with Benson. Even patient Cousin Horace was running out of forensic steam and still Monty continued questioning me.

"So, can you think of anyone else who might have a reason to dislike the deceased?" Monty said, finally. He stared intently at me, as if he suspected I was holding something back. Which I was. For the past half hour I'd been fighting the over-whelming urge to say that if disliking someone was reason for murder, Deputy Monty had better hire a bodyguard if he planned to stay in town much longer. Fortu-nately, Cousin Horace intervened.

"Mrs. Fenniman," he said, glancing up as he scraped little bits of dirt into a plastic bag. "I heard her say at the party that he was a no-good sneak thief, and someone should shoot him down like a rabid dog."

"But he wasn't shot," the sheriff said. "And besides, I don't think Mrs. Fenniman even owns a gun."

"I didn't say she did," Horace said. "But that's what she said."

"She has her grandfather's Civil War sword," Dad put in.

"But what does that matter if —"

"We'll put her down as having reason to dislike the deceased," Monty interrupted, looking up from his notebook.

Monty finally let me change out of my costume, under the careful scrutiny of the waiting female officer. Cousin Horace pro-duced evidence bags large enough to hold the dress, the stays, and all the other parts of my outfit.

"Is it okay if I take my laptop and my cash box with me, for safekeeping?" I asked.

"That depends," Monty said. "Where did you leave them?"

"In one of my storage cases," I said, pointing. "The padlocked one."

The deputy looked at Cousin Horace, who shrugged.

"If it was in a locked case, why not?" he said. "Anyway, we're all finished here."

"Give me the key, then," Monty said, holding out his hand.

I handed my keyring over, with the padlock key separated out from the rest, and watched in exasperation as he let it fall back into the bunch and proceeded to try five or six other keys, including several that any halfwit should have known weren't right. Did he really think Honda made padlocks?

"Ah, that's got it," he said, when he finally got around to the right key. He removed the padlock and lifted up the lid of the case.

"I thought you wanted a computer and a cash box," he said.

"I do," I said.

"Nothing but birds in here."

"Birds?"

I ducked under the yellow crime-scene tape and went to where I could look over his shoulder. Sure enough, the case he'd just opened was filled to the brim with pink wrought-iron flamingos.

"That's the wrong case," I said.

"Only one with a padlock."

I shoved past him, ignoring his protests, and began opening the other cases. Most were empty, their former contents used to stock my booth. But I found the case where I'd stowed the computer and the cash box. The computer was there. The cash box wasn't.

"They've taken my cash box," I said.

"Nonsense, you're just looking in the wrong case," Monty said.

But my cash box wasn't in any of the cases. It wasn't anywhere in the booth.

"Maybe you took it with you when you left the booth."

"For heaven's sake, I know what I did with it," I said, exasperated. "I was going straight from the booth to Mrs. Waterston's party. Why on Earth would I lug along my cash box? I'm very sure I put it and the laptop in this case and padlocked the case to keep them safe till I got back."

"Only you didn't padlock the case," he said.

"Yes, I'm sure I did," I said.

Monty crooked an eyebrow.

"Obviously someone came in, picked the padlock, took my cash box, and — of course! That would explain what happened to Mr. Benson!" I exclaimed. "He interrupted a robbery in progress! The robber killed him, and was so rattled that he put the padlock on the wrong case."

I thought it was a brilliant theory, but Monty looked unmoved.

"That's very interesting," he said. "We'll keep that in mind as we investigate."

Yeah, sure you will, I thought.

"You ask me, the killer only took the money box to distract us," Monty said. "Whoever did it rifled the booth to make it look like a burglary and lucked out, finding you'd padlocked the wrong case. He took the cash box to make it look like a robbery, but not the computer."

"And why not the computer?" I said. "The cash box only had about a thousand dollars in it —"

"Must be nice to be rich enough not to miss a grand when you lose it," Monty said.

"I didn't say I wouldn't miss it," I said, gritting my teeth. "As a matter of fact, if you don't find it, I'll be eating macaroni and cheese till Ground Hog Day. I meant that my laptop's worth at least twice that. Why would the killer take the cash box to cover up his motive and not a much more valuable laptop?"

"Well, maybe a laptop's a lot harder for the killer to dispose of," Monty said. "One bill spends just like another, but if the killer's an amateur and doesn't know how to fence stolen goods, what's he supposed to do with a laptop? Or maybe —"

He narrowed his eyes, and I knew I wasn't going to like what he said next.

"Maybe the killer didn't want to take the laptop because he knew it was more expensive and, what's more, a lot more trouble for you to replace," he said. "Bet you've got all your business records and stuff on the laptop, right?"

I nodded.

"So maybe the killer's someone you know, and didn't want to hurt you any more than he had to."

"That's ridiculous," I said, but I didn't sound very convincing. "Besides, I just noticed something else."

"What?" Monty said, sounding impatient.

"The CD-ROM drive isn't completely closed," I said.

"Oh, for crying out loud," he muttered.

"And someone has definitely been messing with it," I said, wiping fingerprint dust off my fingers and using a corner of my sweatshirt to pull the CD drawer all the way open.

"How can you tell?"

"Look at this," I said.

"Looks like a normal CD to me," he said, giving it a cursory glance. Michael, looking over my shoulder, gave it a closer inspection, then looked up to me with one eyebrow raised.

"It's a perfectly normal CD-ROM, but it's upside down. See?" I said, picking up the CD-ROM by the edges and holding it up. "The label side was down. I was playing this game a couple of nights ago, and that's the last time I touched the CD-ROM drive. I know I didn't put it in upside down; I don't even think it would play in that position."

Deputy Monty didn't seem to find this very interesting, but he had Cousin Horace bag the laptop as evidence, too. I hoped they took me seriously and dusted the CD for prints or something; otherwise, all I'd accomplished was severely inconveniencing myself by the loss — temporary, I hoped — of my computer as well as my cash.

"Don't worry, we know how to take care of these things," Monty said, waving away my anxious questions about what fingerprint powder would do to my CD-ROM drive. "Why don't you folks go along home? We've got a lot of work to do here. And I'd like to finish as much as possible before the press show up."

So about one A.M., Michael and I finally headed back toward the encampment, hoping to avoid the Town Watch, who would probably jump at the chance to book me for running around in jeans and a sweatshirt. If the Town Watch were still awake. More likely they'd gone home like everybody else when they figured out that Monty wasn't letting anyone gawk at the crime scene. Fat lot of good they'd been at guarding things.

"Well, at least we don't have to worry about how to keep Benson from stealing Rob's software," Michael said.

"True. All we have to worry about is how to keep Rob from getting arrested for murder," I said. "Or me, for that matter."

"Surely they'll figure out from the dress that you couldn't have stabbed him," Michael said. "And Rob probably has an alibi, although I can't believe any sane person would think Rob capable of stabbing someone."

"Oh, that's interesting," I said. "I'll be cleared by forensic evidence and Rob by the strength of his character, is that it? Very complimentary."

"I wouldn't say strength of character,

no," Michael said. "More the opposite, really. I think you'd have the gumption to stab someone if you had to — in self-defense, or to protect someone. But Rob? Not likely."

"True, but will a homicide detective believe that? Or a jury?"

"I'm sure it won't come to that," Michael said. "Hey, at least your dad has an alibi. He was with me the whole time you were gone."

"Well, that's a relief," I said. "And that means you have an alibi, too."

"And I'm sure your brother will."

"Which means I'll only have to worry about Faulk, and Tad, and Mrs. Fenniman, and I don't even know who else yet. I'm not sure I'm all that impressed with Deputy Monty's big-city homicide experience."

We stopped talking when we got to the edge of the encampment. Here and there we saw campfires, and when we passed one, we'd nod to the half dozen reenactors gathered around it. But most of the camp had turned in. No wonder. Everyone would have a busy day tomorrow. The men, and the few women who had enlisted in units, would be marching and drilling, firing and cleaning their muskets, and in the late afternoon, participating in a skirmish as a dress rehearsal for Sunday's pitched battle.

179

Meanwhile, if yesterday was anything to go by, the women would air the bedding, cook three square meals, and clean up afterwards, using water that had to be hauled an authentically inconvenient distance. Not to mention minding any children or livestock who happened to have come along, arguing with the Anachronism Police, and hunting down anything the men misplaced — which, thanks to some innate male talent, they seemed to do as easily in a six- by eight-foot tent as in a full-sized house. And quite a few of the women would be giving the tourists demonstrations of buttermaking, soapmaking, candlemaking, quilting, and authentic colonial laundry techniques.

I noticed that none of the stragglers loafing around the campfires were women.

Eventually we left the reenactors' area and reached the crafters' section. I'd done my best to see that everyone followed Mrs. Waterston's detailed instructions on what was and wasn't allowed in camp. But whoever laid out the plan for the tent city had apparently foreseen that the crafters' efforts at authenticity would be just a little more haphazard, half-hearted, and implausible than those of the more experienced reenactors. They'd put us at the back, as far as possible from the road — which wasn't really a hardship; we were closer to the water tanks and the privies.

Michael and I ducked into our tent. An authentic period tent, made of off-white canvas. The rope ties that held the flaps closed on either end didn't do much to keep out the bugs; I had my doubts about whether it was waterproof; and it cost several times what a cheap, modern, nylon tent would have. But it was undoubtedly authentic.

And tiny. About six feet wide at the base, eight feet long, and too short for either of us to stand upright. Michael and I had a hard enough time sharing it, and I felt sorry for the rank-and-file colonial soldiers, who supposedly slept six to a tent of this size.

While I tried to straighten out our bedroll, Michael managed to find and light a small battery-powered lantern.

"Alone at last," he said. "Too bad Deputy Monty insisted on keeping the stays as well as the gown."

17

I glanced up in surprise. Somehow Michael's voice didn't sound as if he were suffering keen disappointment at missing the chance to extract me from my stays. Then again, we'd had a long day.

"They'll give the stays back, eventually," I said. "I can wear them to the next regimental event."

No reaction.

"Test your theory about my needing help getting out of them."

A faint smile. It was too late for this, and I was too tired.

"Michael," I said. "Is something wrong?"

"We need to talk."

I sensed this was going to be one of those "serious discussions" that occur at key stages of a relationship. Usually, in my relationships, at moments when I have neither the energy nor the patience to cope with them. I was opening my mouth to reply, still trying to figure out exactly what I was supposed to say, when I heard a voice through the canvas behind me.

"Do you have to talk right now?" the voice asked. "We've all got an early day tomorrow."

"Oh, hush up," came another voice, from behind Michael. "It was just getting interesting."

I poked my head out of the tent flap. No one was crouched with ears glued to the canvas wall of the tent. All the surrounding tents were dark.

"Maybe it's interesting to you," came the first voice, from the tent to my left. "Some of us need our sleep."

"So buy yourself some earplugs," came the second voice, from the tent to my right.

"Hey!" came a voice from across the way. "Ya'll having a party over there? I've got some beer on ice."

"We need to talk someplace else," I said.

"Definitely," Michael agreed.

We put our shoes back on and began walking through the camp.

I had to admit, the canvas tents did have their charm. From the outside. Looking out over a sea of them, with scattered ones here and there glowing golden from a lamp or a flickering lantern within, you could almost imagine yourself really walking through Washington's camp.

And on a more practical note, the white color made it a lot harder to bump into them in the dark. I wished the same could be said for the astonishing variety of shin-bruising junk people left lying around in front of their tents.

A few yards down from ours, we passed Tad's and Faulk's tent. It looked just like all the other tents, of course, especially in the dark. But I could hear their voices. I couldn't make out more than one word in ten, but I could tell from the tone that they were quarrelling.

"I'd suggest sticking my head in to interrupt that and find out if Tad and Faulk have heard about the murder," I said, in a low voice. "But since you still seem to resent Faulk for some obscure and irrational reason —"

"I don't resent Faulk," Michael said. "Not him particularly, anyway."

"Then why do you frown every time you see him or hear his name."

"He's a symbol right now. Of the whole other side of your life."

"You mean my career?"

"Your career, and everything else that keeps us from spending time together," he said. "Take this weekend. We come down here together, but you spend so much time taking care of your family and your friends that we hardly see each other."

"Michael we've already —"

"I know. We've already talked about this weekend," he said. "And you're right, it isn't a good example. But what about that week we were going to spend together at the Outer Banks?"

"Also not a good example," I said. "You were the one who canceled that, when you had to go to Vancouver to film that part on your friend's TV series."

"I didn't cancel, I rescheduled," he said.

"From a week I'd kept open on my calendar for months, specifically for the Outer Banks trip, to a week when I had a show scheduled," I said. "A very prestigious show that I've been trying to crack for ten years, not to mention the fact that I'd paid a stiff, nonrefundable registration fee."

"I can't believe you're still mad about the TV part," Michael said.

"I'm not mad," I said. "I'm looking forward to seeing the show. I only brought it up because you brought up canceling the Outer Banks —"

"Could you keep it down out there?" someone asked, from a nearby tent.

"Sorry," we both murmured.

We strolled in silence, until we reached

the highway that divided the battlefield in two — and apparently marked the northern boundary of the encampment.

"Weren't there tents above the road?" I said, frowning. "I could have sworn there were people setting up over there this morning, and now — damn!"

I jumped, as the cannon went off, sounding much louder than it did at the craft fair. Though, curiously, it didn't seem to shake the ground any more. Perhaps I was getting used to it.

"The cannon's right over there somewhere," Michael said, pointing off to our left.

"That's right. I suppose they're aiming at the redoubts."

"The what?"

"The redoubts — that's the technical term for those forts on the battlefield. You know, the earth embankments with the wooden stakes sticking out the sides and ditches all around them?"

"Oh, so that's what a redoubt is," Michael said. "My regiment's been talking for weeks about how we're going to storm one this weekend, and I've been too embarrassed to admit I didn't know what a redoubt was. I should have asked you ages ago."

"Redoubt Nine, probably; the French forces actually did storm that a few days before the end of the siege."

I jumped as the cannon boomed again.

"I can guess what happened to the people who used to have their tents over here," I said.

"Yeah, looks like they all moved farther from the artillery. That's why the rest of the camp is so crowded."

"I can't believe they're really going to keep doing that all night," I fumed. "Come on, let's go talk to them."

"Meg, I thought we —"

"Michael, I know you want to have a serious conversation," I called over my shoulder, as I strode over the battlefield toward where the artillery squad had camped. "But I'm half-asleep and cranky and preoccupied with everything that's happened tonight. Having a serious talk right now would stack the deck in favor of an argument I don't want to have. But if you help me talk those beastly gunners into shutting the hell up for the rest of the night, not only is that a subject that I think we can both agree on, but I will probably be grateful enough to — awk!"

I found myself lying facedown on the ground.

"Halt! Who goes there!"

"Oh, for the love of —" I muttered.

"Meg!" Michael called. "What happened?"

"I tripped over something," I said, levering myself up.

"I said, Halt! Who goes there!"

"Gatinois chasseurs," Michael called out to the invisible sentry. "Are you all right?" he said to me.

"Did I ever tell you that there are cactus on the battlefields?"

"Cactus?"

"Approach and be recognized, *Gatinois chasseurs,"* the sentry called.

"Hang on a moment, will you?" Michael called.

"Yes, cactus," I repeated. "Tiny little cactus, only a few inches tall."

"Meg, did you hit your head when you fell?"

"As kids, we all learned not to go barefoot on the battlefield, because of the cactus," I said. "The barbs are so fine you can't even pick them out with tweezers. Have to wait till they work their way out."

"But you're not barefoot now, are you?"

"No," I said, getting to my feet. "But I landed with my face in a clump of cactus. I do hope I didn't trip over something those miserable cannoneers strung up around their camp. We've already had one homicide tonight."

"Maybe we should talk to them later," Michael suggested.

I strode on toward the artillery crew's camp — we were close enough now to see a fire, flickering faintly in the middle of a block of tents.

I heard Michael, behind me, talking to someone. The sentry, I supposed. I'd managed to bypass him, and found myself standing in front of something.

I peered closer and realized I was staring down the mouth of the cannon.

18

Okay, I knew they probably weren't going to fire the cannon again right away, but just to be safe, I ducked well to the side. Then I realized that there was no one standing by the cannon.

Strange. They'd just fired. Before going down to my booth that morning, I'd watched the artillery crew fire the cannon, while the officer in charge gave a running commentary for the audience. It took eight people — and that was pared down from how many they'd have had in a real battle — and they went through more than thirty steps. I seemed to recall that at least a third of the steps involved cleaning the cannon up after firing. So why wasn't someone still scouring the barrel or whatever?

I moved closer again and reached out to touch the cannon's mouth. The metal was the same temperature as the surrounding air. Didn't cannons heat up, even a little, when they were fired?

I was still pondering when a man appeared from behind a nearby tent and came over to stand by the cannon.

"Quite a sight, isn't she?" he drawled, patting the barrel like a favorite horse. "Can you imagine what it must have been like, with over fifty of these babies pounding on the town?"

"Quite a sound, too; and no, I don't even want to imagine what it must have been like," I said. "Are you really planning to keep this up all night?"

He sighed.

"They're from the encampment, Jess — I mean, Captain," the sentry said, as he and Michael came up behind me. "Couldn't sleep."

"No kidding," Captain Jess said. "We're sort of obliged to keep it up all night, ma'am," he added. "Come on; if we're going to keep you awake, we can at least entertain you."

We followed Jess through the tents to the fire at the middle of the encampment. A dozen men and several women sat around the fire. One strummed a guitar. Several held steaming mugs, and some munched toasted cheese sandwiches. My stomach growled, reminding me that I had stormed away from the party, several hours ago, without eating much.

"Would you like something to drink?" Jess asked. "We have beer, hot cider, water, and a fresh pot of our national beverage. No tea, of course."

"National beverage?" Michael asked.

"Coffee," I explained. "After the Boston Tea Party, the Continental Congress made it the official national beverage. I'd love a cup."

"Me, too," Michael said.

"I still say it's an anachronism," one of the men around the fire said. "The coffee may be authentic, but not if you insist on fixing it with filters and a drip machine."

"Well, then, pour me out two mugs of hot anachronism for our guests, Mel," the captain said. " 'Cause I'm not about to spoil good coffee boiling it in the same pot you've been using for the salt pork. Do you folks take your anachronism plain, or with cream and sugar?"

I felt a little more mellow toward the artillery crew once I was sitting by their fire, sipping a cup of excellent coffee, and I didn't say no when they offered me a toasted cheese sandwich. But I couldn't help thinking that every minute brought us closer to the time when they'd feel obliged to fire off the cannon again, and I was bound and determined to stop them.

"Look," I said, when I'd polished off my snack. "I don't want to abuse your hospitality or anything, but what is it with firing the gun, anyway?"

I heard mumbles from several of the people around the fire.

"We were hired to fire it throughout the festival," Jess explained.

"Yes, I know," I said. "To simulate the shelling that began on October 9, 1781, and lasted until Cornwallis finally threw in the towel. I got that much. But why do you have to keep it up in the middle of the night, when there's no one awake to hear you? Or at least there wouldn't be anyone awake if you weren't keeping them awake."

"I'd be happy to knock off at sunset, or midnight, or any old time you like," he said. "But it isn't up to me. You'll have to take that up with Madame Von Steuben."

"Von Steuben?" Michael said.

"The Prussian general Washington brought over to whip the American troops into shape," I explained. "Noted for his harsh discipline, skill as a drillmaster, and ability to curse fluently in three languages."

"You do know your history," the captain said, with a bow.

"I grew up here," I told him, with a shrug.

"And one of this Von Steuben's

descendents is helping out with the festival?" Michael asked.

"Oh, for heavens' sake, Michael," I said. "They mean your mother, of course."

The captain's jaw dropped. Several people around the fire appeared to be choking on their coffee. Michael looked startled, then burst out laughing.

"That's perfect," he said. "Madame Von Steuben!"

"Course we don't call her that to her face," Jess said.

"Of course not," I said. "You're still alive."

"She specifically told us to keep firing sporadically all night," he said. "Said she wanted to make the experience more genuine. Help people understand what our forefathers and foremothers really went through."

"Should have told her no, like you did with the live ammo," Mel said.

"Live ammo?" I echoed.

"First time she saw us fire the cannon, she heard me explain about the recoil," Jess said. "If we were firing real shells, the gun would recoil, oh, about fourteen feet on a piece this size. That's one reason they used a larger crew than we need; about six of the guys just hauled the cannon back in place after it fired. Also the reason we shout 'Stand clear!' before firing; make sure no one's standing behind it, 'cause anyone who was, they'd be toast. If we fired live ammo, that is. When you're just firing powder, you don't get much recoil at all."

"And of course she didn't think that was authentic enough, did she?"

"Thought I'd never get her to see what the problem was," the captain grumbled. "Those shells go a long way. They shelled the town from here, remember."

"You could fire over the river," Michael suggested.

"Oh, yeah, great idea," Jess said. "There're only about five hundred fancy yachts anchored out there right about now, with the festival on."

"Sorry," Michael said.

"Hey, we could aim at the highway," one of the crew suggested. "Course I wouldn't want to waste ammo on small fry like cars. Let's see how many eighteen-wheelers we can pot."

"Tour busses," Mel advised. "You want to maximize your enemy casualties, go for the tour busses."

"Don't mind him," the captain said. "Likes to pull the tourists' legs."

"I hope they don't know where Mom

lives," Michael muttered.

"Getting back to the night firing," I said.

"She doesn't hear gunfire, she'll say we're in breach of contract," Jess said.

"Yes, but she's probably gone to bed by now."

"Yeah, 'bout an hour ago," Mel said.

"How do you know —" Michael began.

"Always good policy, in the army, keeping track of what the brass are up to," Jess said, giving Mel a dirty look.

"I'll make a deal with you," I said. "You cut out the cannon fire until, say, six A.M., and I'll make sure at least a dozen people go up to her tomorrow and complain about the cannon firing all night."

Jess looked thoughtful.

"And I'll even make sure a couple of people are nearby to tell them not to be so fussy. Once you get used to it you don't even hear the cannon, in case she doesn't remember hearing it herself."

"Be nice to get some sleep, Jess," one of his men said.

"And the same thing holds for the rest of the festival, if you stop firing between midnight and six A.M."

"You sure you can manage that?" Jess said.

"Absolutely," I said.

"No problem," Michael added.

"Shake on it then," Jess said. We shook hands, and cheers went up around the campfire. Several people said goodnight and scurried away toward tents, and Mel re-filled everyone else's coffee mugs without a single complaint about the anachronistic preparation method.

"I tell you what," the captain said, winking at his crew. "Let's fire the thing off one more time, just to seal the bargain."

The crew leaped up with such enthusiasm that I didn't have the heart to protest. After all, I decided, it was so soon after the last shot that most people wouldn't have fallen back asleep.

"In fact, you can help us," Jess said. "You can set the whole thing off."

"Thanks, I appreciate the honor, but —"

"We insist!"

Okay, if it kept them quiet the rest of the night, I'd tap dance on the bloody cannon barrel. But to my surprise, instead of leading us to the cannon, Jess stopped in front of a tent at the edge of the encampment.

"What's this?" I asked.

"Go on, look inside," Jess said.

Hesitantly, I lifted up one flap of the tent front — and found myself staring at a huge, gleaming, modern sound system, the kind roadies haul around to fuel rock bands.

"Mel, Frank, run those speakers out," Jess ordered. "Carrie, you make sure the tape is cued up right."

Mel and another soldier dragged out a pair of enormous speakers to flank the tent, while a homespun-clad woman put on a pair of earphones, fiddled with some of the controls of the sound system, and nodded to Jess.

"Earplugs, everyone," Jess ordered. "You might want to put these on, ma'am. Now, on my cue, just hit that button Carrie's pointing to, and we'll give those no-good redcoats one last volley before we retire for the evening."

I pressed the button and jumped back. Through the earplugs, I could faintly hear Jess's prerecorded voice ordering his crew through the steps of the firing drill, culminating in a satisfactorily loud boom.

"That's it for the night, folks," Jess said. Mel and Frank put the speakers away while Carrie, putting the headphones back on, rewound the tape to the proper place.

"That's how come we know your mother had already gone to bed," Jess explained, as we returned to the campfire. "As long as there's anyone here to watch us, we go through the whole drill. We like doing it, but it just seems a waste of time and powder to do the whole thing with no one watching. So we assigned a couple of our guys to take turns shadowing her. She heads our way, one of them uses the cell phone, calls my pager, and we're all correct by the time she gets here."

"Brilliant," I said.

"And so historically accurate," Michael murmured.

"Well, hell, we're not nut cases," Jess said "We're big on authenticity, don't get me wrong. You get some guys, they're not interested in the history."

"Just want to come out, fire off their black-powder guns a few times, then sit around and drink beer," Mel said, frowning at one of the other men lounging around the fire. The man lifted his mug, uttered an improbably loud belch as if it were a toast, and drained the mug.

"Some others, they're so gung-ho they want to come out and pretend the twenty-first century doesn't exist," Jess said, with a glance at Mel. "Want to do everything exactly the way it was done back then, no matter how long it takes or if there's a good reason not to. Dig privies instead of using the chemical toilets. Drink unpasteurized milk. Boil their coffee like eggs. Hell, why don't they just go ahead and bleed people when they feel sick; that's pretty authentic."

"People have a right to do what they like," Mel put in.

"And I respect that right, as long as they don't come over and try to interfere with our right to do what we like."

"Halt! Who goes there?" the sentry shouted.

"Is Meg Langslow up here?" came the reply.

"Oh, God," I said. "Wesley."

"Someone you're trying to avoid?" Jess said. "We could send him back the way he came."

"I wouldn't want to interfere with the freedom of the press," I said. "That's part of what you're all fighting for, isn't it? Let him pass if you want."

A minute later, Wesley Hatcher scuttled over to where I was sitting.

"I've been looking for you all night," Wesley said. "I understand you found the body!"

19

"Body?" Jess said. "You mean all that talk about a murder was real? I thought it was just one of those weekend murder games."

"Oh, it was real, all right," I said.

"By the time they finally found someone to let me out, the body was gone, and there was nothing to see," Wesley complained. "I've got to get an interview with you!"

"Wesley, as Mrs. Fenniman always says, the only thing you've got to do in this world is live until you die. Can I have another cup of your anachronism?" I asked, turning back to Jess.

"Certainly, ma'am," he said. He served out coffee all round, and we studiously ignored Wesley, who paced up and down, whining an occasional complaint. He sounded pitiful, like a dog that badly needed to be let out.

"Halt! Who goes there?" we heard again.

"Place is Grand Central Station tonight," Mel muttered.

"Danny must be loving it," one of the

loungers said. "Usually hard to keep awake on sentry duty this time of night."

"Hey, Jess," said one of the two men who now approached the campfire. "Xavier from the Victory Center wants to know if we could help him out by making some charges."

"Hate to ask, when you're pretty busy all day," Xavier said. "But I'm really in a bind."

"No problem," Jess said. "Thought you made these up way ahead of time, though."

"We did, weeks ago, but we had a burst pipe in the storeroom last night," Xavier said. "Everything is soaked, including the charges."

"Ouch," Jess said, and the men around the fire shook their heads in sympathy.

"You want to learn how to do this?" Jess asked. Michael seemed interested, and I'd gotten my second wind, so Jess showed us how to cut trapezoidal pieces of paper in the proper size, measure the precise amount of gunpowder with a little scoop, roll the paper into a cylinder like a clumsy homemade cigar, and twist the ends closed.

I thought it was a little incongruous that we were making authentic colonial-style musket charges using old copies of the *Newport News Daily Press* and the *York Town*

Crier, but no one else even batted an eye.

Wesley joined in, too, but I'm not sure how useful he was. He kept looking at me, as if hoping I'd reward him with an interview if he made enough cartridges.

"Be real careful not to go over on the powder," Xavier said, not for the first time. "It's better to be a little short than to go over."

"Just what are these cartridges for, anyway?" Michael asked.

"A lot of times, when a reenactment takes place on park land, they arrange for us to hand out the ammo," Xavier said. "For safety reasons."

"You get some of these guys, like to over-charge to get a bigger bang, and that gets dangerous," Jess said.

"Not to mention the fools who do black-powder hunting with the same guns and aren't careful about keeping the live ammo separate from the blanks."

"You mean this is what you'd use if you were shooting for real?" I asked. "With old newspapers and all?"

"Sure," Xavier said. "I do a bit of black-powder hunting myself, and I always use the comics for the live ammo and the rest of the paper for the blanks, to be sure of keeping them straight."

Was he pulling my leg?

"You make the live rounds the same as we're doing it," Jess said. "Only after you've rolled one up and closed off the first end, you'd put the bullet in after the powder before you twist the other end closed. When you come to load the gun, you tear the cartridge open with your teeth and pour the powder down the barrel."

"One of the few physical requirements for the Continental Army," Mel said. "Must have two teeth that meet, so you can tear cartridges open."

"Dental care being what it was, a lot of guys couldn't qualify," Xavier put in.

"Couldn't they just rip the cartridge open with their fingers?" Michael asked.

"Yeah, but it'd be pretty hard, 'cause they'd already be juggling the gun and the ramrod." Jess said. "See, it goes like this."

He took up his musket and demonstrated tearing the cartridge open with his teeth, tapping a small amount of powder in the firing pan, then tucking the paper cartridge into the end of the barrel.

"If I was shooting live ammo, I'd leave the bullet wrapped in this paper, for wadding, which is what made the bullet fit snug in the barrel," he said. "Bullet on top of the powder, of course, or it's not going anywhere. Next I take the ramrod and make sure the charge is all the way down the barrel. And take the ramrod out and put it back in its holder. Last thing we need is ramrods flying every which way in the middle of a skirmish. Now the gun's loaded. If it wasn't the middle of the night, I'd fire her off and show you the cleaning routine, but you get the idea."

"You're not going to leave that thing loaded, are you?" Xavier asked. Jess shook his head.

"You use this worm to snake the charge out," he said, holding up an object like a corkscrew on a two-foot stem. We watched as he dug out the remnants of the cartridge, shook the gunpowder out of the barrel into the general supply, and blew the powder out of the firing pan.

"Most any well-run reenactment either hands out ammo or does an inspection," Xavier remarked as we watched. "And most units do their own inspection, too, just in case."

"Couldn't you tell by the weight of the cartridge that it was live?" I said. "I mean, the bullets are made of lead, right? So the live cartridges have to be heavier."

"Yeah, but in the heat of battle, who notices?" Mel said. "You know what I mean," he added, turning to Michael.

"I'm pretty new at this," Michael admitted.

"Had an incident a long time ago where some fool shot a guy's hat off with live ammo," Xavier said, shaking his hat. "At least he was aiming high like he was supposed to."

"And my guys wonder why the unit's insurance fees for the events keep going up," Jess said. "Even using blanks, you're supposed to aim over the enemy's heads. Blanks aren't harmless, you know; the paper cartridge still gets shot out, and at point-blank range that could put your eye out."

I frowned, and looked over at Michael. Had he already heard all this from his unit, and not told me? Or was this his first exposure to the dire perils of his new hobby?

"Gruesome," Wesley said, a little too eagerly. "Stuff like that happen often?"

"Almost never," Jess said, squelching Wesley's hopes of an exposé on the perils of reenacting.

After a while, Michael spotted me yawning while I was trying to cut a cartridge paper and suggested that we head back to camp. We said goodnight to the cannoneers remaining around the campfire, and to the sentry when we passed him.

"Or am I supposed to say *'Gatinois chasseurs'* like you did when we came?" I asked Michael.

"No, why would you?"

"I don't know. What is *'Gatinois chasseurs,'* anyway?"

"It's my unit," Michael said, sounding mildly hurt. "I was identifying my unit to the sentry."

"Oh," I said. "Sorry. I know how it's spelled, but that's not how I'd been pronouncing it."

"I hadn't noticed that you'd been pronouncing it at all," Michael said, chuckling.

"Well, no," I said. "Not out loud, anyway. But I was working my way up to pronouncing it, and that's not how I would have done it."

"Hey, wait for me," Wesley called, scrambling after us. "I'm going your way, remember."

"Give it up, Wesley," I said. "I'm too tired to talk about the murder."

"Look, I need to know what happened," Wesley said.

"Go see Monty," I said. "He warned us not to talk to the press."

"It's not just for the story," he insisted. "I need to know for myself. I'm worried about my safety."

"Considering some of the articles you write, I don't wonder," I said.

"Hey, you don't have to tell me any details you're not supposed to mention, but just tell me this: could that Benson guy have been killed by mistake?"

"By mistake?" I repeated.

"He was wearing a blue coat, just like mine," Wesley said. "And we're about the same height and weight."

"Wesley, dozens of men were wearing blue coats just like yours," I said. "And a lot of them were about your size."

"Yeah, but how many had people who wanted to kill them?" Wesley said. "I know things. Things I haven't written about yet. Things that could ruin people's lives and stuff. I've had death threats, you know."

"Yes, I know. I made a few myself back when you worked for the *York Town Crier*."

"Anonymous death threats," he said. "And some of them came from some pretty scary people, people who wouldn't just make idle threats."

"How would you know, if they were anonymous?"

"Because I know who knows what I know!"

"Not to mention who's on first base," Michael murmured.

"Look," Wesley went on. "A lot of people saw your friend Tony chasing me off in the direction of the craft fair."

"He's no friend of mine," I said.

"What if one of them followed, intending to do me in, and then got Benson by mistake? If there's any chance that was what happened, I have to take precautions."

"Take them anyway," I said. "You know how people feel about paparazzi. Not ransacking my booth in the middle of the night would be a good precaution; that's what Benson was doing when he was killed. And not ticking off people who can lock you in the stocks. If the killer really was after you, you're lucky I came along, aren't you? Think how easily anyone could have sneaked up behind you and —"

"Don't rub it in. I'm already having nightmares," Wesley grumbled. "I'm going to sue that jerk Tony for every penny he has, see if I don't."

"You'll have to stand in line," I said. "First, I'm going to sue him for copyright infringement."

"You don't let anything go, do you?" Wesley said. "I bet you still blame me for what happened after we went to the prom."

"The prom?" Michael repeated.

"Drop it, Wesley," I said.

"You went to the prom with him?"

"His prom, not mine; and not voluntarily," I said. "Our mothers ganged up on me after he couldn't get a date."

"It wasn't like that at all," Wesley protested. "They asked me to do it as a favor. How many sophomores do you think went to the senior prom?"

"One more than wanted to," I said. "Keep it down, Wesley. We're getting close to camp."

"You do still blame me," he muttered. "And don't try to tell me you didn't wear those heels deliberately."

I suppressed a giggle. Wearing four-inch heels, which made me a good five inches taller than Wesley, had been the only form of retribution I'd dared take at the time of the prom.

I thought Wesley was going to follow us back to our tent and try to interrogate me again, but to my relief, just after we got into the crafters' section of the camp, he waved goodnight and ducked into his own tent.

"Good riddance," I muttered.

"What did happen after the senior prom?" Michael asked.

"Not what you're thinking," I said.

"How do you know what I'm thinking?"

"Because whatever you're thinking, that

isn't it," I said. "Some guys Wesley ticked off decided to play a prank on him. Kidnap him, strip him down to his underwear, and drop him off someplace with no wallet and no idea where he was. I guess they weren't expecting him to have a date along."

"They kidnapped you, too?"

"Yeah, but at least they let me keep my prom dress on. Although that wasn't much of a favor, considering where they dropped us off."

"Okay, I'll bite. Where?"

"The Dismal Swamp."

"You're kidding."

"Unfortunately not," I said. "It's only about an hour and a half from here, you know."

"How did you ever get back?"

"I waited for daylight, then followed a likely looking path until I ran into some bird-watchers. They gave me a ride to Skeetertown, and Dad drove down to pick me up."

"And Wesley?"

"Decided he could do better without me slowing him down, so he struck out on his own half an hour after they dumped us. The bloodhounds finally found him three days later."

"Okay, now I understand why Wesley

isn't exactly your favorite cousin," Michael said as he held up the flap of our tent.

"He isn't even a cousin as far as I'm concerned," I said, as I ducked inside. "Mother's about the only one who puts up with him any more." I winced, remembering Mother's orders to find Wesley a nice story. Well, the murder would certainly qualify, but I wasn't sure I trusted what Wesley would write. I'd worry about it later.

I collapsed onto the bedroll, feeling very grateful for the well-concealed, anachronistic air mattress beneath. I was, I thought, too tired to lift a finger. If Jess and the entire artillery crew rolled their cannon here and shot it off over our tent, I'd probably sleep through the whole thing.

"I'm certainly going to sleep soundly tonight," I murmured.

"Soundly, yes," Michael said. "But not, I hope, immediately."

Okay, so maybe I wasn't quite as tired as all that.

20

Either the artillery crew decided to sleep in, or I really was getting used to the sound of gunfire. When the familiar boom woke me up, I scrabbled in my haversack for my watch and found it was a little past seven.

Michael not only slept through the cannon, he also didn't seem to notice getting kicked or elbowed several times while I struggled into my dress in the tiny tent.

I stumbled outside, stretched, and blinked at the bright sunlight. Another unseasonable steam bath of a day.

"Pardon me, mistress, could you direct me to the necessary?"

"The necessary what?" I asked, turning to see a disheveled-looking man clutching a lumpy haversack.

"The necessary," he said. "You know — the privies?"

"Oh, that's right," I said, belatedly recognizing the colonial euphemism for toilets. And not entirely inappropriate, since the sanitary facilities were a collection of portable toilets and sinks that we all used only when absolutely necessary. I pointed over the tops of the surrounding tents. "Right over there, behind the fences. Men's on the left."

"Thank you, mistress," he said, and galloped off.

I pondered visiting the necessary myself, and decided it wasn't urgent. If I set off now, in fifteen minutes I could be at my parents' house, partaking of the forbidden modern pleasures of running water and flush toilets. And perhaps even a hot shower, if I could get there before most of the visiting crowd of relatives woke up.

Even more important, I could talk to Rob. He'd been conspicuously absent from the party last night, and I had a feeling that, sooner or later, Deputy Monty was going to want to talk to him. And I knew Rob was less likely to push himself to the top of the suspect list if he uttered his first, careless comments about Benson's death to me, rather than Monty.

I made my way through the sleeping crafter section of camp to the more lively regimental section. The camp seemed more authentic today. Yesterday, when everyone was setting up and on their best behavior, I'd decided it was more like a really well-done movie set than an actual Revolutionary War encampment. Everything seemed just a little too clean and well repaired, not to mention a lot less smelly than the real thing. And the reenactors seemed too much on their best behavior, as if to say, "Look how authentic I am!"

This morning, as campers got up and stumbled through pared-down and much-adapted versions of their usual morning rituals, the whole place reeked of authenticity. People had stopped worrying about whether the dogs and children were rolling in the dirt and whether their language was absolutely free of anachronisms, and had just started living. I liked it better this morning.

Until I got closer to the road, where the troops of modern police who'd started searching the encampment at that end spoiled the illusion of walking back into the eighteenth century. I felt a little guilty, since it was probably my cash box they were searching for.

"Don't be silly," I told myself. "It's the murderer's fault they're waking everyone up this way, not yours."

A couple of the more wide-awake reenactors decided to use the police incursion as a teaching tool, and pretended the police were British soldiers looking for wounded rebels. One reenactor got up on a barrel and made an impassioned speech about the colonists' right to freedom from search and seizure, and I could see the local police, who'd had time to get used to this kind of thing, taking the out-of-town police aside and enlightening them.

"You mean the whole town goes crazy like this every October?" I heard one state trooper say. I didn't stick around to hear the answer.

I decided to detour by the craft-fair grounds on the way, hoping the police would have finished messing around in my booth, so I could clean up and get ready for opening. But when I arrived, I saw even more police than before, crawling in and around the place, including a lot I didn't recognize as local.

"Stay outside," Monty called when he saw me. He was talking to a black man, and for an anxious second I thought he was interrogating Tad. Then I told myself not to be silly; the man talking to Monty had no dreadlocks or costume, and was at least ten years older than Tad.

"Well, thanks for coming in," Monty said, shaking hands with the man and guiding him out of the booth. "We'll let you know if we have any other questions."

The man nodded and left.

"You don't look all that grateful," I said.

"Well, I confess, I did like your friend Tad for the murder," Monty said, with a shrug. "He seems to have spent the whole day yesterday quarreling with the deceased, and he certainly has motive. But he might have an alibi after all. Supposedly, he spent the whole evening in a coffee shop with our witness there."

"Well that's good," I said.

"I said 'might'," Monty said. "We still have to check it out. Could be a put-up job. And funny he wouldn't mention it himself, don't you think? You can't come in here," he added, planting himself in front of me with his arms crossed.

"Well, I figured that," I said. "Any idea when you're going to be finished?"

"I can't make any promises," he said. "We got some guys with the Virginia State Bureau of Investigation down from Richmond to help, and they're still examining the crime scene."

"I'll check back a little later, then," I said.

"Hang on," he said. "Where will you be if we need to talk to you?"

"That depends," I said. "Have you found my cash box yet?"

"No," he said. "And if we do, we'll have to hold on to it until the forensic guys have checked it out."

"Okay," I said. "Right now I'm going over to my parents' house to take a shower. Then I'll probably have to go into Yorktown to get some cash, so I can make change for my customers, assuming you finish up with my booth sometime today and I have any customers to make change for. Shall I check in with you when I get back, in case you're finished?"

"Don't count on it. Where will you be later on?"

"I have no idea. I'd planned to be in my booth all day," I said. "If you need to find me, check the medical tent, and if I'm not there, leave a message with my dad."

"Your dad? He's the one running the medical tent?"

"Yes, why?"

He grimaced, and began to massage the bridge of his nose.

"What's Dad been doing to give you a headache?" I said.

"Why, what would you expect him to be doing?" Monty snapped back.

"I couldn't even begin to guess," I said. "That's one of Dad's greatest charms, his spontaneity and unpredictability."

"Are you trying to tell me he's a mental case?"

"No," I said, "I'm trying to tell you that he's a free spirit, and I wouldn't necessarily have any idea what he's been up to."

Although, come to think of it, considering that Dad was an avid mystery buff with a deep and largely unfulfilled yearning to become involved in exciting real-life sleuthing, I could probably make a few guesses.

"If I didn't know better, I'd assume he's trying to convince me that he committed the crime," Monty said. "Which seems pretty impossible, because he's got an airtight alibi, so I have to figure maybe he's one of those cranks who show up all the time when you have a well-publicized homicide, trying to confess and get credit for a crime they didn't do."

"He didn't confess, did he?" I said.

"No," Monty said. "Not yet, anyway. But he's been over here twice this morning already, trying to prove that his alibi has holes in it. There must have been two thousand people wandering around the neighborhood in fancy dress last night, half of them carrying swords and daggers and guns with bayonets, and I'm supposed to worry about one crank with holes in his alibi?"

"You haven't had a lot of sleep, have you?" I asked.

"No," he replied, with a look of surprise.

"Let the SBI take care of themselves for a while, then," I suggested. "And take a nap. You'll be no good to anyone if you're exhausted and irritable."

"Wish I could," he said. "But thanks anyway."

He was looking at me oddly. I realized, with dismay, it was the look of someone who reads too much into a sympathetic remark — perhaps because he scares most people off before they make any.

"I'll talk to my dad when I get the chance," I said, backing away. "He's not a crank, just an avid mystery reader."

"There's a difference?" Monty muttered, to my departing back.

I chose to ignore him, partly because I wanted to hurry over to my parents' house and partly because it was too early for me to remember the exact quote about mysteries being the recreation of the intelligent mind or whatever it was Dad was so fond of reciting.

The neighborhood still slept. I heard nothing but birdcalls, and a persistent tapping that was either a pileated woodpecker hunting for breakfast or Mrs. Fenniman nailing up more campaign posters.

My parents' house was quiet, too. Four out-of-town relatives were breakfasting in the gazebo on the back lawn and throwing scraps to the family peacock flock, which was a bad idea, actually. The peacocks already had their benefactors outnumbered, with more appearing all the time. Had these people never seen *The Birds*?

Dad liked to brag about how well the peacocks were flourishing under his care, but in the past several months we'd begun to realize that perhaps they were flourishing a little too well. We'd only acquired them the previous year, as part of some family wedding preparations, but they'd already quadrupled in number, and the neighbors had grown mutinous. Dad hadn't been able to give away any of the flock, and so far, efforts to turn a profit by selling the surplus birds on eBay had proven strangely unsuccessful. He'd already promised Mother that his next project, after the Yorktown Day festival was over, would be spaying and neutering most of the peacocks.

We all tried to ignore Mrs. Fenniman's occasional ruminations on whether peacocks would taste more like turkey or pheasant. Just to be sure, though, I was planning a brief fling with vegetarianism around Thanksgiving.

Other than the soon-to-be-wiser quartet in the garden, I didn't run into anyone else on my way up to Rob's room. And I was in luck; I could tell from the gentle snoring within that Rob was still home.

Knocking on the door of Rob's room did nothing to interrupt the snoring. Neither did calling his name. I finally had to shake him soundly to get a reaction. Some reaction. He turned over and pulled a pillow over his head.

"Wake up, Rob, I need to talk to you," I said, shaking him again.

"Ohhh," he groaned. "Just let me sleep a little while longer."

"I have to tell you about what happened last night," I said.

"Look, I didn't mean to do it," came his voice, somewhat muffled by the pillow. "I'm sorry."

"Didn't mean to do what?" I asked, and heard a gentle snore. "Rob!"

"I'll go over later to confess," he mumbled.

21

"Confess?" I exclaimed. "Rob, what the hell do you mean, 'confess'?"

"Confess, apologize, whatever."

"Rob, get up and talk to me now!"

"Why, is she here?" he said, sitting up in bed with an anxious expression.

"Is who here?"

"Mrs. Waterston," he said.

"Mrs. Waterston?" I repeated. "No, she's not here; why would she be?"

"Maybe she doesn't know yet, then," he said. "I'll have time to go and find him and take him back."

"Rob, what on Earth are you talking about?"

"Spike," he said. "I lost him."

"Is that all?" I said.

"Is that all? Mrs. Waterston will kill me."

"She may have other things on her mind," I said. "Someone killed Roger Benson last night."

"Oh wow," Rob said, suddenly wide awake. "Who?"

"They don't know yet," I said. "The sheriff put Deputy Montgomery in charge of the investigation, and he's looking at everybody who might have had reason to dislike the dead man."

"Try the immediate world," Rob said, shaking his head. "I know it probably sounds selfish, but I'm a little relieved that at least now I'm rid of him."

"Unfortunately, the same idea has probably occurred to Deputy Monty," I said. "Please tell me you have an alibi for the time between 9:30 and 10:30 last night."

"Damn that dog," Rob said.

"You were chasing Spike," I said.

"Looking for him, more like," he said. "I don't think it counts as chasing if you have no idea where he is. I spent four hours running all over the neighborhood, looking for the miserable little beast."

"That's just great," I said, sitting down on the edge of the bed.

"Meg, how bad is it?" Rob asked. "You don't think they seriously suspect me, do you?"

"I have no idea," I said. "Probably depends on what evidence they find. Maybe we'll be lucky and the murderer will have left his fingerprints on the knife."

"Knife? He was killed with a knife?"

"Yes. My falcon knife."

"The one I was holding yesterday?"

I winced.

"Don't worry too much," I said. "A lot of other people were probably holding it, too. Including me, of course. If it makes you feel any better, I think he suspects me more than you."

"You? Why?"

"It's my knife," I said. "And they found him in my booth."

I decided to leave out the fact that even Michael seemed to think I was more capable than Rob of stabbing someone. Especially since I happened to agree.

"Come on," I said. "Get up and let's go take you over to talk to the police. It'll look better if you go voluntarily than if they have to come chasing you down."

"Yeah," Rob said. "Should I put on regular clothes or do you think I need to wear the colonial — oh, damn."

"What?"

"My costume. It's covered with Benson's blood from when Faulk hit him."

"For heaven's sake, Faulk didn't hit him —"

"Okay, from when he tried to break Faulk's fist with his nose."

I smiled in spite of my anxiety.

"Okay, from when Faulk accidentally hit him," I said. "You're not the only one, though, remember? He probably bled on everyone who was there."

Which meant, of course, most of my friends whom Deputy Monty already suspected. Damn.

"You know what Deputy Montgomery is going to say, don't you," Rob said, glumly. "He's going to say that whoever killed Benson was counting on the blood from the fight to cover up the blood from the stabbing. He might even say that whoever killed him got the idea from the fight, or even started the fight on purpose."

"Don't be silly," I said. "He's not that stupid."

Unfortunately, I was wrong.

"Yes," Monty said, when Rob had handed over the bloodstained clothes. "I'd say this casts a definite suspicion on everyone involved in that fight."

"It wasn't a fight," I said. "It was . . . an altercation."

"An altercation during which one of the participants received a blow to the face of sufficient force to cause exsanguination."

"Oh, for heaven's sake," I said. "He wasn't exsanguinated; he just lost a little blood."

"That's what exsanguinated means," Monty said.

"No, exsanguinated means drained of blood, like what vampires do," I said. "And I seem to recall Benson had enough blood left to walk around for another six or seven hours."

"She's right, you know," Rob said. "Dad paid me a whole quarter for 'exsanguination' when I was eight."

"He means for learning the word," I explained, before Monty could jump to any incriminating conclusions. "Dad's big on improving our vocabulary. Look — Benson got smacked in the face and had a nose-bleed. Big deal. If you ask me, it doesn't cast any more suspicion on the people who were there than on the rest of the world. After all, by nightfall, I'm sure everyone at the festival knew about it, and that means everyone knew there were people walking around with Benson's blood on them, ripe to be set up to take the blame if the police didn't dig deep enough to find the real culprit."

"We'll dig as deeply as we need to, thank you very much," Monty snapped.

"Tell me one thing," I said. "Was he killed here, or just left here?"

The deputy looked at me, unblinking, his mouth fixed in what I suppose he intended as a polite but enigmatic smile. Most guys can't do enigmatic.

"Well, okay, if you haven't figured it out," I said, shrugging.

"Oh, we know all right," he said, continuing to look at me. "But what difference does it make?"

"It makes all the difference in the world!" I exclaimed. "If he was killed somewhere else, then the murderer leaving him in my booth was just a coincidence. And not even a very interesting coincidence, because in case you hadn't noticed, everyone has some storage space for stuff they want to keep out of sight, but my booth's one of the few in the whole fair that has a big enough space to conceal a body in. But if he was killed here, than either he or the murderer came here for a reason, and if you found out the reason, you'd be that much closer to finding the murderer."

"We had managed to puzzle that much out, Ms. Langslow," the deputy said. He was still staring at me with that irritating expression on his face. More of a sneer than a smile, really. Or was it a leer? "What difference does it make to you?" he added.

"It's my booth," I said. "I work here. It matters."

He was still staring at me. I suspected it

was a technique he'd read about somewhere for breaking down suspects. Well, two can play that game, I decided. I put my hands on my hips and stared back, equally unblinking. We stared at each other for what seemed like minutes on end, and for some reason I found myself imagining a nature documentary, with a voice-over by Marlin Perkins, explaining that this was a common behavior pattern in primates seeking to establish dominance or pecking order or whatever they're always going on about in nature documentaries.

Apparently I got to be alpha gorilla this time. The deputy suddenly glanced down at his watch and exhibited the behavior of a primate who badly wanted to be somewhere — anywhere — else.

"Sorry," he said, with a somewhat less-broad version of the snide smile. "I've got a lot to do today."

"So have I," I said. "And I can't start any of it until you let me have my booth back. I don't suppose you have any idea when you're going to be finished here?"

"We'll let you know," he said, looking smug.

"Yeah, right," I muttered, and turned to leave.

"Ms. Langslow," he called.

I looked back over my shoulder.

"I appreciate you bringing your brother over. But now I'd appreciate it if you'd refrain from interfering in my case."

I bit back a sarcastic comment.

"Your dad thinks we're a bunch of bumbling nitwits who need your amateur detective skills to solve all our really important cases."

"I already told you, my dad's a mystery buff," I said. "He loves reading all those books where mild-mannered librarians solve crimes and catch ruthless killers."

"And you don't?"

"Dad's retired," I said. "I work for a living; I don't have time for all that."

"So you're not poking around trying to solve the case?"

I turned and gave him my version of the look Mother always turned on my brother and me when we pulled really stupid, beans-up-the-nose stunts.

"Right now, I'm just killing time, waiting till you finish whatever the hell you're doing in my booth, so I can open up and do my job. About the only thing I can think of to do with myself in the meantime is walk around talking to people, and I'd be astonished if anyone around here wants to talk about anything right now other than the murder. So if that counts as poking around, then yes, I've been poking around, and I'll probably continue poking around. The minute you let me back in my booth, I won't have time to poke around."

He stood there, frowning, for a moment.

"We'll let you know when we're finished," he said, finally.

I found Eileen, delegated the job of replenishing my cash supply to her, and went off to talk to a few people.

I stopped for a minute to watch one of my nieces marching around the town square with the fife-and-drum corps which was rehearsing "The World Turned Upside Down," the tune Cornwallis's musicians had played for the surrender ceremony. Did Cornwallis himself have enough sense of humor to choose that tune, I wondered? Or was it the musicians' in-joke? Either way, it perfectly described my mood as I headed for Faulk's booth to begin my forbidden poking around.

Faulk looked like hell.

22

"What happened to you?" I asked, seeing Faulk's bruised face.

"You should know, you were there," he said. "Although the late and unlamented Mr. Benson's nosebleed was so dramatic, I suppose I shouldn't be too surprised that no one remembers me falling down face first on a set of andirons."

"Ouch," I said. "I do remember, actually. I bet Monty found it fascinating, though."

"Monty," Faulk growled. "The man's not quite an idiot, but he's working on it."

"Please tell me you have an alibi for the time of the murder."

"I wish," he said. "I can't even tell you exactly where I was, and there sure as hell wasn't anyone to give me an alibi. Did you know there's a lake over there, beyond those trees?"

"A pond, actually," I said. "Wormley Pond. What about it?"

"I fell in it," he said. "I was so mad I didn't look where I was going when I left the

232

party. I just took off walking, and eventually I fell into the lake —"

"Pond."

"Whatever. Although I think any body of water deep enough for me to almost drown in deserves to be called a lake. Anyway, when I pulled myself out, I realized I had no idea where I was, and I was standing at this intersection of three dirt roads. I took one, and after about an hour and a half, I came out on Route 17, and I figured out where I was. Took another hour or so to walk back to the camp by way of the highway."

"If you fell in where I think you did, either of the other dirt roads would have brought you back here within fifteen or twenty minutes."

"You have no idea how much better that makes me feel," he said. "Tad came in a little after I did. Said he went down to the river by himself with his laptop and played Doom until his battery ran low, then came back."

"Sounds normal for Tad," I said, trying to ignore the sinking feeling in my stomach. What possible reason could Tad have for concealing the fact that he had an alibi — unless he had some reason for not wanting Faulk to know about the alibi.

"Yeah, very normal for Tad," he said.

"Monty doesn't believe it, though."

I shrugged, wondering how recently Faulk had talked to Monty.

"What were you and Tad arguing about, then?" I asked.

"Don't tell me the whole camp heard us. I was trying to keep it down."

"Michael and I were passing by."

Faulk sighed.

"We were both accusing the other of acting like an idiot about Benson, giving him stuff he could use for the lawsuit," he said. "Wish we'd known he was dead already. We could have stopped worrying about the lawsuit and started worrying about getting arrested for murder."

"Maybe it won't come to that," I said.

"Maybe," he said. "But I wouldn't count on it. And even if we don't, the papers will probably have a field day, chewing over all the suspects."

"And there goes your attempt to keep a low profile till your father gets used to things."

"It's okay," Faulk said. "He'll disown me, but he's already done that about once a year for the past two decades. He'll get over it when all this dies down."

"I wish I believed that was going to happen sometime soon," I said. "The police don't seem to be making much progress. All I've seen them do is loiter around my booth."

"And search everyone else's booth," Faulk said. "They seemed to spend a lot more time in mine than any of the other booths nearby, too. Wish I thought that was a good sign."

I couldn't think of anything encouraging to say about that, so I simply said good-bye and left. Maybe I should have told him about Tad's alibi, but I didn't have the heart. Maybe I was jumping to conclusions. Just because Tad was with someone other than Faulk at the time of the murder, there didn't have to be anything shady about it, right? Or maybe Faulk already knew about it and was concealing it. Why? To save face? What were he and Tad really arguing about last night? And how much did I really believe Tad's alibi, anyway?

Since I still couldn't get into my booth, I took a quick stroll through the fair, trying to spot anachronisms and force the owners to hide them before the Town Watch levied more of the stiff fines that I still had to talk Mrs. Waterston out of charging. The watchmen had begun posting everyone's cumulative fine totals on a board beside the stocks, and after glancing at the totals, I could see why morale in the craft fair was spiraling downward so rapidly.

Halfway through my patrol, I found Michael sitting in Dad's medical tent, along with the sheriff. They were watching Dad do his colonial medicine demonstration for a pair of tourists with a small boy in tow. I could tell the tourists were a little unnerved by Dad's blood-stained leather apron.

"Of course, in those days far more men died of disease, particularly dysentery, than were killed in battle," Dad was saying.

"What's dysentery?" the small boy asked. Fortunately, Dad had turned to greet me and didn't hear the question.

"Good morrow, Mistress Langslow," Dad said, bowing deeply. "Do you need a tonic today? A physic, perhaps?"

"I need my booth back," I said, slumping onto one of the bales of straw he'd set out as seats. "Preferably before the end of the fair; I'd like to at least break even."

"Perhaps you need to be bled," Dad said, picking up a jar of leeches from the rough-hewn table that housed his medical exhibits.

"No thanks, Dad," I said. He was kidding, of course. At least I hoped he was.

"What are those?" the little boy asked.

"Leeches," Dad said. "Bloodsucking leeches," he added — which was redundant, of course, but showed his keen grasp of the way to a ten-year-old boy's heart.

"Real leeches?" the boy asked.

"Of course."

"Ooh, gross!" the boy said, in awestruck tones.

"Would you like to hold one?" Dad asked.

"Cool! Yes!"

"Justin, no," his mother said.

"It's perfectly harmless, madam," Dad said. "They're perfectly fresh leeches. We keep the used ones separate."

"Used ones?" the boy's father echoed, his eyes following Dad's gesture to the jar of used leeches sitting on the table. Business had been brisk, apparently; there were over a dozen used leeches in the jar. I wonder if Dad had convinced anyone other than himself to feed them.

"Once they've taken blood from one patient, you can't reuse them on another, for hygienic reasons," Dad explained. "Of course, they didn't know about microbes in colonial times, but nowadays physicians are very careful to follow proper procedure when using leeches."

"Nowadays?" the boy's father repeated. "You don't mean to tell me you still use leeches down here?"

"Yes, of course!" Dad said, warming to

his subject. "They've discovered a host of medicinal uses for them. They're very useful in cases of impaired venous circulation — with plastic and reconstructive surgery, for example, or cases where limbs have been reattached."

"I see," the man said, glancing involuntarily at the bed of sawdust on the ground beside Dad's authentic period operating table, complete with an authentic period saw and what appeared to be an arm in desperate need of reattaching.

"Of course, even in colonial times, they'd have kept the used leeches separate," Dad continued. "If you put a well-fed leech back in with a batch of hungry ones, they'd cannibalize it for the blood it contained."

"Cool!" said the small boy, digging in his feet to resist his parents' increasingly less-subtle efforts to guide him out of the tent.

"Let's get one out, shall we?" Dad said, taking up a small pair of tongs.

"Fascinating," Michael said, watching so closely that his nose almost touched the jar from which Dad was selecting a leech. "For some reason I always thought they were small and round, instead of long and skinny."

"Well, they're fatter after they're fed," Dad said, as he extracted one slimy brown worm and turned, with a flourish, to perform his demonstration. Alas, at the sight of the leech, the father snatched up his son, and he and his wife ran out of the tent. We could hear the boy's wails of outrage fading in the distance.

"How odd," Dad said. He looked at the leech, squirming in his tongs, sighed, and placed it back in the jar. He looked rather disappointed. As did Michael and the sheriff.

I tried to imagine what wild tales the tourists would take back home with them, about the mad doctor of Yorktown and his cannibal leeches. Ah, well. Just as long as no one complained to Mrs. Waterston. And at least it wasn't an anachronism.

Michael came over to join me on the bale of hay.

"I thought you'd be up to your eyeballs in customers by now," he said, putting an arm around me. "Decided to sneak away for a minute?"

"Everyone else is up to their eyeballs in customers," I said. "All I have is a booth full of police and unsold iron. I have no idea what they're still doing. They've had all night to search the place."

"Sorry," Michael said, and began massaging my shoulders. Which, though I hadn't yet noticed it, were already knotted with tension, despite the early hour. I still wasn't sure I liked it when someone else knew how I felt before I did.

"Are the cactus spines still bothering you?" he asked.

"Shhh," I whispered. "Don't say that in front of Dad. I'll explain later."

"Damn fool way to conduct an investigation," Dad was saying. "No offense," he said to the sheriff, who nodded to indicate that none was taken. "But that deputy of yours wouldn't know a suspect if one came up and shot him."

"Now, James," the sheriff began.

"We've gone over this half a dozen times already," Michael said. "How can you possibly be a suspect when you have three witnesses to confirm your alibi?"

"Well, maybe Dad doesn't want an alibi just yet," I said. "Maybe he wants to be a suspect for a while, and be saved from the gallows at the last minute by a surprise witness."

I could tell from the wistful expression on Dad's face that this was exactly what he wanted.

"Gallows? We don't have execution by hanging in Virginia," the sheriff pointed out. "Only electrocution and lethal injection."

"I was speaking metaphorically," I said. "What is Dad's alibi, anyway?"

"He was standing in the middle of the party, talking to the same three people from the time you had that little disagreement with Mr. Benson to the time we got the word that he was dead," Michael said. "There's no way he could have slipped away from the party, stabbed Benson, and slipped back without those three witnesses noticing."

"So who are the witnesses?" I asked.

"First, one of your aunts," Michael said. "Phoebe, the birdwatcher."

"She's no use as a witness," Dad said. "She never pays attention to anything but birds. Now if you wanted an alibi for a spotted owl —"

"And your Uncle Stanley, the judge," Michael continued.

"He's getting along, Stanley is," Dad said. "His memory could be starting to go, you know."

"Yes, he's only a year or two younger than you are, isn't he?" I said.

"And me," Michael finished.

Dad sighed. He wasn't about to say anything negative about Michael. He was Michael's biggest fan. I could tell, though, that he was disappointed in Michael for spoiling all his fun.

"Are you sure you were with him every second of that time?" I asked. "You didn't leave to go to the bathroom or the bar or anything?"

"You went to fetch us drinks," Dad said, brightening. "I remember that now."

"We were standing right beside the bar," Michael said, giving me an exasperated look. "I seem to remember that we kept right on talking while I was waiting for our drinks."

"Yes, but you would have been distracted by your interaction with the bartender," I said.

"Not that distracted," Michael said.

"Tell you what," I said. "We could re-enact it later. Scare up Aunt Phoebe and Uncle Stanley, run through the whole thing, see if there's any possibility that Dad could have gotten away with it."

"Perfect!" Dad said, beaming. "I'm sure when we run through it you'll realize how flimsy my alibi is."

"We'll see," Michael said. He was obviously still convinced of Dad's alibi, but somewhat mollified by the word "reenact" and the dramatic possibilities it suggested.

"Meanwhile, I hate to change the subject, but I have a question," I said, turning to the sheriff.

"I can't tell you what's going on with the investigation," he said, nervously.

"This has nothing to do with the investigation," I said. "At least I hope it doesn't. What does Wesley Hatcher have on you that he thinks would swing the election if he published it?"

23

The sheriff flinched.

"That's . . . that's personal," he said, finally.

"Well, I assumed it was personal," I said. "I couldn't imagine anything job-related he could possibly hold over you."

"Thank you, Meg," he said, patting my hand. "Thank you for that vote of confidence."

I decided it would spoil the good impression I'd made if I explained that I knew it couldn't possibly be job-related because the whole county knew he never did any police work at all if he could help it.

"Okay, so it's personal," I said instead. "What is it? We'd like to help you, but we can't if we don't know what's wrong."

"That young man had evidence of an unfortunate . . . lapse in judgment I made a while back," the sheriff said. "Nothing illegal, nothing unethical or immoral. Just . . . well, stupid. Something stupid I did that would look bad if folks found out about it.

He's been trying to hold it over my head, trying to get me to tell him something he could use in a story."

"What did he want to know?"

"I don't think he had anything in particular in mind," the sheriff said. " 'Something juicy,' that's all he said. I told him I didn't know anything juicy, and I wouldn't tell him if I did. Of course, now he wants all the details about the murder. That's why I'm staying so far from the investigation. I can't tell him what I don't know."

"Of course, he may not believe you."

"Well, if he doesn't, I'll just have to live with that. I'll just have to tell him to — to —"

"Publish and be damned!" I suggested.

"Yes, that's the ticket," the sheriff said. "You have such a way with words. Only . . . do you think it's all right to say 'damn' with the election and everything?"

"Mrs. Fenniman says much worse," I said.

"That's true," he said. "But she's not actually carrying the burden of public office. I'll say 'publish and be darned,' just to keep on the safe side."

Just then Cousin Horace stuck his head through the flap of the tent.

"The fresh tomatoes just arrived," he said.

"Not too fresh, I hope," Dad said.

"Oh, no, they're plenty squishy," Horace said.

"I'd better go, then," the sheriff said. "Got to keep up appearances while I can."

He got up, put his tricorn hat on, and ambled out.

"The burdens of public office," I said, shaking my head.

"So what are you up to while Monty's occupying your booth?" Michael asked.

"Doing Monty's job for him," Dad suggested. "Solving the crime."

"Oh, no, Dad," I said. "Monty very specifically warned me against trying to do that. I'm just walking around, hunting down anachronisms, and talking to people."

"I don't suppose the topic of the murder ever comes up, does it?" Michael asked.

"Strangely enough, it does," I said.

"Well, Monty's doing the best he can to make sure no one forgets it," Dad said. "He came through here just after I opened, demanding to search the place, and confiscated a lot of my instruments. Then he brought them all back, about a half hour ago."

"That's odd," I said. "Did he say why?"

"Not a word," Dad said. "Of course, not being from around here, I don't suppose he understands how valuable the insights of the local population can be in solving a case like this."

"Probably not," I said. "So, Michael, want to stroll around with me and tap the keen insights of the local population? Unless your unit has something planned."

"Not really. Remember what Jess said last night about some units being more gung-ho than others?"

"Don't tell me your unit is one of those that just shows up to fire off your guns and drink beer?"

"I beg your pardon! The *Gatinois chasseurs* are not anything like that."

"I'm sorry."

"We're French; we just show up to wave our swords around and drink champagne."

"Much better," I said. "When will you be opening the champagne?"

"Not till after the 4 P.M. skirmish," he said, offering his arm. "Until then, I'm at your disposal."

"We'll see you later, Dad," I called, as Michael and I strolled out of his tent.

"Come back and tell me what you find," Dad called. He sounded a little forlorn, so I was relieved when we ran into a couple of reenactors outside, working up their nerve to enter.

"Is this the doctor's tent?" one asked. "I mean, he's a real doctor, right, not just doing an impression of one?"

"Oh, he's real, all right," I said. "What's wrong?"

"Poison ivy," the man said.

"I'm sure he'll have something for that," I said, and watched as the patients ventured inside.

"Of course, with the festival on, he'll want to give them an authentic period salve," I remarked to Michael when they were out of earshot. "That's why I didn't want him to know about the cactus spines."

"The authentic period salve wouldn't work on cactus spines?"

"The authentic period salve is lard and sulfur ointment, which works just fine if you don't mind me smelling like a crate full of rotten eggs for the next two days."

"I see your point," he said. "I'll try to keep my face out of the shrubbery until he's back in the twenty-first century. *Enfin, ma chérie, où allons-nous?*"

"I have no idea what you're talking about, but it sounds nice," I said. "Feel free to say more charmingly incomprehensible things to me as we stroll around interrogating suspects."

"Actually, what I said was —"

"No, no! Don't spoil my illusion that you just said something witty, complimentary, and ever-so-slightly risqué! Haven't you ever experienced the letdown of hearing a favorite opera sung in English? Besides, there's Mrs. Fenniman; let's go interrogate her."

"Is she a suspect?"

"Of course, and even if she wasn't, she knows more about what goes on in town than anyone other than Mother."

Mrs. Fenniman stood at the edge of the town square with a frown on her face, watching the sheriff.

"I need a better campaign platform," she complained. "He's killing me with those damned tomatoes. I thought you were going to think of something, Meg."

"Just because they're throwing tomatoes at him doesn't mean they're going to vote for him," I said. "Could mean just the opposite, in fact."

"Maybe," she muttered.

"I think public opinion's more likely to hinge on how his department handles this murder investigation," I suggested.

"Well, that's a relief," she said. "Because, if you ask me, that Monty fellow isn't handling it worth a damn. Be a lot different when I'm elected."

"Just what is he doing, anyway?"

"He's got his troops searching all the booths for your cash box," she said. "Didn't occur to them that all these folks have cash boxes of their own, so they got a little over-excited, first half-dozen booths they searched. Don't see what he thinks he's accomplishing; cash is cash. And do they really think a thief would keep around any checks made out to you?"

"I doubt it," I agreed.

"Seems to be searching for something else, too, but he's not letting on what," she added. "Something smaller than a cash box, anyway. And he's got a bee in his bonnet about weapons. Some of those reenactors complain that they can't walk ten feet without some cop wanting to see their swords and bayonets."

Now that was interesting. They already knew my dagger was the weapon — so why were they so interested in other peoples' swords and bayonets? There was something fishy going on, but I didn't think Deputy Monty was going to give away any details. I wondered if I could pry anything out of Cousin Horace.

"I swear," Mrs. Fenniman said, shaking her head. "If you'd told me Roger Benson would cause more trouble dead than alive,

I'd have called you a liar. But that's what's happening."

"Just what trouble did he cause you when he was alive?" I asked.

"What makes you think he caused me some particular trouble?"

"Horace said you called him a no-good sneak thief who should be shot like a rabid dog."

"I did, and I meant every word of it," she said. "But it wasn't something he did to me in particular. Before he went into the computer racket, he was one of those merger-and-acquisition crooks. I had some money in this pulp mill company up near Richmond. Cooper and Anthony. It was starting to diversify, might have gone someplace, except that Benson and his crooks engineered one of those slash-and-burn leveraged buyouts."

"What's that, anyway?"

"They bought the company by running up a lot of debt, sold off all the assets that had any value, and shut the company down," she explained. "And somehow, even though they'd sold off the assets for a mint, there didn't seem to be a whole lot of money left over to pay the stockholders. Not when they finished paying off the debt and their own salaries and bonuses, anyway.

Some mighty clever bookkeeping, I'll give 'em that. Mighty clever all round. Anyway, it cost me a pretty penny, but I wasn't the worst hurt. Some people lost everything they had."

"Anyone around here?" I said. "Anyone who might be holding a grudge?"

"No idea," she said. "Made a bigger stink up in Richmond than it did down here, and anyway, that was seven or eight years ago. Anyone going to do anything, I think they'd have gone and done it by now."

"I think you're underestimating how long most people can hold a grudge," I said. "But speaking of 'gone and done it' — do you have an alibi for the time of the murder?"

"Not a bit of one," she said, cackling. "I had a long day of campaigning, so I left early and went home to bed. So I can't prove I didn't do him in."

"You're not going to try to get arrested for this, are you?" I asked.

"Hell, no," she said. "I might have done it if I'd thought of it, but I didn't; and I'd hate to take the glory away from whomever actually had the gumption."

"That's good," I said. "I'm not sure getting arrested would be a good campaign tactic."

"Actually, it might be, under the circumstances," Mrs. Fenniman said. "Good thinking, Meg. I'll have to consider that."

She strolled off, looking thoughtful.

"Oh, dear," I said. "I hope she isn't going to start badgering Monty about her lack of alibi," I said. "Dad's already driving him crazy enough."

"Yeah, I noticed," Michael said. "That's why I was trying to keep your dad distracted, instead of coming to look for you."

"Thanks," I said. "Oh, damn, there's Wesley again."

"Relax," Michael said. "He doesn't seem to be looking for you."

"No," I said. "But he's certainly looking for something."

As we watched, Wesley stumbled along, his eyes on the ground. When he got to a booth, he'd walk in, ignoring customers and crafters alike, scanning the floor and every horizontal surface. Then he'd walk out, stumble on toward the next booth, and repeat the whole routine.

"He's been doing that all morning," Michael said. "Well not quite that; he was a little less frantic earlier. He came into your dad's tent and looked high and low, badgering us all the while about whether we'd found something of his."

"Found what?"

"He wouldn't say. We figured maybe he was snooping around everywhere the cops have been, but from the way he's acting, I think maybe he really has lost something."

"And I bet I know what it is," I said, fishing in my bag, and turning my back to Wesley. *"Voilà!"*

"CD-ROMs?" Michael said. "He's lost three CD-ROMs?"

"I bet he's lost one," I said. "He was waving one at me when he said that he could swing the election. I bet he dropped it in my booth, and I picked it up without thinking."

"I think I'd notice if I picked up a stray CD-ROM; they're not exactly something I use every day."

"I would notice, normally, but everybody was handing me CD-ROMs yesterday — Tad brought by a CraftWorks patch, and Rob gave me his CD-ROM of the game to keep. I probably thought I'd dropped one of those and put it in my haversack."

"Or maybe I shoveled it into your haversack along with all the rest of the contents when I kicked it over."

"That's right, you did," I said.

"So should we give it back?"

"Later," I said. "When we get my laptop back and can figure out which one is Wesley's."

"I suppose we'll have to inspect the contents pretty thoroughly to do that."

"Naturally," I said. "Wesley will just have to suffer a little longer."

"Okay," he said. "Where to next?"

"Well, I thought —"

"Meg!" Mrs. Waterston said, from behind us.

"Morning, Mom," Michael said.

"Good morning," she said, rather perfunctorily. "Meg, that sheriff's a relative of yours, isn't he?"

"A distant relative, yes," I said, wondering what she was going to complain about. I knew, from experience, that no one ever asked if people were relatives of mine if they were going to pay them extravagant compliments.

"Then can't you get him to do something? That is how you get things done in this . . . town, isn't it?"

I wondered, briefly, what adjective she'd swallowed. "Crazy," maybe? "Backwards?" "God-forsaken?" I'd heard them all; sometimes even said them myself, but she knew better than to say them aloud. And I knew better than to ask.

"What is it you want him to do, anyway?" I asked instead.

"I want him to finish this investigation,"

she said, "before it ruins the festival."

"Ruins the festival?" I echoed.

"Look how many tourists there are today!" she exclaimed, with a sweeping gesture. "Hundreds! And what are they seeing? Are they seeing an authentic colonial encampment? A thriving market full of period crafts? A little slice of Yorktown's history? No! All they see is dozens of modern police running all over everywhere."

"Actually, I think most of the tourists are rather enjoying the excitement," Michael remarked.

"Well, that's not what I brought them here to enjoy," Mrs. Waterston said. "What are the police doing, anyway?"

"Trying to solve a murder, I suspect," I said. "Questioning suspects and searching tents and booths."

"Well, they could question people out of sight of the tourists, couldn't they?" Mrs. Waterston demanded. "And what are they searching for? They have the murder weapon, don't they?"

"Well, yes," I said. "But they still haven't found my cash box."

"Your cash box?" Mrs. Waterston said, in a surprisingly faint voice.

"Yes, my cash box. It seems to have disappeared from my booth between the time I left for the party and the time I found the body, and while our local police may not have the extensive experience with homicides you get in a big city, they can put two and two together. They think it's pretty obvious that whoever killed Benson also took my cash box."

"But . . . but . . . that's impossible," Mrs. Waterston stammered.

"And just why is that?"

"Because I took your cash box," Mrs. Waterston said. "And I assure you, I'm certainly not the murderer."

24

Michael recovered first.

"Mom, why on Earth would you steal Meg's cash box?"

"I didn't steal it," she snapped. "I just took it for safekeeping. I thought she needed to learn a lesson about carelessly leaving her cash box lying around, in plain sight, in an unlocked booth."

"Gee, thanks," I said. "But for your information, I didn't just leave it lying around. I left it locked in one of my metal storage cases."

"Well, when I came by your booth, it was just sitting there on the table."

"And when was that?"

"I left the party for a little while about nine thirty or ten," she said. "I hadn't seen Spike all day, so I was going to bring him back with me. Your . . . brother was supposed to have dropped him off at my house and fed him. Which he hadn't done properly, of course; he must have let Spike slip out when he left the house, and I found the poor little thing cowering in the yard, trembling with hunger. I fed him, and I was heading back to the party with him. But on the way he managed to slip his leash and ran off into the craft-fair site. I thought perhaps he'd detected a prowler."

"More likely a prowling cat," I said.

"So I followed him," she said.

"Even though you thought there might be a prowler about?"

"I thought some of the Town Watch would be about, too, instead of carousing themselves into a stupor at the party," she said, in something closer to her usual tone. "But never mind; we won't see that happening again."

I briefly felt sorry for the Town Watch.

"I'm holding you responsible for their behavior for the rest of the fair."

My sympathy for the Town Watch evaporated.

"Anyway, I finally cornered Spike in your booth, barking at something."

"Probably the murderer," I couldn't help saying.

"Oh dear!"

"Meg!" Michael exclaimed. "Mom, it was probably only the body."

"Oh, that's *so* reassuring, Michael," Mrs. Waterston said. "Not a murderer; only a dead body. How silly of me to be upset."

"So what happened when you found Spike?" I said.

"I picked him up, and I noticed your cash box, just lying there on the table. I didn't know anything else had been happening; I just thought you'd been careless. So I took it away for safekeeping. I locked it in the safe, where I keep my own jewelry," she said. "It was perfectly safe, and I was going to tell you so today. With the murder and all, it slipped my mind."

"And it never crossed your mind that it might have had something to do with the murder — after all, you found the cash box in my booth, the murder was in my booth."

She shook her head.

"The booth had been ransacked," I said. "Didn't that strike you as odd?"

"It didn't look that messy for your booth," she said.

"Mom," Michael said, shaking his head.

"I'm sorry," she said, looking stricken. "I didn't mean —"

"Never mind," I said.

She glanced up at Michael, looking very upset, and for the first time I could remember, I felt — could it be sympathy? For Mrs. Waterston? Yes, definitely sympathy, and perhaps just a little bit of something that might resemble affection. She was so clearly upset by Michael's disappointed tone of voice — more upset by that than by the possibility that she'd barely escaped an encounter with our knife-happy murderer or with his victim. Call me a softie, but it's hard to keep on disliking someone who cares so much about the man you're in love with. Why couldn't she have shown more of her doting maternal side before?

Later, Meg, I told myself. Aloud, I said, "You'll have to talk to the police, you realize."

"Oh, dear," she said. But then she squared her shoulders and lifted her chin.

"We'll go with you, if you like," I said.

"Thank you, Meg, but there's no need to trouble yourselves, really," she said, as she began marching off. "I'm sure you both have a lot to do."

"Well, I'm going that way anyway," I called after her. "I don't have all that much to do until they let me have my booth back, which I hope they might possibly be ready to do. It's almost noon, after all."

But Michael held me back as I started to follow her.

"Meg — what if they suspect Mom?"

"Don't worry — they may suspect her at first, but she's in no real danger of getting arrested or anything."

"Why not?" he said. "She was in the booth around the time of the murder — how can she prove she didn't do it? Spike certainly can't give her an alibi."

"She has a better alibi than anyone at the fair," I said. "See the guy following her?"

"Which guy?" Michael asked, frowning.

"The guy in the blue uniform with the gold trim — the one who's sauntering just a little too casually down the lane behind her."

"Who's he?"

"One of Jess's men, no doubt — gold trim means artillery, remember? And Jess said he had someone following her around every minute."

"That's right!" Michael exclaimed, his face lighting up. "I'd forgotten about that; thank goodness you didn't. I'll just run up to the artillery camp and find out who was following her last night. The sooner we get that straightened out, the better."

"Good idea," I said. "I'll go down to my booth and make sure they don't haul her away to jail in the meantime."

"Thanks," he said. He gave me a quick kiss on the cheek and turned to go. But after about two steps he turned and looked back.

"Meg — I know she's irritating as hell,

but she means well," he said, and then ran off toward the hill where the cannon-crew members were working. At least I assumed they were working; we'd heard the boom of the cannon at irregular intervals all morning, and I doubted they'd try the tape-recording ploy in broad daylight.

I headed back to the town square, where the sheriff again sat in the stocks while Cousin Horace did a brisk business selling half-liquid tomatoes. Today, I noticed, a lot more of the aspiring pitchers were craftspeople — probably reacting to the turmoil the sheriff's underlings were creating throughout the craft fair. Or maybe they thought the sheriff was in charge of the Anachronism Police.

"Hey, Horace," I said, joining him behind the table. "How's it going?"

"Your brother Rob's supposed to spell me in fifteen minutes," he said. "Have you seen him?"

"He could still be talking to Monty," I said, pitching in to make change for a customer while Horace handed out the tomatoes. "Want me to go look for him?"

"Please," Horace said.

"Okay," I said. "But before I do, tell me something. When was Monty going to get around to telling me that my dagger wasn't the murder weapon?"

"How did you — ? But that's — No one's supposed to —"

Horace stood, his mouth hanging open, each hand gripping a tomato with such force that the juice was running down into his sleeves.

"Hand the man his ammo, Horace, and stop gaping,"

"I don't want those used-up tomatoes," the customer complained.

"Two nice, fresh, rotten tomatoes, coming up," I said.

Horace, looking dazed, dropped the squashed tomatoes and fished out two less-damaged ones.

"Don't try to tell me it's not so," I told Horace, in an undertone. "And if Monty finds out I know, you can tell him I deduced it, partly from what the police have been up to all morning and partly from something he said himself, and I'll say that in public if he tries to take it out on you. But just tell me: what makes them think it wasn't my dagger?"

"Shape of the wound," Horace muttered, as another customer stepped up. "Coroner said your dagger couldn't have made it."

"So what did?" I said, out of the side of my mouth, while smiling at a man who handed me a dollar bill.

"Something bigger," Horace said, while counting out ten tomatoes.

"Bigger how? Longer? Wider?"

"Blunter. Like an unsharpened dagger. Unsharpened something, anyway."

"So that's why they were inspecting everyone's weapons?"

"Yeah, and not getting anywhere," Horace said, looking a little less nervous now that all the customers were busy pelting the sheriff. "Some of these reenactors keep their weapons sharp; we found that out the hard way."

"You'd think cops would know to treat weapons more carefully. Did anyone get seriously hurt?"

"No. Used a few Band-Aids, though."

"Please tell me Monty is wearing one of them."

"Most of them," Horace said, snickering. "Anyway, that's why they're back to searching the craft fair so hard, especially the blacksmiths. Looking for unsharpened weapons."

"Thanks, Horace," I said.

"I didn't say anything," he said.

"Of course not. Thank you for your eloquent silence."

I strolled on back to my booth. The police

presence had shrunk to Monty and two other officers, and both were listening to Mrs. Waterston. Michael was there, too, with Mel from the artillery camp.

"Are you sure there's no way she could have shook you off?" Monty said, turning to Mel.

Without changing his expression, Mel reached inside his coat, took out his wallet, and held it out. Monty tilted his head to inspect it, but I noticed that he didn't take his hands out of his pockets. And he reacted as if a skunk had lifted its tail at him.

"So you're a damned bounty hunter," he said.

"I'm a private investigator," Mel said. "And yes, I'm presently working for a bail bondsman. It's legal, and I'm damned good at it. So I can guarantee you, she didn't shake me off."

Michael beamed at me as if I were personally responsible for putting his mother under surveillance by a genuine private investigator for the duration of the murder inquiry. Mrs. Waterston looked less enchanted with the whole thing.

"You down here to haul some lowlife back to Richmond?" Monty asked.

"I'm down here for the reenactment," Mel said. "It's my hobby."

I didn't like the way they were glaring at each other, so I decided to distract them.

"Look, you're not doing much with my booth right now, other than interrogating people in it," I said. "Any chance you could find a more private place to do that so I can actually start doing some work here?"

"I was just going to send for you," Monty said, with a scowl. "Now that we've cleared up the disappearance of the cash box, we're finished here."

He went off, taking Mrs. Waterston, Mel, and the rest of the police with him.

I looked around my booth. If I were a deputy whose job probably depended on my boss getting reelected, I'd be a little more careful how I treated voters' relatives. Obviously, at some point, the police had stopped considering my booth an active crime scene and started using it just as a place to hang out, judging from the number of coffee cups and doughnut boxes stashed in the corners.

"I'll get rid of these," Michael said, grabbing a stack of the rubbish. "And I think I saw Eileen down the lane; I'll let her know you're opening up. Anything I should bring back?"

"Some customers would be nice," I said.

"I meant to help with the cleanup," he called over his shoulder.

"I take it back," Amanda said from across the lane. "He cleans; he's a keeper."

With Michael pitching in to help, the booth was ready for business far sooner than I'd expected. And to my astonishment, Cousin Horace even showed up with my laptop a few minutes after the police had gone.

"No real need for us to keep this around, and I thought you could use it," he said, and disappeared before I could thank him.

"That was nice," Michael said.

"I hope he had permission to give it back," I fretted. "Not that I'm going to ask Monty, of course. But at least now, when things are quiet, I can check those CDs."

"I could do it now," he said, "if you don't mind. We've pretty much finished the cleanup."

"Go right ahead," I said. "Just let me know if you find anything juicy."

"Grisly as it sounds, I should probably take this anachronism behind the curtain," he said.

"Be my guest," I said. "But no practical jokes. No dying elephant screams, no clanking chains, no blank shots."

"I'll be a perfect lamb," he said, and disappeared behind the curtain with my laptop.

25

Nothing like a homicide on the premises to draw in customers. People began swarming in even before we finished the cleanup. Okay, they spent a lot of time staring at the curtain behind which, as everyone had heard, I'd found the body, and starting whenever Michael made the slightest noise. Some even asked me to tell them about what had happened. But after milling around taking up space for a while, enough of them would feel sufficiently guilty to buy something. I began to hope I'd make up for lost time after all.

If I'd had a chance, I'd have tried to dust the fingerprint powder off every surface of the booth before letting people in, but I quickly realized that the lingering signs of the investigation proved more of a selling point than a tidy booth.

"Looks like you're catching up," Amanda said, popping across the lane during one of the few quiet moments we both had.

"Hope so," I said.

"I've been wanting to ask — where did

you get that outfit you wore last night?"

"Michael had Mrs. Tranh make it," I said. "Why — do you want one?"

"I think I might look pretty good in a dress like that, with a set of those stays," she said, looking faintly sheepish. "And heck, if I'm going to do any more of these costumed fairs, I think I should get the right outfit."

"To tell you the truth, yesterday I'd have said you were crazy, but today — I feel kind of frumpy in this dress," I said, shaking my head in surprise. "By the way — you live in Richmond, right?"

"All my life," she said. "Even went to college there. Why?"

"Ever heard of a company called Cooper and Anthony?"

"Yeah, heard too much about it," she said. "Why?"

"What is it?"

"What was it, you mean," she said. "Small, family-owned business outside of Richmond. Started out making paper after the Civil War, then expanded into other stuff. Managed to expand themselves out of business about seven years ago."

"I heard they had help going out of business," I said.

"I've heard that, too," she said. "Mostly from men who lost their jobs when the place closed down. I always figured, they were so bitter, maybe it made them feel a little better to blame outsiders for their problems."

"I just talked to someone who lost money investing in Cooper and Anthony, and those bitter men just may be right."

"Damn, does that mean I have to go back home and apologize to Daddy and my uncles for thinking all these years that they were paranoid?"

"Oh, no; please don't tell me it's your family we're talking about."

"Not just my family; must have been six or seven hundred people lost their jobs when the place finally shut down."

"Any of them still bitter enough after all these years to do something about it?"

"We're talking about Benson, aren't we? He had something to do with the shutdown?"

"Engineered it, according to Mrs. Fenniman."

"This'll make Daddy's day, hearing the man responsible for him losing his job has passed over."

"Make mine; tell me you have an alibi for the time of the murder."

"Oh, don't you worry," Amanda said. "I have a real good alibi, and if Monty looks at me the way he was looking at you, my alibi damn well better punch his lights out if he wants to alibi me again tonight. I just hope that bunch of sorry old men up in Richmond were playing their usual Friday night poker game last night, or the cops'll be looking real hard at them. Couple of them caused some trouble already, back when the plant shut down."

"That's too bad," I said.

"Keep an eye on my booth, will you?" she said. "I think I'll wander over and tell Deputy Monty all about Cooper and Anthony."

"No problem," I said. "I'm sure Monty will be thrilled to know all about his six or seven hundred new suspects."

Of course, Monty might decide that the demise of Cooper and Anthony was too long ago to be relevant, but just imagining those hundreds of people up in Richmond, only an hour's drive away, lusting for Benson's blood, made me feel a little less anxious about our local suspects.

"That's not accurate," someone said behind me.

I turned to see a woman wearing a Town Watch badge frowning down at the table where I kept the small iron goods.

"I said, that's not accurate," she repeated, taking a sheet of paper out of her haversack. "They didn't have nails in colonial times."

"Actually, they did," I said, picking up one of the nails on display. "They looked different from our modern nails, of course, since they were made by hand. The shaft was usually square, and the head was either square or pyramid shaped because —"

"Nonsense," she said. She had taken out a quill pen and a bottle of ink — ready to write me up a summons for anachronisms. "They didn't have nails at all; they just used wooden pegs to hold things together."

"Well, maybe you should tell that to the blacksmiths up in Colonial Williamsburg," I said, with growing irritation. "I spent quite some time up there, learning about eighteenth-century hardware, and I can tell you —"

"They're wrong," she insisted. "Wooden pegs. That's all they ever used. Wooden pegs."

"Look, lady," I said, losing my temper completely. "They had nails long before 1781. How do you think they put shoes on horses — with Scotch tape?"

Her mouth fell open as she pondered this. Then she recovered.

"Well, I never!" she exclaimed, storming

out. "Just for that, I'm going to double your fine!"

As I was counting to ten, I heard someone slowly clapping. I turned to see Jess, the artillery captain.

"Good job," he said. "She doesn't believe you, of course. You should have reminded her they had nails at Calvary."

"I should have kept my temper," I said.

He shrugged.

"Who cares," he said. "Bunch of morons, the Town Watch. Not a one of them knows a rifle from a musket."

"I'm not sure I know, either."

"Yeah, but you're not running around telling people their expensive, well-researched, reproduction frontier rifles are anachronisms, are you?"

I groaned.

"I'll speak to them," I said.

"Thanks," he said. "They've been all over us, ever since Madame Von Steuben found out about the loudspeaker trick. And after the fiasco last night with their losing the key to the stocks, they're all trying to get out of the doghouse by putting us in it. Say, you know that cousin of yours?"

"Which one?" I asked. "I have about a million of them around here."

"The reporter guy, the one who got

locked up. He wants to interview some of our people. Is he trustworthy?"

"Not in the slightest," I said. "He'd sell his grandmother to get a scoop."

"We'll be careful what we say, then."

"You don't have to talk to him at all, you know," I said.

"Well, I feel kind of sorry for him," Jess said. "All the other reporters who weren't even here all day got their stories, and he didn't get out of the stocks in time to make his deadline."

"He should be thankful. If he hadn't been locked up, maybe he'd have been *in* the stories," I said. "As a prime suspect, or maybe even the victim."

"Yeah, this way he's one of the few people in town who's in the clear," Jess said, turning to leave. "Him and the guy who passed out after locking him up."

As Jess strolled away, I suddenly wondered if Tony's drunkenness was such a good alibi. He'd been lying where Wesley couldn't see him, after all. He could have locked Wesley up, gone down to my booth to kill Benson, and then come back to lie down where I'd found him. For all I knew, he could have been awake when I stumbled on him.

Tony as murderer. I liked the idea.

I'd have to talk to Wesley — find out exactly what he remembered and see if my theory held water. And if it did, I'd make Monty listen if I had to knock him down and sit on him.

I ducked behind the curtain to tell Michael and found him laughing at something on the laptop screen.

"Okay," I said. "What's so funny?"

"Well, not the first CD; that's just the latest copy of Rob's game," he said, holding up one of the white paper envelopes, which he'd labeled LAWYERS FROM HELL. "Not of general interest."

"Well, not to us, anyway," I said. "Although for Rob's sake, I hope it's a runaway success."

"As long as I never have to play it again," he said. I knew how he felt. Rob had drafted me as a beta tester so often I'd begun dreaming about the game, and I'd picked up so much miscellaneous trivia about torts and writs and habeas corpus that I could probably do a pretty believable impersonation of an attorney if I had to.

"What about the other disks?"

"Well, I suspect the one I've got in the machine now is Wesley Hatcher's disk," he said.

"The one with the incriminating evidence about the sheriff?"

"Exactly. Incriminating photos, to be exact."

"How bad is it?"

"Take a look," he said, starting to turn the laptop so I could see the screen.

"Michael," I said, backing away slightly, "I do not want to look at a bunch of dirty pictures, especially not of someone I know. Someone I'm related to, if you come right down to it. And besides —"

"Don't worry," he said. "Just look."

I glanced down at the screen. There was the sheriff, all right. And he was with a woman. They were seated, one on either side of a white, Formica-topped table, in front of a window. Outside the window you could see the storefronts of a shopping center, including a Farm Fresh supermarket.

"They're in a fast-food restaurant," I said.

"A McDonald's, I think, from the color scheme."

"You're right," I said. "In fact, I think I know exactly which McDonald's — it's on Route 17, in Gloucester, about four or five miles north of Yorktown. I recognize the shopping center behind them.

"You're probably right," he said.

"Is that it? Him sitting with a woman in Mickey D's?"

"Well, not just sitting with her," Michael said. "Here he is shaking her hand when she arrives at the table . . . opening up his box of Chicken McNuggets . . . opening the mustard sauce. And look — he's offering her some fries."

"And she's taking one," I said, shaking my head. "Heavy stuff here."

"Hey, maybe that's it," Michael said. "Maybe it's the fast food that's incriminating. Did he make a campaign promise to go on a diet and shape up?"

"Not that I've heard," I said. "Why would he? I can't imagine anyone would care. And who is she, anyway? She looks vaguely familiar."

"Not someone you know, then?"

I peered close, and had Michael run through the whole picture sequence again.

"Like I said, she looks vaguely familiar, but that could just be because I've been staring suspiciously at her face for fifteen minutes now," I said, finally. "Unless — Michael, she could be the same woman we saw talking to Benson last night. The one driving the Jaguar."

"That's what I thought," he said. "I wasn't sure, though."

"Go back a couple — there. The profile. It's definitely her; I got a good look at her profile when she drove past. It has to be her."

"Of course, since we have no idea who she is, I'm not sure that helps much."

"Do you think you could figure out how to crop one of those so it shows just her? I've got my little printer in the van; we could print out a copy of it."

"Great idea; then we could show it around, and find out if anyone knows her. Although that's going to take an awful lot of time," he said. "And I suppose we ought to give this to Monty, come to think of it."

"Don't worry about showing it around," I said. "We'll show it to Mother; if she doesn't know who it is, the odds are no one else in town will, either, and if she does, we can give it to Monty along with the information about who she is."

"Good point," Michael said. "I'll see what I can do about the cropping. One other thing — what do you make of this?"

He opened up a file. A letter, from Wesley to the Canton, Ohio, Police Department, inquiring about one Ranulf Brakenridge Montgomery.

"He's suspicious of Monty," I said. "Do you think this has anything to do with the blond McHussy?"

"I don't see how. Looks more like he just saved it by accident in the same folder as the photos. I do it all the time."

"But since we don't know what he found out from the Canton PD, we don't really know, do we?"

I went back to helping customers, while Michael fiddled with my laptop. I wished I could help, but sales were brisk, and after having my booth occupied all morning by the police, I needed to make up for lost time.

At one point, I made a run back to my van for another load of stuff, including the printer. When Michael saw me return, with one of my handy metal storage cases on the dolly, he put the laptop aside and stood up, ready to help me carry the ironwork into the booth.

"Hang on a second," I said. "I need to do something first."

Michael watched in astonishment as I took out a large canister of black pepper and shook a generous amount of the contents over the metal in the case.

"Okay, you can haul it in now," I said, with a sneeze. "Try not to knock off any more than you have to."

"What's the pepper supposed to do?"

"It's all for show," I said. "The minute

the first customers noticed the fingerprint powder, they started buying like crazy. Bought nearly everything in the booth. So I brought out the stuff that had been behind the curtains — of course the police had dusted that, too, and all of it sold."

"So now you're shaking pepper on stuff that wasn't even in your booth, and telling them it's fingerprint powder."

"I'm not telling them anything. If they want to leap to the conclusion that it's fingerprint powder, well that's their problem. If anyone ever asks me, I'll tell the truth. But they don't; they just swarm in like jackals, looking for souvenirs of a murder. So I'm giving them souvenirs."

He chuckled, hauled out the ironwork, and set to work hooking up the printer to the laptop. He was doing it all wrong, but I bit my tongue. I'd realized long ago the futility of telling Michael how to do computer tasks, so I left him to figure it out and went back to selling my dusty ironwork.

But the next time I saw Wesley pass by outside, I ran out to him. He was so preoccupied I had to grab his arm to get his attention, and when I did, he yelped and jumped away as if I'd stabbed him.

"For heaven's sake, calm down," I said. "What's wrong with you?"

"Sorry," he said. "I'm a nervous wreck. I can't believe that idiot deputy won't even consider the possibility that Benson wasn't the intended victim."

"Well, consider the source," I said, seeing an opportunity to wangle information. "I mean, what do we really know about Monty's detective abilities?"

"Not much," Wesley said. "And the sheriff doesn't either. If he did, he wouldn't have put a glorified meter maid in charge of a homicide investigation, would he?"

"Glorified meter maid?"

"Well, what would *you* call 'parking enforcement'?" Wesley said. "That's what he was — not any kind of a detective. And to think, my very survival could be in his hands."

"And who knows?" I said, "That could be like asking the fox to guard the hen house."

"What do you mean?"

"The more I think about it, the more I wonder how Monty managed to get to the crime scene so fast," I said. "He claims he was on his way here to silence the artillery when the call about the murder came in — but what if he was already here for another reason?"

Wesley looked pale.

"You don't really think —" he began.

I shrugged my shoulders.

"I should never have come here," Wesley said, and scuttled off. I ducked back into the storage area to tell Michael what I'd learned.

"Of course, now I'm feeling guilty," I said. "Poor Wesley really seems to believe he was the intended victim, and now he's more paranoid than ever."

"Well, what if he isn't just paranoid?" Michael said, looking thoughtful. "It is pretty hard to tell people apart when they're all wearing the same thing. I keep embarrassing myself, mixing up a couple of the guys in my regiment, for the same reason."

"True," I said, remembering how I'd accidentally blasted poor cousin Horace, thinking he was either Wesley or Benson.

"If the murderer really was after Wesley, that opens up a whole new set up suspects," Michael said. "I'd feel better if I thought the police were at least considering the possibility."

"I'd feel better if I thought the police didn't have something to hide," I said. "Between those blackmail photos of the sheriff and now this news about Monty — maybe there's a good reason why Monty keeps ordering me to keep my nose out of his investigation."

"Well, that and the fact that he resents you trying to do his job," Michael said. "Let's not let him know we're snooping — at least not until we find out if Wesley's scoop on Monty is true."

I nodded, and went back out to mind my booth. I tried to think how we could check on Monty's background without waiting until the weekend was over. My only idea was to ask some computer-savvy person to do an online search — and the only person I could think of was Tad. Who wasn't above suspicion to me, even if Monty had managed to confirm his alibi. Damn.

At any rate, the fair was in full swing now, and I couldn't very well abandon it to go snooping, so perhaps Monty's suspicions would be lulled by closing time. Between serving customers and keeping the Anachronism Police in line, I had my hands full. What criteria had Mrs. Waterston used to recruit the Town Watch, anyway? Not knowledge of history, that much I knew. I'd already uncovered one watchman who thought we were commemorating D-Day.

Rob dropped in eventually. From the tomato stains on his clothes, I deduced that he'd kept his promise to help out Horace.

"Have you seen Mrs. Waterston?" he asked.

"Yes, and it looks as if you may be off the hook," I said.

"Really?" Rob said, his face lighting up. "They figured out who killed Benson?"

"I meant off the hook with Mrs. Waterston," I said. "She has no idea you lost Spike for four hours; she thinks you committed the far lesser sin of letting him slip out the door when you took him home."

"I guess that's an improvement," Rob said.

"Then again, maybe if you told her what really happened, she'd decide you're too irresponsible to take care of Spike."

"Oh, I am! I am!" Rob exclaimed. "I should never be given responsibility for a helpless animal. Someone should tell her that!"

"Someone like your sister, I suppose," I said. "Grow up, Rob; if you don't want to take care of the damned dog —"

"I've come for my flamingos," Mrs. Fenniman announced, marching into my booth.

26

"Flamingos?" said one of the browsers, looking up from a candleholder.

I winced. I was hoping to deliver Mrs. Fenniman's flamingos a little more privately. Not that I was exactly ashamed of them. I'd worked very hard, trying to make them — well, "a work of art" might be a slight exaggeration. "Aesthetically pleasing," anyway. Each flamingo was formed from a single, unbroken bar of metal, shaped into a slightly stylized outline. I was proud of how well I'd captured the light, airy feeling of the birds, the grace of their long, slender legs. I rather enjoyed the creative tension between the delicacy of the subject and the strength of the iron. And I'd made each one slightly different — some feeding, some walking, some lifting up their heads, some looking backwards. I'd taken pains to see that there were no child-endangering sharp points on my flamingos — the bills weren't all that sharp; it was an optical illusion created by narrowing the line of pink on the bills and filling in with matte black. And even the fluorescent pink finish had grown on me. Although I'd made fun of it when describing them to Michael, there was something oddly magical about the muted pink glow they took on at twilight.

Still, they were pink flamingos. And I had no desire to be stereotyped as "that lady blacksmith who makes those cute pink flamingos."

"Well," Mrs. Fenniman said, tapping her foot.

"I'm really busy," I said, "Maybe I could bring them over to your house after the show? If you're out campaigning, I could leave them on the back porch."

"Nonsense. You don't have to go to all that trouble; and besides, I want to see them now," she said. "You just keep doing what you're doing — I'll get them out and look them over myself. And Rob here can help me carry them," she added, reaching out an arm to snag my brother as he tried to sneak past.

I knew better than to argue.

"Take them out back, then," I said. "They're not in period."

I showed her where to find the metal storage case with the flamingos, gave her the key — Monty had carefully locked them up again, of course — and let her get on with it. She and Rob dragged the case outside my booth and a little to the side, and began setting the birds up in the lane. In front of my booth.

"I said take them — oh, never mind," I muttered. "It's a lost cause."

"How much are you selling those for, anyway?" a customer asked.

I stifled a groan, counted to ten, and quoted an astronomically outrageous price.

The customer began writing a check.

"I'm doomed," I whispered, ducking behind the curtain when the customer had gone.

"What's wrong?" Michael said, jumping up from where he was playing with the laptop.

"I've just sold two more flamingos," I said.

"Congratulations," he said. "But I thought you only made the dozen, for your aunt."

"It's a commission," I said. "She paid in advance."

Michael looked at the check I was holding and did a double take.

"You're charging that for just two flamingos?"

"Without the family discount, yes."

"I do hope you'll give me the family discount when I order some for my mother."

"Of course," I said. "You even can get the much larger thoughtful-boyfriend discount if you lie, and say someone else made them."

"I'll keep that in mind," he said, chuckling. "So, do you want to see what's on the third CD-ROM?"

"Something juicy?"

"I have no idea," he said. "It keeps asking me for a password."

"Let me see," I said.

I tried to click on the CD-ROM's icon to open it. A gray box popped up, saying, "Please enter the unbreakable top secret password."

"That's definitely Tad's sense of humor," I said. "In case we had any doubt which CD-ROM was his."

"I tried everything I could think of," Michael said. "Including all the Greek words I know.

"Why Greek?"

"There are Greek letters written on the CD-ROM — see?"

He pushed the button to pop the CD-ROM drawer open, and pointed to the tiny characters scrawled around the circumference of the disk.

"You know Tad better than I do; maybe you can guess the password," he said.

"I don't have to guess," I said. "That writing just told me. That's not Greek, it's Elvish."

"Elvish?"

"Or maybe Elven; I forget which is correct. It's been years. Ever read Tolkien?"

"Yes, but as you said, it's been years," he said.

"Remember the scene where they kept trying to guess the password to the door of Moria, and realized that it was right there in the inscription — 'Speak friend and enter'?"

"Vaguely," he said.

I pushed the CD-ROM drawer back in, clicked on the icon, and when the password box popped up, I typed "the unbreakable top secret password" into the space.

The words "Welcome, Meg!" appeared in large, bright red letters.

"Bingo!" I said. "Tad's sense of humor plus Faulk's long-standing love of Tolkien equals one password. Not a real password that would do anything to stop a hacker, of course; just something to slow down amateur snoops."

"Call me amateur, then," Michael said. "It sure stopped me cold."

The words then disappeared in a highly artistic slow fade, to reveal a rather mundane screen full of the tiny icons that indicated files and folders.

"Where do we start?" I muttered.

"Maybe with the file named 'Read me first'?" Michael suggested.

Okay. I'd have gotten around to that in a minute. The read-me file contained a note. Addressed to me.

"Dear Meg," it said. "I'm giving you this CD in case something happens to me, or even worse, to me and Faulk, because I know you'll figure out how to use it.

"I've been gathering evidence against a guy named Roger Benson. I started out doing it for a lawsuit I was going to file, because Benson stole CraftWorks and had his company put out a pirated version. The more I look, the more evidence I find that I'm not the only one he's done this to, and it's scary how often the people who try to fight back have been having fatal accidents. CraftWorks is pretty minor, compared with some of the stuff he's stolen, so I'm hoping he won't go after me, but if he does, please see that this gets to the FBI or someone who can do something with it."

It was signed "Thaddeus R. Jackson" and below the note, in typically organized Tad fashion, he'd listed phone numbers and addresses for the regional and national FBI offices and half a dozen other law-enforcement agencies.

"Oh, great," Michael said. "He gives you a bombshell like this, and makes sure he does it so publicly that Benson knows exactly where to come looking for it."

"I assumed Benson was looking for Rob's game disk," I said. "He knew I had that; I don't really think he knew Tad had passed along his evidence."

"But you don't know that for sure," Michael said. "And no offense to Rob and Tad, but I can't imagine either CraftWorks or Lawyers from Hell is worth killing people over."

"No, but according to this next file, Tad thinks Benson's company was using games and programs like CraftWorks as a cover for laundering cash for the Russian mafia."

"Sound plausible to you?"

"How do I know?" I said, with a shrug. "I mean, Faulk's an old friend, but I haven't really known Tad that long, and only because of Faulk. He always seemed like a nice guy."

"A little excitable," Michael said.

"You could say that," I said. "In fact, if I'd only met him this weekend, I think I'd say he was a loose cannon with a hair-trigger temper and a serious grudge against Roger Benson."

"Yeah, frankly, that matches my first impression," Michael said. "Doesn't he seem to be overreacting just a little to the software piracy?"

"Not if he and Faulk are going deep into debt to fund the legal battle against Benson, which is what I gathered from talking to Faulk."

"Ouch. Meg, I hate to say it, but if I were Monty, Tad would look awfully suspicious to me."

"You don't have to be so tactful," I said. "He looks awfully suspicious to me, and I'm supposed to be his friend, dammit. Or at least his boyfriend's friend. He supposedly has an alibi, but I don't know if it's any good. This is great; we have to figure out if the stuff on this CD means Tad is in danger, or if he's just being melodramatic, or maybe trying to cover up a murder."

"For the sake of argument, what if Tad decided it was a mistake, giving you the CD-ROM, and went back to try to collect it, found Benson ransacking your booth, and attacked him?"

"Or what if he went back to my booth to collect the CD-ROM, and Benson followed him and attacked him?"

"Also possible. He could have killed Benson in self-defense, or at least what he thought was self-defense."

"Then what about the alibi?" I said.

"True," Michael said. "If the alibi is genuine. Then again, if it isn't genuine, doesn't arranging it suggest premeditation?"

"I hate this," I said. "I really hate this. I know how hurt Faulk will be if he finds out we suspect Tad, and that's nothing compared to how hurt he'll be if Tad turns out to be the killer. Michael, don't tell anyone we looked at this. If Tad's alibi's a phony and he did kill Benson, and realizes that he handed me his motive on a platter —"

"Understood. The less we know the better," he said, and began closing the windows Tad's program had opened. "I tried to look at it, but there was a password; I couldn't do anything with it. I know you probably won't want to hear this, but I think we should give this to Monty."

"I don't want to hear it, but I agree. But we do it in front of witnesses. And not till we've made a copy of the data. Remember, we're not sure Monty's even qualified to investigate this."

"Okay," he said. "I'll start on the backup."

"Meg," Eileen said, sticking her head behind the curtain. "Someone else wants to ask about the flamingos."

"I'm doomed," I muttered as I went back out into the booth.

I'd sold another flamingo and was deep in negotiations with a customer who wanted some wrought-iron cranes when Mrs. Fenniman came storming back into the booth.

"I'm only paying for twelve flamingos," she announced.

"Well, that's fine," I said. "I only made twelve."

"Then you need to learn to count, girl," she snapped back. "There're thirteen of them."

"There can't be," I said.

"Come see for yourself."

I followed her out into the lane, where a crowd of tourists were inspecting the flamingo flock at close range.

"Clear the area!" Mrs. Fenniman boomed out, and the tourists did; or at least enough that I could see the whole flamingo herd.

I took a quick count. She was right. There *were* thirteen.

"You see," Mrs. Fenniman said, noticing my frown.

"Yes, I see," I said. "But I only made twelve flamingos, so one of these has to be a ringer. And it's not hard to see which," I added, zeroing in on the runt of the litter.

Oh, it was made along the same general lines as my flamingos. Same method, approximately the same size. The workmanship was far inferior, though. Where my birds flowed in long, graceful curves, this one had an awkward, squarish shape. The color was ghastly, not a pure pink at all but one with mottled brown and gray overtones, and the finish was peeling off in great leprous patches. The edges were less-finely finished — knowing how many small neighborhood children went to visit Mrs. Fenniman, I'd worked hard to see not only that the bills were blunt but that none had any rough places, sharp edges, or dangerous points. But every corner of this bird was a laceration waiting to happen, and it had a beak so sharp no responsible person would put it anywhere near small children. In fact —

"Call Monty," I told Michael. "There's blood on this flamingo's beak."

27

"Blood?" Mrs. Fenniman trumpeted. "On one of my flamingos?"

"No," I said. "You're only paying for twelve, remember? The blood's on the one you're not buying."

"I haven't picked mine yet," she grumbled. "What if I like that one?"

I glowered at her and she retreated, clutching one of the unstained flamingos.

Using some clean rags, to avoid getting fingerprints on the flamingo — or at least any more fingerprints on top of what Mrs. Fenniman and dozens of passing shoppers had already made — Michael and I hauled the bogus flamingo back into my booth. And one of mine, for comparison. Mrs. Fenniman would just have to get along with eleven for a while.

When Monty showed up, he looked harassed, and not all that pleased to see us.

"So what's this nonsense about a blood-stained flamingo?" he said.

"I think I've found the missing murder

weapon you've been hunting for," I said.

"What gives you the idea we're missing a murder weapon, Ms. Langslow?" he said, a little too loudly. "We found the victim with your knife stuck square in his back."

"Yes, but you've known for quite some time that my knife didn't kill him, haven't you? Probably since about five minutes after the coroner saw the wound. When we were talking about my dad this morning, you said something about how many people were running around with knives and swords and bayonets. Why would you care, if you had the murder weapon? And it's no secret to anyone that you've been scouring the camp and the fair all morning for weapons; hell, you even confiscated some of my dad's surgical instruments for a while."

"So what makes you think you've found this so-called missing weapon when we couldn't?" Monty said.

Was it just his typical stubbornness, or was there some more sinister reason for him to act so obtuse?

"Oh, for heaven's sake, just take a look at the thing, Monty," I said, jerking a thumb at the bird in question. "It won't kill you to look."

He lost the mocking air when he inspected its beak, keeping his Band-Aid—

decked hands well away from it, I noticed.

"Damn, you made that thing sharp," he said.

"I didn't make it," I said. "This is one of the ones I made."

I indicated my flamingo.

"Looks pretty similar to me," he said.

"Similar? Are you crazy!" I exclaimed, and I pointed out the finer features of my bird and the shortcomings of the imposter.

"Still looks pretty much the same to me," he said.

"They're right," I muttered. "Justice really is blind."

"But you're right about one thing. This fellow's beak couldn't stab butter," he said, indicating my flamingo with a disparaging air. "You'd have to use him as a blunt instrument. This other one, now — that's a lethal weapon. Where'd you find the damned things, anyway?"

"Here, in my booth," I said. "They've been here all along."

A couple of spectators tittered.

"They couldn't have been," he said.

"Don't you remember when I was looking for my cash box?" I said. "You opened the case they were in yourself, and said there was nothing but birds inside. Then you locked it up again, with the murder weapon inside."

More titters.

"You've been searching all morning for something that's been right here under your nose the whole time. Gee, maybe if you'd let me back in my booth a little sooner you'd have found the murderer by now."

"If I find you've been withholding evidence and obstructing justice —" Monty began.

"Then you can arrest me," I said. "Do I get a discount if I pay my bail in quarters?"

Monty's face turned pale, and then went blank and stony.

"I'm afraid we'll have to ask you to vacate this booth while we check this out," he said, with narrowed eyes.

I should learn to keep my mouth shut.

"I guess we should make ourselves scarce for a while?" Michael said. I was glad to see he'd had the foresight to pack the laptop and sling it over his shoulder while I was alienating Monty.

"Guess so," I said. "Hang on a moment. If I'm going to turn into the wrought-iron-flamingo lady, I don't want to lose sales momentum. Rob, don't get lost."

I wandered over to Amanda's booth, with Rob and Michael following.

"Remind me to commit all my crimes down here from now on," Amanda said, as she watched Monty. "If I lived here, I think I'd vote against that sheriff of yours, no matter who was running against him."

I shrugged.

"He only got the job because of necrophilia, anyway," Rob said. "It runs rampant down here, you know. You get used to it."

"You don't say," Amanda said, looking at him over her glasses.

"He means nepotism, of course," I said.

I *think* she believed me.

"Mind if I put a sign up in your booth for a while?" I asked.

"Be my guest," she said. "Your booth is already drawing me more traffic than I've ever seen. Need some paper?"

I took one sheet of the offered paper, wrote "SIGN UP HERE FOR INFORMATION ON THE WROUGHT-IRON FLAMINGOS" and taped it to the front of her booth, then cleared a small space on the table and left the remaining sheets stacked there.

"Feel free to tell really outrageous stories to anyone who asks where I am," I said.

"You got it, hon," she said. "Have fun."

As I walked by, I heard Monty snarling into his police radio.

"Then send someone out looking for them. No, I don't know his last name. We only have one Horace —"

"Hollingworth," I said.

He glared at me, but repeated Horace's full name into the radio.

"That's right. And the coroner. No, we don't have another dead body; never mind what I want him for, just —"

Michael, Rob, and I strolled away. We passed through the town square, where Horace was selling tomatoes. I made Rob take his place and told Horace to run along to my booth. We took a detour through the tent where the Lions' Club was advertising a colonial pig roast, interrupted the coroner in his task of dishing out barbecue sauce, and dispatched him to Monty, too.

"Okay, you're my witness," I said to Michael. "We have now done our bit to help the minions of the law, right?"

"So now we have some barbecue and relax until Monty's finished at your booth?"

"No, now we go to see a man about a flamingo."

We passed by Dad's booth, where I deduced, from the squeals of childish laughter, that he and his troupe of performing leeches were entertaining a crowd of small boys.

"Doesn't it hurt?" I heard one small boy ask.

"No, the leech's saliva contains a mild anaesthetic," Dad said. "As well as an anticoagulant."

I only hoped he and the leeches weren't playing Rogue Elephant, which, according to Rob, involved Dad attaching the longest available leech to his nose and lurching around the room trumpeting like a wounded pachyderm. Rob still swears that Dad did this to entertain him when he was sick with the chicken pox. I prefer to believe that no one from whom I had inherited DNA could be capable of doing such a thing, and have always put the whole episode down to Rob's vivid imagination and the fact that he was running a fever of 102 degrees at the time. Still, I decided not to peek into Dad's booth. One likes to keep a few illusions intact.

"Should we ask your Dad along?"

"He sounds happy," I said.

"So where are we going?"

"To see Tony, of course," I said. "The only person at this whole fair with a known history of copying my ironwork. Not to mention the fact that I just realized something about Tony that makes him — well, you'll see. It all points to Tony."

Well, except for the stuff that pointed to Monty. I'd worry about that later.

We stopped in the lane, near Tony's booth, and observed him from a distance for a few minutes before approaching. He looked badly hung over, and he didn't have many customers to distract him.

"Shouldn't we tell Monty about this?" Michael asked.

"You really think he'd listen?"

"Okay, so what's our plan?"

"He's spotted us," I said. "Come on."

If I hadn't already decided that Tony was guilty of something, I could have guessed from the way he reacted to seeing us. He retreated behind his counter when we drew near, and when we stepped into his booth, he glanced behind him as if planning to duck out the back.

"Going someplace, Tony?" I asked.

"I . . . uh, I need to restock," he said.

"Good idea," I said. I walked behind the counter and picked up the book Tony had stashed beneath it.

"*The Complete Book of Locks and Locksmithing*," I read, holding it up. "Interesting choice of reading."

"Business is slow; I'm thinking of branching out," he said.

"I'm sure you are," I said, grabbing his

arm. "Come on, Tony, we need to talk. Let's go someplace more private."

"I can't leave my booth," Tony said, as Michael grabbed his other arm.

"I thought you were going to restock. Don't you have a CLOSED FOR RESTOCKING sign? Well, people will figure it out. Come on, let's talk while you restock."

His booth was on the outermost edge of the fair, only about eight feet from the lightly wooded area that surrounded the field on two sides. We led Tony a few yards into the trees, where we wouldn't be overheard, and sat him down on a fallen log. I stood over him, hands on my hips, and Michael leaned against a nearby tree, his arms folded, and assumed a fierce, bloodthirsty expression that I recognized from having seen him play Richard III a few months before.

"Okay, Tony," I said. "The game's up."

28

Tony winced and glanced up at Michael, who gave him a lovely menacing smile.

"We know you went down to my booth after you locked up Wesley," I said.

"That's ridiculous," Tony said.

"We know about the flamingo, Tony," I said.

"Oh, no," he whispered.

"We know what you did with it," I went on. "So why don't you just go along with us to the police and come clean?"

"God, no!" he cried. "They'll think I did it! And the killer will know that I know something!"

Michael and I looked at each other.

"Yes," I said, carefully. "You could be right."

"Then you've got to help me!" he said. "I know I shouldn't have done what I did, but when I saw my flamingo sticking out of his back, I panicked; and I thought I heard the guy that did it coming back and —"

"Slow down, Tony," I said. This wasn't

turning out the way I had planned it. Not at all. "Start from the beginning."

"Start from why you went to Meg's booth in the first place," Michael said.

"Okay," Tony said. "Okay, I guess you figured out I was trying to make a flamingo like yours."

"Not very much like mine," I couldn't help saying.

"Well, what do you expect? — I only got glimpses of it at the last fair, when you were showing it to the old lady," he said. "I knew I had the shape down pretty good —"

I bit my tongue and nodded.

"But I was having trouble with the finish. It just didn't look right. I thought maybe I could figure out what was wrong with the finish on mine by looking at yours, or if not, maybe you'd have some notes on how you did the finish. So anyway, after I got your cousin in the stocks, I realized that there was nobody else around, and it was a good time to sneak over to your booth. I pretended to pass out, and then I got up, went over to my booth for my flamingo, and then to your booth."

"So much for parallel development."
He shrugged.

"Anyway, I got into the case with your flamingos, and I took some Polaroids, but I couldn't tell much about the finish from just looking. And I figured anything valuable would be locked up, so I'd brought along my tool kit, and it didn't take me five minutes to open that padlock. You really should get a better lock; I could sell you a —"

"Later, Tony. Get back to your burglary."

"I didn't steal anything."

"What did you do with my cash box?"

"I didn't do anything. Just took it out of the case when I was searching. Anyway, I didn't find any papers, so I was starting up your laptop. When I heard someone coming, I dived under one of the tables."

"Just like that?" I said. "You didn't try to hide what you'd been doing?"

"I put the laptop in the case and shut the lid," he said. "I figured anyone who came in would think the flamingo was yours."

"Then what happened?"

"Someone came in."

"Who?"

"I'm not sure," he said. "There was a cloth covering the table that went right down to the floor. I found a crack, but all I could see was his shoes."

"Okay, then what?"

"Then another guy came in, and one of them said 'What the hell are you doing here?' and they argued for a while."

"About what?"

"I couldn't tell. After those first words, I think they tried to keep their voices down, and the tablecloth muffled the sound. I could tell they were angry; that's about all."

"And that they were both men," Michael put in.

"Yeah, definitely both men."

"Go on," I said.

"Okay, so they were arguing, and I heard one of them say something about 'that damned dog.' I could see both sets of feet heading for the back of the booth, and I heard a lot of clanking and grunting, and one of them came back, and I saw the table-cloth on the other table move, so I figured maybe there wasn't enough room for both of them behind the curtain, and the one guy had lost out and decided to hide under the table."

"It's like a French farce," Michael muttered.

"Only they rarely kill people in French farces," I added.

"Anyway, then that little dog came in and started barking, like he couldn't figure out which one of the three of us to attack. You know, the little hairball that's always trying to bite people."

"Spike," I said. "I should have known. Where Spike goes, trouble follows."

"Yeah, well this time that harridan who runs the fair followed."

"Mom?" Michael exclaimed.

"Uh . . . yeah," Tony said. "I could tell it was her. When she reached down to put a leash on the mutt, I caught a glimpse of her face and that big, white, fright wig. And she dragged him out, still barking. You could hear them all the way out of the fair grounds."

"And you just sat there under the table all this time?"

"I figured if I sat tight, maybe they wouldn't catch me," Tony said. "And a damned good thing, too, considering that one of them turned out to be a murderer."

"So what happened next?"

"The guy under the table came out and looked behind the curtain, and he blew out of there, real fast. I waited a bit, to see if the guy behind the curtain was coming out, and I decided maybe he'd gone out the back of the booth. So I came out, and peeked behind the curtain, and there was this guy, dead, with my flamingo in his back. It was freaky, really, seeing him lying there — I couldn't tell who he was, just that he was wearing a blue coat exactly like the one I was wearing."

"And that's when you panicked."

"Yeah. I figured they'd blame me, you know? I mean, it was my flamingo. So I pulled the flamingo out and wiped the blood off its beak with my handkerchief, and put it in the case with yours. And I saw the knife and I stuck it in his back so they wouldn't wonder how he'd died."

"Great thinking, Tony. Only my knife and your flamingo's beak were just a little bit different in size. They figured out almost immediately that the knife wasn't the weapon."

"Okay, so I wasn't thinking too clearly," he said. "I really was pretty drunk. And do you have any idea what it's like, finding a dead body like that?"

"You seem to forget that Meg found the same dead body a little later on," Michael pointed out.

"Well, she wasn't a witness to his murder," Tony said.

"Some witness you are," Michael said.

"Yeah, Tony," I said. "Once you tell the police all of this, everyone in town will know you were an earwitness to the murder. The killer will probably go after you, just in case you could identify him to the police, which is a real laugh, because so far you haven't remembered a thing that could possibly help identify him."

"I know it's a guy."

"Wow. You just eliminated fifty percent of the human race," I said. "Only — how many billion people left?"

"Give me a break," he said. "I was pretty drunk. And all I saw was his shoes."

"Okay, concentrate, then. Tell us about his shoes."

Tony concentrated.

"They were dark," he said.

"Black or brown?" I asked.

"Yeah," he said. "Or maybe dark blue."

"What kind of shoes?"

"I don't know. They had buckles on them; I couldn't see what was under the buckles."

"Let me guess: one buckle on each foot."

"Ha, ha," Tony said. "Look, I told you I didn't see anything."

"No kidding."

"One of the buckles was kind of odd."

"Odd how?"

"It had a kind of a dent in it," he said.

"Would you recognize that buckle again?" I asked.

"I don't know," Tony said. "Maybe."

"Come on," I said. "We're going to find the buckle."

We went back to Tony's booth, recruited

a neighbor to watch it while he was gone, and set out dragging him up and down the aisles of the craft fair.

At first, we tried to be subtle. We'd wander into peoples' booths, and I'd stand chitchatting with the owners while Michael and Tony inspected their shoes and the shoes of anyone else in the booth. If the crafter was behind a counter, we'd think of some stratagem to lure him out where we could see him.

Dad joined the party after we passed through the medical tent, and after that, all hope of subtlety went out the window.

We walked up and down the lanes, our eyes fixed on passing shoes, and we spent a lot of time apologizing to the people we bumped into. Four or five times, when we were all waiting for Tony to make up his mind about a shoe, people jumped to the conclusion that one of us had lost a contact, and within seconds we had a swarm of eager helpers combing the ground.

Although we gave Dad the gist of what Tony had said, so he knew that we were almost certain to find the buckle on a man's shoe, he kept getting carried away. After the third time he managed to get slapped or swatted for trying to twitch up some poor woman's skirts, we invented an important job for him — keeping a list of who had already passed inspection, which kept his hands busy scribbling and prevented him from being hauled away on some kind of morals charge.

The list was already lengthy when we left the fair grounds and moved over to the encampment, roaming up and down the ad hoc streets, peering and scribbling.

By the time we'd been at this for an hour, everyone had figured out something was going on. Dad invented a cover story that Tony and I were trying to find a buckle that we both wanted to use as a model for our own work, which was pretty flimsy, but after that we were stuck with it. Most of the crafters we met thought Michael and I were inflicting some obscure penance on Tony for his well-known plagiarism of my best designs, and the reenactors had gotten so used to strange behavior from the locals that they didn't really seem curious.

Of course it was only a matter of time before Monty found out what we were up to, jumped to the unfortunately accurate conclusion that it had something to do with the murder, and sent out a couple of officers to bring us back to the operations tent where he'd set up his on-site headquarters.

He wasn't in a good mood.

29

"Give me one reason why I shouldn't arrest you for withholding evidence and obstructing justice," Monty said.

I decided to assume this was a rhetorical question and changed the subject.

"We've found an important new piece of evidence for you," I said.

"Yes, and you've been running all over the fair, looking at people's belt buckles, and concealing this evidence from the police for how long?" Monty demanded.

"Shoe buckles," Dad corrected him.

"We wanted to bring you complete information," I said.

"Wanted the glory of solving this yourself, you mean," he said.

I bit back my quick answer, which would have been that, no, I just didn't want to give the information to someone I feared would misuse it to build a stronger case against one of my friends — especially since I wasn't quite sure I trusted Monty. So I sat, trying not to interrupt, as Monty took Tony through the same catechism I had been through. No, he didn't remember any more about what the shoes looked like. And, no, he hadn't seen the odd buckle anywhere around the fair.

"So you don't remember anything else?" Monty asked.

"Not about the shoes, no," Tony said.

"Do you remember anything that's not about the shoes?" Monty asked.

Tony thought.

"I remember the socks a little," he said. "I think it was the socks, anyway."

We all sat upright.

"What about the socks?" Monty demanded.

Tony thought again. Or maybe just paused, for effect.

"Red plaid," he said, finally.

"He was wearing red plaid socks?" Monty said.

Tony nodded.

"You didn't see any pants cuffs?"

"No, just a glimpse of red plaid," Tony said.

"You idiot," I exploded. "You dragged us all over the fair looking for slightly dented buckles, and didn't think to mention that the guy was wearing red plaid socks! We could have searched people's tents for the socks!"

Tony looked at me and smirked.

"You didn't ask about his socks," he said. "Just his shoes."

"I think that just about settles it," Monty said. "And don't be too hard on Tony here," he added, turning to me. "We'd have figured it out sooner or later anyway."

"Figured out what?" I asked, although I had a sinking feeling I knew.

"Well, there were a lot of interesting costumes at that shindig," Monty said, looking at me with one eyebrow raised, as if to imply that he'd found my costume particularly interesting. "But I only remember one red plaid costume, and by an odd coincidence, the person wearing it was the person I was planning to arrest anyway. So don't be too mad at Tony here, Ms. Langslow. His evidence was just one more nail in the coffin. Ah, here we are."

Faulk walked in, followed by two of the deputies. He glanced at the rest of us, then looked at Monty.

"You wanted to see me?" he said.

"Oh, no," I murmured.

"I certainly did," Monty said. "Read him his rights, Fred."

"He was the one in the kilts," Tony said.

"And red plaid socks," Monty said. "Which you saw."

"Yeah, or it could even have been part of the kilt," Tony said. "I was looking through this really small hole."

"You're arresting me for wearing a kilt?" Faulk said, pretending a lightness I could tell he didn't feel. "May I call the Celtic Antidefamation League now?"

"No, actually we're arresting you because your fingerprints are on the murder weapon," Monty said.

"The flamingo," Faulk said.

"Aha!" Monty said.

"Aha, yourself," I said. "It's all over the fair that the flamingo was the murder weapon. Even the tourists are talking about it."

"But none of the tourists managed to leave their fingerprints all over the flamingo in question," Monty said. "Bloody fingerprints."

"Well, of course my fingerprints are all over it," Faulk said. "I handled it."

"Aha!" Monty said again. Irritating habit.

"It had nothing to do with the murder," Faulk said. "I waited till he was away from his booth and I went over and snooped around, after that dustup with Benson. So I guess I did have some blood on my hands. And I found the flamingo."

"Why didn't you tell me?" I exclaimed.

318

"If you saw the flamingo and knew he was copying it —"

"Dammit, I'm asking the questions here," Monty said. "Why were you snooping around, anyway? What business was it of yours?"

Faulk sighed and rubbed his face with his hands, the way people do when they're too exhausted to think.

"I wanted to see what he was making. He's been copying his stuff from me, and Meg and — oh, I don't know how many other blacksmiths. The man doesn't have a creative bone in his body. I wanted to see what he was ripping off."

"What, are you suing him or something?"

"Well, maybe," he said, glancing at me. "Meg and I have been talking about it. But mainly I wanted to see who was going to try to dismember the little weasel. I've had to pull other blacksmiths off him the last four or five shows we've been at together, to keep them from beating him to a pulp. I wanted to see who was going to try to k— hurt him this time. That's why I didn't tell you," he said, turning to me. "I know you'd only get ticked off."

"I think I had a right to know," I said.

"Yeah," he said. "You did. And I was going to tell you after the fair. I figured you'd be upset at first, but if he wasn't around, it would be okay. I mean, you hated making the flamingos so much; I figured once you got past your first reaction, it would be okay. You wouldn't mind as much."

"No," I said. "I hated making them, but they were my flamingos. I'd have minded."

Faulk nodded.

"Minded enough to go after him?" Monty interrupted.

"Me?" I spluttered.

"No," Faulk said, smiling faintly. "I can't imagine Meg going in for physical violence when she can do a lot more painful damage with that tongue of hers."

"Gee, thanks," I muttered.

"And, of course, you've never gone after him yourself, have you?" Monty said.

"No," Faulk said, keeping his voice even.

"Yeah, I figured you'd say that," Monty went on. "Everyone around here says you don't fly off the handle easily, but when you do lose your temper — watch out. So who knows? My information says you were about to go bankrupt, supporting your little friend's lawsuit against Benson. Then again, maybe you mistook this Benson fellow for Tony here, who was ripping you off. He's about the same size and build, and

320

like that reporter keeps saying, everyone looks alike in these damned blue uniforms. I don't really care which one you had it in for. You had reasons to hate 'em both; I'll let the DA sort it out which one you thought you were killing. Fred, read him his rights and slap a pair of cuffs on him."

A craft fair's like a small town — whenever something interesting happens, everyone seems to find out all at once, as if by telepathy or jungle drums. So I suppose I shouldn't have been surprised to find quite a few people lurking in the vicinity of the operations tent when we came out to watch Faulk being led off to the squad car. And since Faulk was generally well liked, I could hear shocked and resentful murmurs running through the crowd.

"Meg — break it to Tad, will you?" Faulk said, over his shoulder. "And see if you can convince him that now is not the time to be stiff-necked, and he should call my parents about finding a lawyer. They might even offer to pay; God knows I'm going to have a hard time doing it."

I nodded.

"Uh . . . can I help?" Rob said, stepping out of his place in the watching crowd. "I mean, you at least need an attorney with you for the arraignment. Or I could go get one of the uncles if you'd rather."

"No, you'll do fine, Rob," Faulk said. "And maybe you can figure out how to arrange bail, so I don't have to spend the rest of the weekend in durance vile."

"I don't think our durances are all that vile," I said. "It's a pretty new jail."

"Yeah, right," Faulk said, as the police went through the ritual of holding his head so he didn't strike it on the doorframe while getting into the car. "See you, sword lady."

"I can't believe you're stupid enough to think Faulk is the killer," I blurted out to Monty as he was getting into the front seat of the car.

"Yeah, well, I was thinking it was your friend with the braids until his alibi came forward," Monty said.

"Alibi," Faulk echoed, from inside the car. "Tad was off by himself, playing Doom on his laptop when the murder happened."

"Yeah, well, I guess he would say something like that," Monty said, with a sly smirk. "But the guy he was with came in a couple of hours ago and alibied him. Hey, there's another possible motive," he said, turning to me. "Mr. Cates here found out his boyfriend was two-timing him and killed the next person he met in a jealous rage."

With that, he ducked into the car and

slammed the door, just in time to save me from a charge of assaulting a police officer when I impulsively hurled my haversack at his head. It bounced harmlessly off the car instead.

"Well, that was stupid," I muttered, as I bent to pick it up and check the contents for breakage.

"I'm sorry, Meg," Michael said. "I know Faulk's your friend."

"And he's not a killer, no matter what that idiot Monty thinks," I replied. "And I don't believe Tad did that to him, although now Faulk has gone off to jail thinking he has, and — oh, damn!"

"I believe you," Michael said. "Look, tomorrow we can —"

"Michael, I have a copy of our battle orders," said another French soldier, coming up and handing him a paper.

"Sorry," Michael said. "This'll just take a minute."

He joined a group of white-clad *Gatinois chasseurs*. Apparently something about the battle orders upset some and made others laugh, but you could tell that overall they were getting excited about the coming skirmish.

Mrs. Waterston hove into sight, flanked by a man in an officer's uniform who was carrying a quill pen, a bottle of ink, and a flat board that seemed to be a colonial-style version of a clipboard.

"Does anyone else want to fight in the skirmish?" Mrs. Waterston called. "Last chance; come forward if you want to fight in the skirmish!"

I watched as she signed up a number of men, including Cousin Horace, and told them to report to Mrs. Tranh to be outfitted with their uniforms.

What the hell, I thought. Make an effort to share Michael's interests.

I strolled over to where Mrs. Waterston stood.

"If you need bodies, I'd be happy to pitch in," I said.

"Oh — Meg," Mrs. Waterston said, as if she wasn't quite sure she recognized me. "I'm terribly sorry, but you know, women didn't go into combat in those days. I'm afraid we can't allow it."

She smiled and looked past me, searching the crowd for more male volunteers.

I was about to point out that there were a few other women already fighting, regular members of various units. But then it occurred to me that perhaps Mrs. Waterston hadn't detected this, and would go and insist that they be kicked out. I didn't want to cause anyone any trouble.

"You can watch from the sidelines, you know," Mrs. Waterston said, noticing that I was still there. "With all the other camp followers."

30

Camp followers?

She's Michael's mother, I told myself, as I forced my hands to unclench, bit back several stinging replies, and walked away. You don't want to get in an argument with Michael's mother. And however seductive it might seem right now, killing her would be a bad idea. The police were still swarming all around, and Michael would be upset. I glanced over to where Michael was standing with his unit. He hadn't heard what she said. Maybe she hadn't meant it as an insult. Michael saw me looking at him, said something to his comrades, and headed my way.

"Meg, are you okay?" he asked, as he rejoined me.

"Thank goodness the police have finally arrested the murderer," I heard Mrs. Waterston say to the officer at her side.

"Not as far as I'm concerned," I muttered.

"She doesn't mean it that way," he said.

"She's so focused on her festival; it's not as if she's even thought about whether Faulk's guilty or not."

"I know," I said. "Look, I've got to get back to my booth; you have to go rehearse. I'll see you at the skirmish."

"Meg, are you sure —"

"Michael!" Mrs. Waterston called. "Why aren't you with your regiment? We're getting ready for the rehearsal skirmish."

"You're right, I've got to run," Michael said. "We'll figure out what to do later."

I nodded and moped off, back to my booth.

The craft fair was open for another hour, and I got through it on autopilot, fending off questions from people who wanted to know more about Faulk's arrest with the not inaccurate claim that I was too busy to talk. On the bright side, I realized I wasn't going to go broke from the weekend's adventures. Eileen and Amanda had taken care of the booth in my absence, and had done well. I could gauge how tired I was by the fact that I couldn't instantly calculate in my head exactly how well, but I suspected I'd have a record weekend, even if I sold nothing on Sunday — not that there was much left to sell. And I'd taken a slew of orders for special commissions, which meant future income during the normally slow winter season. Of course, the bad news was that most of the commissions were for wrought-iron flamingos. I decided to get depressed about that later, so I could concentrate, for the moment, on feeling depressed about Faulk's arrest.

When the fair closed for the day, I headed over toward my parents' house for a short visit. I'd probably miss the beginning of the rehearsal skirmish, but I didn't think anyone would miss me, and I needed a break.

A break from portapotties. A break from the questions everyone had been throwing at me. And a break from the close proximity of the cannon, which had been booming quite vigorously ever since having to give Mrs. Waterston an alibi had revealed the crew's ploy with the speakers. Even at this distance, I thought, the cannon was giving me a headache. Or was it just stress? And I was very much afraid that our deal for some peace and quiet at night would be off.

I ran into my nephew Eric as I walked down the driveway.

"Meg!" he said, his face lighting up. Nice to know someone was glad to see me, although he looked uncharacteristically anxious.

"What's wrong?" I asked.

"Duck's brooding again," he said. "Can you help?"

"Brooding?" I asked. Weren't we all? But then, Eric's pet duck was a cheerful, gregarious creature who followed him around like a pet dog. What could she possibly be brooding about, and what was I supposed to do about it — quack knock-knock jokes?

"Brooding," Eric repeated. "Sitting on her eggs. Can you help?"

Oh. Of course.

"Why does Duck need my help with that?" I asked.

He sighed.

"She keeps laying them in all the wrong places, and people break the eggs accidentally, or they have to chase her away. I thought maybe if we moved the eggs just right, she would go on sitting on them in the new place."

"Okay," I said. "We can give it a try."

I could see what he meant about all the wrong places. Duck was sitting on the hood of Dad's car. Evidently Dad hadn't driven it for the past day — no, two days. I could see two eggs under Duck. And Dad might not get around to driving his car until after the festival was over, but even a bird-lover like Dad was unlikely to give up driving for however many days it took duck eggs to hatch. Assuming they ever did hatch, which was unlikely, since Duck was, as far as we knew, the only duck for miles around.

I sent Eric in to get a bit of deviled egg, Duck's favorite food, and studied the situation. I had been struck by what seemed like an inspiration, and I was testing it to see if it had any cracks.

When Eric returned with the food, we managed to lure Duck off the car hood long enough for me to grab the pair of eggs she was sitting on. She didn't like it much, though; she began quacking and making little dashes at me with lowered beak. But she didn't seem to mind Eric holding them.

"Eric," I said. "How far do you think you can lead Duck?"

"She'll follow me anywhere," he boasted. "At least when she's not sitting on her eggs, that is."

"Good," I said. "You know those guys who are firing the cannon out on the battlefield?"

I watched as Eric went down the driveway, carefully holding the eggs, with Duck following behind. With any luck, if Eric could find a moment to deposit the eggs on top of the cannon, we'd have another night's reprieve from the cannon fire.

And the cannon crew would, I knew, take good care of Duck.

Probably overfeed her, but then, so did Dad and Eric.

"Remember," I called. "Wait until the skirmish is over. And try not to let anyone see you."

Eric nodded, not even looking back, so fiercely was he concentrating on the eggs.

When I got to the house, I found Mother and Mrs. Fenniman moping on the porch as neglected glasses of lemonade sweated small puddles onto a tile-topped table.

"Hello, dear," Mother said, faintly, as I sat down.

Mrs. Fenniman merely grunted.

I thought of going to the kitchen for a glass so I could pour myself some lemonade, but it seemed like too much trouble. I sat down on the glider and rocked for a while in silence. From time to time, either Mother or Mrs. Fenniman would sigh.

I don't know why I didn't succumb to the contagious atmosphere of gloom and depression, but I didn't. Okay, I'd arrived ready to whine a little and extract some sympathy, but seeing the two of them pining away like lost souls ticked me off. It was okay for me to get depressed, dammit, but a world in which neither Mother nor Mrs.

Fenniman was out causing some kind of mischief was truly a world turned upside down.

"So what's wrong with you?" I finally asked Mrs. Fenniman.

"I feel worse than a snake with a pot-belly," she said. "That low-down polecat of a sheriff has stolen the damned election with his sneaky tomato toss."

"Then go out and do something sneakier," I said.

"Can't," she said.

"Yes, you can," I said. "I have every faith in your superior guile and cunning."

"I thought you were going to think of something for me," she complained.

"Okay, borrow the dunk tank they use at the county fair and have them set it up in front of the courthouse," I suggested. "Or go hand out your grandmother's recipe for stewed tomatoes. Better yet, go down to the garden-supply store and buy up all the tomato seeds you can find and hand them out."

Mrs. Fenniman chuckled faintly; then more vigorously as she started thinking about it.

"I might," she said. "I just might do that. I think I'll go down there right now."

She got up, drained her lemonade, and

strode off down the driveway.

"It's October," Mother pointed out. "They probably don't have a lot of seeds at the garden-supply store."

"Well, by the time she gets there and finds that out, she'll be so fired up she'll think of something better," I said. "What's wrong with you?"

"Nothing, dear," Mother said.

"Well, it's too dull for me around here," I said, standing up. "I'm going down to the battlefield to watch the rehearsal. Mrs. Waterston sure does know how to put on a festival. I think she'll be a shoe-in to chair next year's committee."

Mother sniffed.

"And I bet the battle's going to be the most exciting thing of the whole weekend," I went on. "Yes, I bet people will be talking about that battle for weeks. Months, even."

"Nonsense," Mother exclaimed. "It's going to be a complete disaster. You should hear some of the ridiculous things she's said about it. That woman knows nothing about how to plan a battle."

"And how much do you know about planning battles?" I asked.

"As much as Mrs. Waterston, thank you very much," Mother said. "And a great deal more about the Battle of Yorktown. After all, I grew up here. She's going to spoil everything."

"Well, there's not much you can do about that now," I said.

"We'll see about that," she said. She got up, went into the house to repowder her hair and top it off with a huge flower-trimmed straw hat, and set off down the driveway at a brisk pace.

As I followed, more slowly, I didn't know whether I'd done a good deed or just stirred up trouble, but I felt better now that only one of us was moping.

Out on the battlefield, chaos reigned. Rope barriers now divided the battlefield proper from the sidelines, where workmen had begun erecting bleachers for the spectators. Mrs. Waterston, in yet another fabulously ornate period dress, was running up and down the sidelines like a football coach, barking out orders with an anachronistic megaphone that the Town Watch were studiously ignoring. I could tell from some of the comments of other people in the watching crowd — friends and family of some of the reenactors, from the sound of it — that they resented her. I could only imagine what the troops felt about the whole thing.

Especially since a lot of the participating

reenactors had been to Yorktown Day before and knew a lot about what actually took place back in 1781. I figured out, finally, why so many reenactors tolerated Mrs. Waterston's unpopular decisions — she had somehow convinced the National Park Service to allow her to stage the reenactment on the actual battleground, an unheard of feat in recent memory. Still the troops obviously didn't like her plans as detailed on the official instruction sheets the Town Watch handed out. A few people were shouting mad and a lot more simply muttered mutinously.

And yet the show went on, and Mother appeared to have something to do with it. To my surprise, she was acting as a peacemaker. After Mrs. Waterston passed through a group, stirring up discontent and making herself about as popular as the tax on tea must have been, Mother would follow in her wake and leave even the surliest soldiers smiling. The rehearsal skirmish got started late, but it did start, with Mother, sitting at the edge of the battlefield, smiling and waving a handkerchief at the participants whenever ill will seemed about to erupt.

"It's too good to be true," I muttered, as I sat on the bleachers with Dad, watching another column of troops march out onto the field for the rehearsal. "She's up to something."

"Who's up to something?" Dad asked.

31

"Never mind," I said, knowing Dad would never find fault with anything Mother did, however outlandish. "Monty looks very cheerful."

The deputy was standing a few feet away, talking very enthusiastically to a group of people.

"Who's that he's talking to?" Dad asked.

"Reporters, probably," I said. "Yeah, I recognize one of the guys from the *Daily Press*. And Cousin Wesley, of course."

"A complete cover-up," Wesley said, leaving the group around Monty to sprawl on the bleachers just below us. "Well, they'll see. You can't get away with trampling on the First Amendment like that."

"And I wish I thought they'd done a really thorough investigation," Dad said. "I just think they're in danger of overlooking something."

"Yeah," Wesley said. "Like the very real possibility that Benson wasn't even the intended victim. They're absolutely ignoring the danger to other potential targets."

"Like you, for example?"

"I have enemies; I keep telling them that."

"They haven't even tried to investigate my alibi," Dad said. "For all they know, I could have sneaked away from the party and killed Benson, and they would have the wrong guy locked up."

"This is ridiculous, Dad!" I said. "If it's not Wesley whining about how he was the intended victim, it's you saying they ought to consider you a suspect. Well, here's your chance, Dad. There he is — go for it. I'll even lend you a flamingo."

Both Wesley and Dad looked startled.

"Yeah, make fun of it," Wesley said. "How would you feel if I turned up in your booth tonight with a beak in the back, huh? Your own cousin?"

"I think I could cope," I said.

"Now, now," Dad said, "Look, there's Michael's unit. He looks nice in his uniform."

Well, actually "nice" wasn't quite the word I would have used, but he was well worth looking at. I followed him with my eyes, but thanks to Dad and Wesley, my mind had drifted back to the murder, Faulk's arrest, and my fear that if I didn't do something, the real killer was going to get away.

"So what do you think, anyway?" Wesley said. "Deputy Monty seems to be pretty sure he's got the right man. Do you think Cates did it?"

"He's wrong," I said. "And we'll prove it, as soon as that stupid Monty stops preening himself and listens."

At least I hoped we would prove it.

"What, have you got like a witness or something?" he asked.

"Something like that," I said.

Or maybe it would be just me trying to prove it, I thought, smiling back as Michael caught my eye. He seemed to be enjoying himself, clowning around with several of the guys from his unit. Somehow I didn't think he was going to be up for more sleuthing.

Okay, I'd do it by myself. Scour the camp for anyone else who wore a kilt — there had been a few. And wasn't there a whole unit of highlanders coming down for the battle tomorrow? Maybe some of them had come early. And I could find Mel, the bounty hunter, and pick his brains. Maybe he'd seen something while tailing Mrs. Waterston. Then again, he was from Richmond. What if he was another Cooper and Anthony victim seeking retribution?

And what if I'd too easily dismissed Wesley's insistence that he was the intended victim? If he was right, that opened up the possibility of additional suspects — Tony, for example. What if Monty was right about him faking drunkenness after killing Benson?

And what if Wesley was right about Monty having as much to hide as anyone? I had to find a way to check on him. And what about the mysterious blonde in the Jaguar?

And I needed to find Tony again and interrogate him some more. Maybe I could shake him on the sock story. Then again — we knew he'd been at my booth; we only had his word that he was hiding under the table. Maybe he was only making up the story of the socks. Maybe we'd all dismissed him as a suspect too easily. Roger Benson had made more than enough enemies. Maybe I should snoop around and find out if Tony was one of them. Why weren't his fingerprints on the flamingo, anyway? Or maybe they were, and the police dismissed them as irrelevant because they knew he'd made the bird. I recalled that both he and Benson had used the phrase "parallel development" in referring to their misdeeds. Did that suggest that they knew each other?

And while I was at it, I was going to find

Tad — I hadn't seen him to tell him about Faulk's arrest — and get at the truth about this alibi business.

I turned to leave, still brooding over the possibilities. I glanced over at Wesley, hoping he wouldn't tag along. It was going to be hard enough trying to talk to people without Wesley underfoot.

Wesley was watching the troops with a speculative look in his eye. In fact, he seemed to be staring at Michael. I suppressed a giggle. When he'd asked about witnesses, I'd been looking at Michael. What if Wesley had jumped to the conclusion that Michael was the witness?

Well, let him, I thought. Michael's going to be too busy to bother with Wesley, and if chasing around after Michael keeps Wesley out of my way, all the better.

I noticed with some surprise that Mother was leaving, escorted by a dozen officers, all from different units, to judge by their uniforms. What was she up to?

I was about to follow her to find out when I ran into Jess, from the cannon crew.

"Hey, thanks for sending the kid with the duck," he said. "Looks like we might all get another good night's sleep after all."

"So Madame von Steuben bought the eggs as a reason not to fire the cannon."

"Hell, no," he snorted. "She was for making an omelet right then and there, and maybe duck *à l'orange* for dessert. But then — well, come take a look."

I followed him upstream, against the departing crowd, and onto a small rise, where he stopped and pointed toward the cannon emplacement.

I could see Duck, comfortably settled on the back end of the gun, with her head tucked under one wing. Perched on the muzzle of the cannon, like a living gargoyle, was Mrs. Fenniman. In her right hand she held one of my pink flamingos — well, okay, I suppose they were her flamingos now — and I could just make out a sign dangling from its beak.

"And the sign says . . . ?"

"SAVE OUR FEATHERED FRIENDS," Jess said. "Hell of a nice old lady, even if she is a bit of a fruitcake."

"Most of my family are."

"I was only kidding about the fruitcake bit."

I shrugged.

"Just one thing," he asked. "What is the other egg, anyway?"

"Other egg?"

"Yeah, I can tell one of those eggs the duck is sitting on is hers, but the other's way too big. What is it?"

"Ah," I said. "I bet Eric broke one of the duck eggs and had to replace it with a peacock egg. Did Madame Von Steuben notice?"

"No, we kind of stood in front of it so she couldn't get a real good view. Are you serious — a peacock egg? Can I keep the chick if it hatches?"

"Sure," I said. "In fact, if you want some peacocks, talk to my Dad in the medical tent. He has a lot of peacocks."

"You think he might be willing to sell a pair?"

"Good chance."

"Cool," Jess said.

"I just hope Mrs. Fenniman doesn't have to perch there all night," I fretted.

"Heck, no," Jess said. "We've got Mel back on the boss-lady's trail. As soon as she turns in for the night, we've got a bed all made up in the tent for the old lady. She'll be fine. Wish I could say the same for the rest of us. Lord, would you look at that!"

He pointed to an area of the battlefield where several veteran reenactors had begun drilling a collection of Mrs. Waterston's new recruits. Including, to my surprise, Wesley, who normally avoided anything that resembled work. The recruits were marching up and down, holding boards sawed into roughly musket-shaped pieces — three feet long, two inches square on one end, and widening to two-by-four at the other to simulate the stock. I suspect they'd borrowed them from the Victory Center, which used them to demonstrate colonial drill tactics to the tourists.

"Amazing," Jess said, shaking his head, as we watched how hard the drill instructors had to work to get the recruits to form two straight lines, one a few feet behind the other. "First time I've ever seen a bunch who could figure out more than one way to mess up 'Right face!' "

"Are you really going to give those guys muskets?" I asked.

"If I had my way, we wouldn't even give them sticks," Jess said, as the recruits pretended to fire their imaginary muskets, and about a third of the men in the back line managed to whack their neighbors over the head. "They're sure not getting ammo. Or bayonets, for that matter," he added, as several fist fights broke out between the front and rear lines. "I'm going to go down and see if I can help out with this."

I wished him luck and returned to camp — which had grown even larger; more reenactors had arrived for the rehearsal and tomorrow's battle. I could hear at least two competing live musical groups playing English folk dances, and the camp rang with laughter and the shouts of people greeting old friends.

I wasn't in the mood for a party, so I strolled on past the camp, toward the deserted craft-fair grounds.

Okay, considering what I found the last time I went back to my booth after dark, maybe it wasn't a particularly brilliant idea, but I needed the peace and quiet, and I figured it was only in the movies that murderers spent the rest of their lives lurking suspiciously around the scene of the crime. Still, I jumped a foot when I saw movement in one of the aisles I had to pass on the way to my booth.

So, of course, in defiance of all the rules of common sense, I went to see what was going on.

32

I crept down the lane, acutely conscious of how much my skirts and petticoats rustled, but it wasn't as if I had time to go back to the tent and change into more suitable skulking clothes.

The intruder, whoever he was, had entered Faulk's booth. Probably someone who figured that Faulk's incarceration gave him a chance to steal things, I thought, grimly. I took advantage of every bit of cover, hiding one minute behind the canvas that covered a quilt display and the next in the shadow of a tall reproduction corner chest. As I passed by one booth, I spotted a hammer on the counter and snagged it — I felt better with some kind of weapon in my hand. Finally, I darted behind the holly bush just outside one corner of Faulk's booth. I could definitely see someone moving about in the booth.

"Stop where you are!" I shouted, leaping out from behind the bush and toward the entrance of the booth, where I ran head on into someone else, trying to do the same thing from the other direction.

We both shrieked and jumped away. I swung the hammer, missed, and hit myself on the leg just as I landed in the holly bush. The other figure — I could see now that it was Tad — fell with a clatter in a display rack filled with tall iron pot-hooks and lamp-stands.

By the time we picked ourselves up and confirmed that our injuries were minor, the intruder had long gone.

"If there even was an intruder," Tad said. "Maybe it was just your shadow."

"Or your shadow," I said. "The shadow I saw wasn't wearing skirts."

"We were probably seeing each other's shadows," Tad said.

"No," I said. "There was someone here, I'm sure of it. We need to search the booth."

"I'm not sure I'd notice if the intruder took anything," Tad said.

"That's okay," I said. "I think it's more important to make sure that he hasn't left anything behind. Like supposedly incriminating evidence."

We searched but found nothing that looked suspicious — no bloody handkerchiefs hidden in the trash can, no phony notes making it appear as if Faulk had arranged to meet Benson. Nothing much out of the ordinary.

In the next lane over, I saw a watchman's staff lying outside one of the booths, but there was no way to tell how long it had been there. Mrs. Waterston had already chewed me out once about the watch carelessly leaving their staffs lying around.

"Maybe one of the Town Watch was investigating a suspicious noise and ran off in panic when we jumped out yelling at him," Tad suggested.

"Maybe," I said. "Or maybe it was just a souvenir hunter."

"Probably," Tad said. "Let's forget it. I can just pack this stuff up and take the booth down, and it won't matter if anything's left behind."

"Pack the booth up?" I said. "Why? The fair's supposed to be open again from ten to two tomorrow."

"Do you really think I want to stand around selling Faulk's hardware when he's in jail?" Tad asked.

"Can you afford not to?" I said. "I thought you guys needed every penny you could get for legal fees. Even more so now."

"You don't think his getting arrested for murder's going to affect sales just a little?"

"You're right, it'll affect sales a lot," I

said. "We've got to change all the price tags tonight. Mark everything up — I think about fifty percent."

"You're crazy," Tad said.

"Hey, you said yourself that the intruder could be a souvenir hunter — have you seen my sales today?" I asked. "And my iron was only at the scene of the crime, not made by the hand of the actual suspect. Maybe fifty percent's not enough; maybe we should double everything."

"I think fifty percent should do fine," Tad said, chuckling.

He cheered up a bit while we did the marking, and by the time we'd finished, he obviously felt much happier. Of course, I had no idea how much of his improved mood came from my promise that I was going to do everything I could to catch the real murderer.

While we were marking things, I uncovered something that gave me pause. A large key — it had to be one of the keys to the padlock on the stocks. Had Faulk kept a key? Or was this what the intruder had come to find? Or to plant?

Tad didn't even blink when he saw me holding the key. I waited until he wasn't looking, then tucked it into my haversack.

"With you on his trail, that poor killer

hasn't a chance," Tad said, as we put away the pens and price tags.

"Maybe," I said, taking a deep breath. "But before I go off chasing the killer, I want you to level with me. Who were you with the night of the murder?"

"Oh, damn, not you, too," Tad said, slumping. "That damned deputy had to say just enough in front of Faulk to make him think the worst, and it's all perfectly innocent, not to mention having nothing to do with the murder."

"Convince me," I said.

"Okay," he said. "You probably won't believe me, but I was meeting my brother."

"Your brother? Tad, I thought you told me you were an only child. And an orphan."

"I lied," he said. "My dad's gone, but my mother's still around, and I have two brothers, three sisters, and lord knows how many aunts and uncles. I hadn't seen any of them in seven years, until my brother came down here to meet me last night."

"What happened? Seven years ago, I mean."

"I don't know," he said. "When I came out, they didn't handle it well. Then again, maybe I didn't give them much time to figure out how to handle it. The whole thing was a mess. So when I got out of college, I didn't give any of them my address, and I rewrote my autobiography. I know that sounds tacky."

"Maybe," I said. "But I found out recently that when we were in high school, both Rob and I had recurring fantasies about finding out we'd been switched at birth in the hospital, and that our rich, glamorous, normal, real parents would show up any day to claim us."

"You?" Tad exclaimed. "Why? I mean, your family's fantastic."

"Try growing up with them," I said. "So, yeah, maybe what you did was tacky, but I understand. What made you change your mind?"

"I don't know. Maybe it's being with Faulk — family's so important to him, even though he doesn't get along that well with his. I sort of got homesick for mine, and I contacted one of my brothers. Only then I couldn't figure out how to tell Faulk. That's why I arranged to meet my brother at a coffee shop in town. I figured if it worked out, I'd tell Faulk and introduce them tomorrow. Only with the murder and everything . . ."

He shook his head.

"And Faulk doesn't know this yet?"

"No, I can't get in to see him till visiting

hours tomorrow. Unless your brother can arrange to get him out on bail, which may not be possible. We're having trouble scraping up the deposit."

"We'll take up a collection at the fair tomorrow," I said. "I can't imagine anyone who knows Faulk thinking he's a murderer; and if they do think it, they'd better not let me know they do."

"Thanks," he said, sounding relieved.

"And speaking of tomorrow, we'd both better turn in."

"Do you think it would help if I staged a protest?" Tad asked, as we turned to leave the booth. "I could put on my runaway-slave outfit and chain myself to the steps in protest. I bet I could generate a lot of publicity."

"I don't think Faulk wants publicity," I said. "I think he wants bail and a good lawyer."

"You're probably right," he said, with a sigh.

"There is one thing you can do," I said. "It might help Faulk, although I can't make any promises."

"Anything," he said. "You name it."

"Find out exactly what Monty did on the Canton PD," I said. I gave him Monty's full name, and the approximate date he'd arrived in Yorktown.

"I'll start as soon as we get back to camp," he promised. "I've got my whole computer setup in the van."

Back at the tent, I tried to work up a show of enthusiasm for the coming battle, but I didn't think I was fooling Michael. He didn't remember whether the key had been in the booth when he'd been minding it, but then I didn't expect him to.

Fortunately, he seemed as exhausted as I was, and didn't try to reopen the discussion on the state of our relationship. He fell asleep almost immediately, while I tossed and turned, trying to put the pieces of the day together in some fashion that wouldn't end with Faulk being arrested. And trying to think what I could do tomorrow to set things right.

I doubt if Michael appreciated it when I finally couldn't stand it any longer and dug out my cell phone to make a late-night phone call and fix the one thing I could do something about.

"It's past midnight," he mumbled. "Who on Earth are you calling?"

"The jail," I said. "Hello, who's this? Hey, Fred. Is Horace there? Okay, what about Ricky? Great, could I talk to him?"

"Why are you calling the jail?" Michael asked.

"I need to get a message to Faulk," I said, covering the mouthpiece. "I don't want him thinking the worst all night. Hello, Ricky? Hi, it's Meg. Look, could you do me a favor?"

"You don't really think you can talk the police into giving a prisoner a message at this time of night, do you?"

"You know the prisoner Monty brought in? Right. Could you tell him something? I know, but Monty did something just to upset him, and I want to clear things up. Yeah, I agree, a total jerk. Just tell him that Monty wasn't straight with him; Tad's alibi was really his brother. Yeah, can you believe it? The man's a slime ball."

"I can't believe you actually talked him into it," Michael said.

"Thanks, Ricky. Give my love to Aunt Alice. Good-bye."

"Another cousin," Michael said, as I put away the cell phone. "Is there anyone in Yorktown who's not your cousin?"

"I'm not claiming Wesley," I said. "Or Monty either, for that matter."

"Just hope he doesn't come around to claim you've interfered with his investigation," Michael grumbled.

"He'll never find out," I said.

At least I hoped not.

33

The next morning was Michael's turn to rise at dawn and attempt the feat of getting dressed in a two-person tent without waking the other person. He didn't succeed either, of course, and by the time he finally went outside to deal with his boots and weapons, I'd given up hope of getting back to sleep and was only trying to figure out why he had to be up so early, anyway. We still had several hours until I had to be at the craft fair, and the battle didn't start till three.

Well, if I couldn't sleep, I could make good use of the time. I rummaged through the clutter until I found my cell phone. Then I curled up in the sleeping bag and spent the next hour calling relatives and neighbors to ask if they could lend me any ironwork they'd bought from me. Most agreed, and promised to drop the stuff off at my booth. Since I hardly had enough stock left to sell, I planned to put tags on the borrowed stuff saying "for display only; order now for delivery before christmas" and see how many more commissions I could score.

It worked fairly well; I took dozens of orders, and whenever I dashed over to check on how Tad was doing, Faulk's booth was full of customers and increasingly lower on ironwork. The bail fund grew steadily until Mrs. Fenniman came by and offered to put up the balance in return for Faulk making her a gazebo that looked like his booth.

"Of course, if they convict him, he might not be able to make your gazebo for quite a while," Tad reminded her.

"If he's convicted, he won't need the booth for quite a while, so you can give me that," she replied. Practical as usual.

The Anachronism Police had the bit in their teeth and were writing citations right and left. Luckily, my fellow crafters took my word that I'd do something to erase the rapidly mounting fines, so morale was high. Even mine. A night of tossing, turning, and fretting hadn't produced any brainstorms about the murder, but I had come up with a way to handle the fines, and enlisted Tad and my nephew Eric to help me carry it out.

We didn't see much of the reenactors. Except for Wesley, who strutted by, resplendent in a scarlet British officer's uniform, all the reenactors were busy making last-minute preparations for the battle.

"And sleeping off the beer, some of them," one soldier's wife told me, shaking her head. "Seems some of the boys must have gotten a little soused and went around playing pranks."

"Pranks?" I said. "What kind of pranks?" Call me paranoid, but I couldn't help jumping to the conclusion that anything out of the ordinary had to be connected with Benson's murder.

"Oh, stupid stuff," she said. "Someone going around pilfering stuff — just for the hell of it, as far as we can tell, because most of what was missing wasn't valuable. And this morning all the pilfered stuff has started turning up in places some drunk would think was funny. Like we found one woman's missing stays run up a flagpole and a stolen bayonet stuck in the wall of the privy for a toilet-paper holder. Juvenile stuff like that. So everyone's on edge, expecting to find the missing musket balls in the stew, or maybe someone's stolen long johns."

"Must be a Y-chromosome thing," I said, and we both laughed as she wrote a check for the iron pot rack she was ordering.

"Whoever did it better steer clear of the Royal Welsh Fusiliers," she said, as she turned to go. "Their regimental standard still hasn't turned up, and those boys are hopping mad."

Maybe that was why Michael hadn't dropped by all morning, I thought. Maybe he was helping soothe frayed tempers and recover purloined items. Or, more likely, maybe he was simply having too much fun marching around in the white-and-gold uniform.

Two o'clock came, and the crafters who didn't want to see the battle began their loadout, while the rest of us headed out to the battlefields. I lagged behind. If Michael and half the men in my family hadn't been participants, I think I would have gone back to the tent and curled up for a ten-hour nap. I'd been questioning people all morning, whenever I could steal a moment away from my booth, and I hadn't turned up a single useful bit of information, or thought of a single plan for helping Faulk. To top my mood off, the first person I ran into when I got to the battlefield was Mrs. Waterston.

"Oh, there you are, Meg," she said, in a voice that implied she'd been searching frantically for me all day.

"What's up?" I asked, warily.

"I don't suppose you know where that brother of yours has gone," Mrs. Waterston said.

"Off to join whatever unit he's fighting in, I should think."

"Oh — he's fighting?" she said, sounding surprised.

"Well, he's a man; they're all allowed to fight, no matter how useless they are at it," I grumbled.

"Bother," she said, without appearing to hear me. "Well, here, you watch him for a while."

With that, she handed me Spike's leash and sailed off. He looked up and wagged his tail as if glad to see me. I sighed, and decided to find a portapotty before the battle got going. Preferably one that didn't already have fifty people in line, which was how I ended up going back through the rapidly emptying camp to use the relatively out-of-the-way portapotties there.

When I got out, I looked over at the tree where I'd tied Spike and saw only his leash and his empty collar lying on the ground. He'd escaped again.

"As soon as this bloody festival is over, I am buying that dog a proper harness," I fumed, turning around to scan the surroundings. "Maybe a straitjacket."

I strode down the lanes of the camp, calling Spike's name, which was probably a mistake. He might not even want to be found.

I passed Cousin Horace, who was struggling with a pair of dark blue overalls.

"Have you seen Spike?" I asked.

"No. Could you help me with these?" he said.

"Stand still then."

He didn't exactly stand still, but at least he stopped wiggling his legs, and I was able to undo the misbuttoned overalls and do them up again properly. Meanwhile, above my head, he was struggling into a coat.

"There," I said, standing up. "That's a nice uniform, Horace."

"I'm fighting with the Third Virginia State Legion," Horace said, proudly, turning so I could admire his hunter-green coat.

"Won't catch me in one of those dandified uniforms," drawled a voice nearby.

Tony Grimes. Who seemed to have regained some of his courage since fingering Faulk for murder, the rat. Although when I got a little closer, I suspected it was Dutch courage. Hair of the dog.

He was sitting outside his tent, wearing a filthy set of buckskins, trying to tie the laces of a pair of buckskin shoes, and making a poor job of it.

"Nice outfit, Tony," I said. "I guess you usually just keep them around for gardening and changing the oil in your truck."

"Don't forget your hat, soldier," Tony said to Horace. "Madame Von Steuben's on a tear; she's court-martialing anyone who's missing part of his uniform."

"Oh, dear, where did I leave it?" Horace moaned.

"If you don't know, go see Mrs. Tranh, quick," I said. "She brought spares of everything, if she hasn't run out."

"Better hurry," Tony said, as he reached back into his tent for something. "All the redcoats were supposed to be on the field half an hour ago."

Horace hurried off. I stopped.

"All the redcoats?" I repeated, under my breath.

Horace's uniform was green. Bright, hunter green.

I turned and walked back to Tony. He was struggling to tie a knot in a broken buckskin lace.

"What did you say?"

"I just told your wimp of a cousin to hurry," Tony said. "Mrs. Waterston wanted all the redcoats in the redoubt half an hour ago."

"Only Horace's not a redcoat, you slimy little weasel!" I exclaimed, leaning over, pulling Tony up by the front of his buckskin shirt, and shaking him. "You're colorblind, aren't you?"

"What difference does that make?" Tony said, trying to pull away.

"You told Monty the killer was wearing red plaid socks," I said. "How the hell did you know they were red plaid? They could have been green or blue or even purple plaid for all you knew."

"I'm only red-green colorblind," he said. "I can see most other colors, and I've gotten very good at telling what kind of brown means red and what kind of brown means green."

"Yeah, you did a great job of matching the color of my flamingos," I said. "Pink's just like red for you, isn't it? And I bet you're a little shaky on anything even close to red or green. Admit it," I snapped, giving him another good shake.

"Okay, maybe I could be wrong on the color, but they were definitely plaid," he said. "How many people were wearing kilts at that party? Just Faulk."

"Yeah, but there were plenty of people wearing plaid underneath their costumes," I said. "Plaid shorts, plaid socks, all kinds of things. And the killer could have changed out of his costume by the time he went to my booth. Maybe the killer wasn't even at the party in the first place. It could be any-body, you idiot."

I let go of his shirt. Okay, I shoved him a little while I was doing it. He landed hard on his backside, then rolled over and scuttled into his tent.

"It could be anybody," I repeated. I should have felt relieved — surely this would clear Faulk, or at least cast serious doubt on the case against him. Why did I have such a nagging feeling of anxiety?

Maybe because I was in close proximity to the real murderer. Tony had lied time and again about what he'd done on the night of the murder. Why was Monty so unwilling to consider him as a suspect?

Well, if Monty wouldn't tackle him, I would.

"Damned mutt," came a mutter from inside Tony's tent.

Spike scrambled out through the tent flap, dragging a muddy piece of cloth. No, not just a piece of cloth. A British flag. The one stolen from the Royal Welsh Fusiliers, perhaps?

I bent down and opened the tent flap. The odor hit me first — a mixture of beer, sweat, and vomit, like a frat house. Holding my breath, I peered in to see Tony, sitting on a tangled wad of blankets, gulping something from a bottle wrapped in a paper bag.

"You want me to take this flag back before they catch you with it?" I asked.

He raised his head, looked at the flag, and frowned.

"Damn," he said. "Where'd that come from?"

"The whole camp was buzzing this morning about a series of daring midnight robberies."

"Daring midnight robberies?"

"A flag, a cannonball, some poor woman's stays run up the flagpole."

"Oh, yeah," he said, with a sickly smile. "That's right. Hell of a prank. But don't tell anyone. You don't want to get us in trouble."

"Us?"

"Me and Wes."

"You and Wes?" I said. "Since when did you guys get to be such buddies? I thought you hated him."

"He's not so bad," Tony said. "He agreed not to write the article about me. And I apologized for locking him up. So we had a few drinks together."

Quite a few, from the look of him, but I held my tongue.

"So all is forgiven and you're friends now."

"I have to get to the battlefield," he said. He started to sit up, but I shoved him down again. Something bothered me.

"Tell me one thing, Tony," I said, fishing in my haversack. "And then I'll leave you alone."

"Yeah, right," he said.

"What did you do with the key?"

"What key?"

"The key to the padlock. This key," I said, holding up the key I'd found in Faulk's booth. "This key. The one you used to lock Wesley in the stocks."

"I never had that key," he said.

"Then how'd you lock him in?"

"It was a padlock, for Pete's sake," Tony said. "You don't need a key; you just snap it shut."

With that, he pushed past me and staggered toward the battlefield.

Tony never had the key. He hadn't even known that the padlock needed a key.

But Wesley had. He'd known it since Thursday night, when he'd tried to play his prank and lock me in the stocks. He knew about the padlock, and he even knew we kept the spare key on a nail under the platform. The spare key that wasn't there when I found him. The spare key he'd used to lock himself in to fake an alibi.

If Tony had left the town square to go to my booth, why not Wesley? And then, back at the stocks, all he had to do was loosen a few bolts and slip in after securing the padlock. I'd checked that the padlock was locked — I'd never thought to see if the other end was loose.

"Come on," I told myself. "You're not going to accuse your own cousin of being a murderer, are you? What possible motive could he have?"

Good question.

I pulled Spike behind me as I strode through the camp to Wesley's tent. When I found it, I tied Spike's leash to a tent peg and crawled inside.

It smelled strongly of unwashed Wesley, with grace notes of stale grease, thanks to a stash of fast-food bags crumpled in the corner. And a tantalizing hint of a scent I couldn't identify but knew I'd smelled recently.

I began to search — hastily. He was supposed to be in the British lines, but then Wesley wasn't famous for being where he was supposed to be. I was looking for discarded plaid, which wasn't as easy as it sounded. Dirty clothes — most, I suspected, on their fourth or fifth reuse — covered every surface. I lifted one pair of graying briefs and uncovered a file folder. I was about to put the underwear back when I noticed the name "Cooper" on a piece of newsprint sticking out of the folder.

I opened the folder. It contained a small collection of articles on Roger Benson and his works. I scanned them, briefly. Most were about the fall of Cooper and Anthony, and I nodded without surprise when I realized that Cooper and Anthony had owned the *Virginia Commercial Intelligence*, whose closing had cost Wesley his dream job and, as he'd said himself, destroyed his journalism career.

"That's a good enough motive for me," I murmured.

The last article in the folder came from the *York Town Crier* a few weeks ago — a puff piece about Rob and Lawyers from Hell, mentioning Benson's firm as one of those vying to market the game. No wonder Wesley had suddenly reappeared in Yorktown.

Finding the orange plaid socks stuffed into one of the McDonald's bags was just icing on the cake.

I grabbed the bag, planning to take it, with the file folder, straight to Monty — better yet, the sheriff. I still didn't trust Monty — and ducked out of the tent.

But as I stood up, the greasy paper of the bag gave way and something heavy landed on a sensitive part of my foot. Several somethings.

"Damn!" I said, jumping back. Spike gave chase to one of the small objects as it rolled in front of him, and growled when he found that musket balls are inedible.

Musket balls. Four of them. And a trickle of black powder followed them out of the bag. That was the half-familiar scent, I realized; the strong, acrid tang of old-fashioned gunpowder. What was Wesley doing with the missing musket balls and a residue of gunpowder? I didn't remember him seeming that interested in black-powder shooting when Jess and his crew had shown us how to make cartridges. Then again, he'd helped; he knew how to make cartridges.

"And how to make live ammo," I said, aloud; and suddenly I remembered how Wesley had looked at Michael last night, when he'd gotten the false impression that Michael was the witness Monty was talking about.

"Michael," I exclaimed. "He's going after Michael."

34

I set off for the battlefield at a dead run, with Spike charging ahead of me, clearing a path by barking and snarling furiously at everyone we passed. Unfortunately, when I reached the barriers that separated the battlefield from the spectators' area, I ran afoul of the safety monitors.

"We're sorry, ma'am, but we can't let you out on the battlefield," the man kept repeating, ignoring my attempts to explain. "Only participants allowed on the battlefield."

"There's someone on the battlefield who's got live ammo," I said.

"Impossible," he said. "We did a safety inspection before the battle began. Took an hour and a half, with this many participants. I guarantee you, no one took any live ammo out by accident."

"It's not an accident," I said. "He's trying to kill someone!"

But he wasn't listening. I saw him gesturing for several other monitors to haul me away, and I decided to retreat while I could still do so under my own steam.

By this time, of course, all the safety monitors up and down the line had me flagged as a possible troublemaker. As I strolled along the barrier, seeking a more sympathetic ear, I could see other monitors coming to attention as I approached.

Okay, I thought. You're only letting participants past; I'll become a participant.

I picked up my skirts again and jogged over to Mrs. Tranh's costume booth. I found her fitting Horace with a hat.

"It's too big," he complained, as it fell over his eyes.

"Only hat I have left," Mrs. Tranh said. "You want hat, take this one. You want hat that fits, come here two hours ago."

"Mrs. Tranh," I said. "Do you have any uniforms left? Any at all, I don't care what unit. I don't even care what army."

"Sorry, all out of uniforms," Mrs. Tranh said, frowning. "You should have told me you need uniform."

"I didn't need it until just now," I said. "Horace, take off your uniform. I need to borrow it."

"No," he said. "I'm wearing it."

"Horace —"

He turned to walk away, and I grabbed his arm.

"Hey, girlfriend, what's wrong?" Amanda said, strolling up. "You look all hot and bothered."

"Horace, take off the uniform," I repeated.

"Leave me alone," Horace whined.

"I'd stick with blue-eyes, hon," Amanda said.

Horace continued to squirm, trying to free his arm.

"I need his uniform to save Michael!" I said.

"What wrong with Michael?" Mrs. Tranh demanded.

"Well, why didn't you say so in the first place," Amanda said, grabbing Horace's other arm.

"Sorry," Mrs. Tranh said to Horace, and deftly tripped him. Amanda sat on him while Mrs. Tranh and I stripped him of his uniform and began stuffing me into it.

"You can't do this," Horace said, looking miserable in his cotton boxers and sleeveless undershirt.

"Here," I said, handing him Spike's leash. "Go find Monty and the sheriff, Horace. We'll need them."

Fortunately, Horace and I were much the same height, and he was pudgy enough that I could fit into his uniform, despite the differences in our shape. The trousers were a tight fit, though.

"Don't sit down," Amanda advised.

"Here," Mrs. Tranh said, tying back my hair with a bit of ribbon while Amanda jammed Horace's tricorn on my head. "Pull hat low."

"And keep the musket in front of your chest," Amanda added.

"Right — oh, and could you hang on to this file folder and the McDonald's bag?" I said, cramming them into my haversack as I spoke and handing it to Amanda. "Give them to Monty and the sheriff when Horace finds them. But not unless they're both together."

"Sure thing," she said, hanging the bag over her shoulder.

I set out again for the battlefield.

This time, the monitors let me pass, after inspecting Horace's musket and cartridge bag, and told me to hurry — the skirmish was already beginning. I kept the brim of my hat pulled low, nodded my thanks, and trotted off in the direction they'd pointed. And hit the ground almost immediately when a volley of musket fire rang out somewhere to my left.

"Only blanks," I told myself, as I scrambled up. "Pay no attention to them. They're only blanks."

Except, if I was right, for one gun, and I didn't think Wesley knew he had any reason to shoot me. Yet.

I began working my way through the outskirts of the battlefield, trying to figure out what was going on. Damn, I thought, if only I'd paid more attention to the rehearsal skirmish last night. All I could see around me was a milling herd of sweating, panting men in uniforms whose color the ubiquitous dust was slowly but surely trying to obscure.

"At this point in the battle," came Mrs. Waterston's voice over the bullhorn. "The colonial forces on the left wing begin massing for a sortie. I repeat, the colonial forces on the left wing begin massing for a sortie."

"Who the hell does she think she is?" a nearby soldier fumed. "Napoleon?"

"Aunt Margaret says to stay put," announced another soldier, joining him. "She'll just wave her handkerchief when we're supposed to make our sortie."

He pointed to something behind us, off the battlefield. Mother was sitting in a Chippendale chair, surrounded by a bouquet of different-colored uniforms. She seemed to be issuing orders. In the few seconds I watched, several soldiers ran off and others arrived.

"Left wing, were you planning on doing anything soon?" the bullhorn blared.

The soldiers (I recognized one as a cousin) glanced back at Mother and stood their ground.

I moved on.

I came abreast of some soldiers crouching behind some bushes. Instinctively, I crouched with them.

"Third Virginia State Legion troops are over there," one said, pointing.

"I know," I lied. "Courier. Where are the *Gatinois chasseurs?*"

"The what?"

"Left wing, get a move on!" came the bullhorn.

"Like hell we will," the soldier muttered. "We've been fighting this war since before you ever heard of Yorktown, lady! We'll move when we damn well feel like it! Sorry," he said, turning back to me. "Who were you looking for?"

"*Gatinois chasseurs.* The French who're supposed to storm Redoubt Nine," I added, seeing from his puzzled face that either he hadn't heard of them or I still wasn't pronouncing them right.

"Outside the redoubt already, I think," he said. "At least that's where they're supposed to be. Who knows? Madame Von

Steuben there has managed to screw up the whole thing already. No one's where they're supposed to be at this point in the battle."

"No, actually we're fighting the Battle of Cowpens, only she forgot to tell us," another soldier said.

They all laughed.

Great. There were three thousand men on this field, none of them where they were supposed to be; not that I knew where they were supposed to be anyway. How on Earth was I going to find one homicidal redcoat?

Well, I could start by going where Michael and his unit were supposed to be. And at least, having grown up around the battlefields, I knew where Redoubt Nine was. More or less, anyway. I stood up, got my bearings, and began trotting toward it.

I quickly gathered that it wasn't quite the thing, even in a reenacted battle, to just take off across open ground toward your destination. Open ground is open for a reason — usually that people are firing across it. And even when they're shooting blanks, muskets produce a remarkable amount of smoke. I got turned around several times, and found myself near a group of Hessian mercenaries, from which I deduced that I'd managed to wander behind enemy lines.

"You're a casualty, soldier," someone told

me, as I passed his unit. "I just shot you."

"Fine," I said. "I'm shot; I'm a ghost; I'm going over to haunt Redoubt Nine for a while. Which way is it?"

The Hessians pointed, and I corrected course and set out again. But my erratic pilgrimage had not gone unnoticed.

"Someone tell that soldier in the green coat to stay with his unit," Mrs. Waterston snapped over the megaphone. "And get those animals off the battlefield!"

I turned, curious, and saw that Horace, deprived of his uniform, had donned his beloved gorilla suit and was loping across the battlefield in my wake, shaking his fist. At me, probably. He still held one end of Spike's leash, though, and Spike was having a fine time, barking his head off and trying to bite passing soldiers.

I could hear tittering from the bleachers.

"Get my dog off the field of battle, you moron," Mrs. Waterston screeched, so loud that she set off a small shriek of feedback from the bullhorn. She then treated us to a pungent summary of Horace's intellectual status and ancestry — well worded and effective, no doubt, but not something I'd have shouted in public through a bullhorn.

Some of the soldiers were smothering laughter as well.

I decided it would be the better part of valor to lose myself in a crowd, so I took off running for the nearest mass of men, only to realize, when I had nearly reached them and they all began shooting over my head, that I was approaching a group of redcoats. Tony Grimes might have trouble spotting me, but I wasn't going to fool Mrs. Waterston.

"Meg! I didn't know you'd joined a unit."

I turned to find Dad standing behind me, holding on his shoulder what looked like a small barrel. I wondered, briefly, why anyone would run around in the middle of a battle carrying a powder keg, then I saw the flash of the videocamera lens through a hole in the front of the barrel.

"Your unit's over there," he said, pointing. "You should —"

"Never mind that now," I said. "Where's Michael? I've got to find Michael! Where's Redoubt Nine?"

"Relax, you're *in* Redoubt Nine," Dad said. "Michael's unit is going to be storming us in a few minutes, so just stay here with me and —"

I took off running again, and began scanning the faces of the redcoats for Wesley. Some were lying down, pointing their guns through the gaps in the redoubt, where they could shoot, while others, from the direction they were looking, seemed to be waiting for something to come over the top of the redoubt.

"Meg, what's —"

"Find Wesley, Dad," I called over my shoulder. "Quick!"

I started as a volley of musket fire rang out, and I heard shouts from outside the redoubt. I continued to search for Wesley, earning more than a few curses when I grabbed soldiers and turned them around to see their faces.

The first white-clad French soldiers began appearing over the tops of the redoubt. The British shot at them, though I could see that they were actually careful to aim over their heads.

"Allons, mes amis!"

I looked up to see Michael standing on top of the redoubt, looking impossibly tall, waving his sword, urging on his men.

I looked down at the redcoats below him. I could see several aiming over his head. And one aiming much too low. . . .

"No!" I shrieked and launched myself at the redcoat in a flying tackle.

The gun went off about the time I hit him, and I could tell that he was driven not only sideways from the impact of my tackle but also back from the recoil of the gun. Which shouldn't have happened, of course, since you don't get recoil when you fire a blank, so he'd definitely been firing live ammo.

As I hit the ground, I looked up to see Michael, clutching his chest. The growing red stain looked incredibly vivid against the white of his uniform. Then he fell to the ground coughing.

35

"Killer," I snarled at Wesley. I kicked him in the face, quite deliberately, while scrambling up, and shoved my way through the mass of white- and red-clad soldiers to throw myself down at Michael's side.

"Michael!" I cried. "Can you hear me?"

"Ma'am, we're trying to have a battle here —"

"Call an ambulance!" I shouted. "Dad, put that thing down and get over here. Dammit, Michael, hang on!" I cried, as I tried to figure out whether I should cradle his head or whether moving him was a bad idea. "I'm sorry; I've been awful to you. Just hang on, please. I promise if you just hang on —"

He opened his eyes. This was a good sign, right?

"Meg, will you do something for me?" he gasped.

"Anything, Michael, but don't try to talk now," I said. "Dad, where the hell are you?"

"Meg, you're spoiling the filming," Dad

said, looming over me with his camera-filled powder keg."

"You're filming this!" I said, looking up at him. His videocamera was whirring away. He didn't seem upset. I noticed that a couple of the soldiers around us were smothering giggles. I looked down at Michael. The red stain didn't seem to be spreading. And it looked very red. Almost unnaturally red.

"Michael?"

He opened one eye and winked at me.

"You're all right?"

He opened his hand to reveal a plastic bag that still contained a few drops of stage blood.

"Do you want me to keep filming this?" Dad asked.

"Shh," Michael said, closing his eyes again. "I think she's about to say something I want to hear."

"Michael, you jerk!" I shouted.

"No, that's not it," he said, shaking his head.

"I thought you were dead!" I shrieked, snatching off my cocked hat and hitting him with it. "I thought the little weasel had killed you!"

"And you came running to save me," Michael said, pulling me down on top of him.

"I'm overwhelmed."

"You're overwhelmed!" I said. "I'm furious. Do you realize —"

"Hey, you're in my light," I heard Dad say to someone. "I'm trying to film."

I looked up to see Dad's powder keg pointed at Michael and me.

"We can discuss how grateful you are later," I said, pulling myself up again. "Right now —"

"Meg Langslow!" came Mrs. Waterston's voice through the bullhorn. "Why are you ruining my battle? Get out of there immediately!"

"Ma'am," a nearby soldier said, obviously fighting laughter. "If you're finished having hysterics now —"

"Laugh all you want," I said, standing up and dusting off my uniform. "But one of your soldiers — make that someone pretending to be one of your soldiers — is using live ammo here. He tried to kill Michael."

"Meg Langslow! Get off my battlefield this minute!"

"Her battlefield," someone muttered.

"She's not kidding," another soldier said. "I've been hit! Someone put a round right through my canteen!"

"There he is," I said, pointing to the other end of the redoubt, where Wesley was trying to slink away. "He killed Benson and now he's trying to kill the only witness! Catch him!"

Fortunately, Wesley did his best to convince them I was telling the truth by bolting out of the redoubt the second he heard me. And I gather even the suspicion of live ammo on the field really ticked people off. The soldiers gave chase — a few at first, and then both units of French and British, when the word of what Wesley had done had made the rounds.

In fact, within a few minutes, half the soldiers on the field were merrily running up and down the battlefield, chasing Wesley — several hundred soldiers, not to mention assorted camp followers and stragglers, Dad with his camera, Horace in his gorilla suit, and Spike, barking happily.

I heard the sound of cannon fire and whirled around to see if anything had happened to Duck and Mrs. Fenniman, but they were both still calmly perched on their proper ends of the cannon. Jess and his man had hauled out the speakers and punctuated the chase with an almost nonstop series of cannon blasts.

"He's pretty fast," Michael said, as we watched Wesley temporarily outpacing his pursuers — although from our vantage point we could see a group of buckskin-clad riflemen and Indians crouching behind some bushes, waiting to ambush him.

"Used to run track and field in high school," I said. "Never was good at contact sports, though," I added as Wesley, cut off by the frontier unit, made the mistake of trying to break through a flanking unit of Highlanders and ended up at the bottom of a small plaid mountain.

By the time someone found Monty and dragged him out onto the battlefield, Wesley had been rescued from the overly enthusiastic Highlanders and tied up, while a picked honor guard of American, French, British, and German soldiers watched over him.

"What's going on here?" Monty snapped. "Why is this man tied up?"

"Because he's the one who really killed Roger Benson," I said.

"And you have some kind of evidence?" he said, with a sneer.

"Hold your horses, you miserable carpet-bagger," Amanda said, as she came trailing after him.

"Wrong period, ma'am," a soldier said. "How about miserable Tory?"

"That'll do just fine," she said, handing me my haversack. I pulled out the McDonald's sack and the file folder and presented them, with a flourish, to Monty.

He still looked a little dubious after I'd showed him the loot I'd found in Wesley's tent, but he began looking interested after the redcoats showed him the second live round they'd found in Wesley's cartridge case, not to mention the newly ventilated canteen. And after Tony Grimes showed up, escorted by a squad of the Virginia militia, confessed to his color blindness and his ignorance of how colonial-era padlocks worked, Monty looked positively triumphant.

"Well, it looks as if we have this thing wrapped up," he said. "I think —"

"What is going on out here?" Mrs. Waterston demanded, storming up to Monty. "We're trying to have a battle here! I've been working for nearly a year to arrange this event and you're ruining everything. And you —" she said, turning to me. "It's all your fault! What do you mean, running out here and —"

"Mom, shut up," Michael said.

Her jaw dropped. I heard scattered applause from the ranks, followed by a lot of shushing.

"The man who killed Roger Benson was planning to kill me under cover of the battle," Michael said. "Meg found out and rushed out here to risk her own life to save me."

"She did?" Mrs. Waterston said.

Gee, I thought, you don't have to sound quite so surprised.

"But I thought you put the killer in jail," she said, turning to Monty.

"That was only a ruse to lull the real killer into a false sense of complacency," Monty said, ignoring the catcalls and raspberries from the soldiers.

"Well, then who is the killer?" she asked.

"Him," chorused several dozen soldiers, pointing to Wesley — who managed, despite being tied hand and foot, to give a fairly convincing impression of snide villainy.

"Then he's banned from participating in this festival," Mrs. Waterston announced, turning on her heels. "Permanently," she added, more loudly, over the chorus of laughter that accompanied her departure.

"Oh, I'm crushed," Wesley muttered.

"Yeah, you've got bigger things to worry about," Monty said, gesturing for two of his officers to help Wesley up. "Like whether the DA goes for the death penalty."

"It was an accident," Wesley said. "Yeah, I know it was stupid to try to cover it up, but

I wasn't thinking clearly."

"An accident?" I said.

"He fell on the flamingo!"

"Wesley, Wesley," Dad said, shaking his head. "You know they're not going to believe that. How could he possibly have fallen on the flamingo four times?"

"Four times?" I repeated.

"At least," Dad said. "According to the autopsy report, anyway. I wasn't given the chance to examine the deceased myself," he added, in an injured tone.

"Take him away, boys," Monty said.

"Attention," came Mrs. Waterston's voice on the bullhorn. "Please excuse the interruption to the battle. Our local sheriff's department has apprehended the parties responsible, and as soon as they have been removed from the field, we will start the battle over."

"She's got to be kidding," one soldier muttered, but he and the others turned and began ambling off in various directions to retake their starting positions.

"Oh, good. I can get some different angles this time," Dad said. He popped open one end of his powder keg, ejected a tape from the camera, replaced it with a fresh tape from his cartridge bag, shouldered the keg, and ran off after the *Gatinois chasseurs*.

"I think I'll sit this one out," I said, heading for the barriers that marked the edge of the battlefield. "I did enough damage for one day in the first skirmish."

"Or possibly to the first skirmish," Michael said, falling into step beside me.

"Uh . . . Meg?"

I turned to see the sheriff, resplendent in buckskins with a coonskin cap, trying to catch up with us.

"When you searched that fellow Wesley's tent, did you happen to find . . ."

"Hang on," I said, digging into my bag. "I have the pictures here."

"Thanks," he said.

"Just tell me one thing," I said, as I handed over Wesley's CD-ROM. "What were you doing talking to her?"

He winced.

"You may not believe me, but as God is my witness, I was trying to talk her out of that damned fool project," he said.

"And why is that?" I asked, trying very hard to pretend I knew who the woman was and what project he was talking about.

"People around here don't want a Yorktown theme park," the sheriff said. "Can you imagine it — cartoon characters walking around in tricorn hats, a phony early American village, colonial-style rides in the amusement park! I paid attention just fine in school, and I don't recall anything about our forefathers building roller-coasters and selling corn dogs, for heaven's sake. I don't care how many jobs her company promises, that stuff never turns out the way they promise; and even if it did, it's a trashy idea, and I don't want any part of it. And I told her so."

"Bravo," I said. "I agree."

"And that Wesley took pictures of me telling her, and he threatened he was going to make it look like I was in cahoots with her," the sheriff said.

"I can't swear those are the only copies," I said. "But even if they aren't, I doubt if anyone's going to believe anything Wesley has to say for a while."

"Well, that's true," the sheriff said. "Thanks."

He saluted. Remembering I was technically in uniform, I saluted back, and he shambled off.

"Meg!"

"Suddenly I'm Ms. Popularity," I said, seeing Tad and Rob running my way.

"Do you still have my CD-ROM?" Rob asked.

"And mine?" Tad added.

"More CDs, coming up," I said, handing

each of them the proper little square envelope.

"Okay," Rob said. "It's a deal."

He and Tad exchanged CD-ROMs, and they shook hands formally.

"Okay, I'll bite," I said. "Now what are you both up to?"

"I'm going to find a reputable company to develop and market Lawyers from Hell," Tad said, as he stowed Rob's CD-ROM in an inside pocket of his velvet coat. "Maybe make a few tweaks to it first. I've got a few ideas that'll jazz it up; make it run like a scalded dog."

He smiled, started to leave, then turned back.

"Oh, you know that deputy guy you wanted me to check on? He only worked for the Canton PD for about a year. Parking enforcement."

"So the evil Wesley was right about something; Monty's *not* a detective," I said.

"Well, he was in Cleveland," Tad said. "But they kicked him out for sexual harassment. That's how he ended up in Canton. And eventually in Yorktown."

With that, he sauntered off toward the bleachers.

"So he's not a phony," Michael said. "Just a male chauvinist pig."

"I could have told you that part," I said.

"Should we tell the sheriff about this?" Michael asked.

"Or Mrs. Fenniman?" Rob added.

"Or maybe both?" I said. "So, Rob, what are you doing with Tad's disk?"

"I'm going to talk one of the lawyer uncles into taking Tad's case against Benson's company on spec, and help out with it," Rob said, tucking the CD-ROM into his haversack. "I've decided I want to specialize in some kind of computer-related law, and this looks like a good way to get started."

He began to leave, then stopped, reached into his pocket, and handed me a sheet of paper.

"Mother told me to give you this," he said.

"Sauce au poivre," I read. "Well, let's hope it's close to the way Le Rivage does it."

"Actually, it's from Le Rivage," Rob said. "And Mother said to tell you to call Didier and let him know when you're coming in to measure for the wine rack."

"Wine rack?"

"Yeah, don't you remember? You're making him some kind of custom wine rack in return for the recipe."

With that, he ambled back onto the battlefield.

"How on Earth did Mother know I

wanted the recipe?" I wondered.

"I told her," Michael said. "Although I thought she'd find some way to get the recipe without trading who knows how many days of your work for it."

"I'll manage," I said. "And it'll be worth it."

"Definitely," Michael said, as we resumed strolling. "My mouth waters just thinking about that sauce."

"Actually, I meant 'worth it,' knowing I can give your mom the recipe so she'll stop hounding me."

"Well, that, too," he said. "Anyway, everyone's happy."

"Not quite everyone," I said.

"True," he said, as we ducked under the barrier at the edge of the battlefield and began shoving our way through the crowd.

"Monty!" I called, seeing the deputy ahead of us.

"I can't talk now," he said. "I have to go down to the jail to book our suspect."

"And to release Faulk, I assume," I said. "You won't be holding Faulk now that you have the real killer, I hope?"

"And have every lawyer in your family breathing down my neck and yelling about false-arrest suits? Are you kidding?"

"That's good," I said. "And while you're

at it, make sure your boss knows why you left Cleveland."

"He knows all right," Monty snapped, turning to face me with his hands on his hips. "And also about all the damned diversity training I had to take to get hired anywhere. You are looking at the most culturally enlightened, diversity-sensitive law-enforcement officer this misbegotten hick town will ever see."

With that, he stomped off toward his waiting squad car.

"I can tell he's a changed man," Michael said.

"If that's the post–diversity training Monty, I can see why Cleveland canned him," I said. "Ah well — he's the sheriff's problem now."

"Or perhaps, in a few weeks, Mrs. Fenniman's," Michael added.

"Ms. Langslow?"

I turned to see three members of the Town Watch, holding several long sheets of authentic-looking old-fashioned paper.

"All the crafters who check out have been saying that you're taking care of their fines," one said.

"Naturally," I said. "How much does the bill come to?"

"Seven thousand, eight hundred and

forty-five dollars," he said, with a sharklike smile.

"Here," I said, reaching into my haversack and hauling out a wad of bills. "This should cover it."

"What's this stuff?" he said, frowning down at the bills.

"Colonial currency, of course," I said. "You wouldn't expect me to pay you in anachronisms, would you? Oh — and you can keep the change."

"Colonial currency?" Michael asked, as we walked off, leaving the watchmen staring with astonishment at the bills.

"Tad did some research on the Internet this morning, and ran the stuff off on his color printer," I said. "And Eric spent several hours staining the bills with tea and drying them with Mother's hairdryer. I owe them one."

We'd shoved our way past the crowd, and I breathed a sigh of relief.

"Any other loose ends you need to tie up?" Michael asked.

"Not that I can think of," I said.

"Well, I have just one," he said. "Now that all that's over with, I hate to sound like a broken record, but —"

"We need to talk," I said. "Somehow I predicted that."

36

"Seriously," Michael said. "Were you or weren't you going to make some rather extravagant promises out there on the battlefield when you thought I was dying?"

"Yeah, I was," I said, rather sheepishly. "I was already feeling terrible that I'd neglected you all weekend, and on top of that, put you in danger. I mean, I was the one who let Wesley think you were the witness who could put him away."

"No harm done," he said. "You rescued me. Of course, if I could make one small suggestion, I think maybe next time I'm being stalked by a cunning, ruthless assassin, could you maybe figure out a way to rescue me without putting yourself in such danger?"

"I suppose, but the problem is, if we could rewind the weekend and start all over again, I'd do the same thing, all along the way. If my family or my friends are in danger, I'm not going to just stand by. I'm going to do something."

"And you're going to charge in and do it yourself."

"Probably," I said. "I can't change who I am."

"I'm not asking you to change who you are," Michael said. "I love *who* you are; it's *where* you are most of the time that drives me crazy. I don't want you to change, just relocate."

"I can't just pack up and move to-morrow —"

"You could come down next weekend, and we could do some househunting."

"I have a craft fair next weekend," I said.

He rolled his eyes in exasperation.

"We'll have to do it during the week," I said. "You've got some time during the day without classes, right?"

"All right!" Michael exclaimed. He threw his hat into the air, grabbed me, and swept me into the kind of passionate, dramatic kiss you see on the cover of romance books — although on the book covers, usually, at least one of the participants is wearing skirts.

"Huzzah!" shouted some passing troops, sensing a celebration of some sort, and Michael retrieved his hat to bow to them.

Okay, the idea of relocating still scared me, but the shock of thinking Michael had been shot affected my attitude. Commitment still made me nervous, but maybe nervous was better than losing Michael. I was just going to have to get used to the idea of uprooting my life and moving to Caerphilly.

I decided to postpone a decision on whether to actually move in with Michael or just relocate nearby until I saw what our house-hunting search turned up. Of course, given the tight housing market in Caerphilly, I probably wouldn't have to make the actual leap into moving right away. In fact, I decided, the difficulties of househunting could take weeks — months, even — which would drive Michael bananas, but would be a boon for me. I'd probably have more than enough time to get used to the idea of moving by the time we actually settled on a place.

A bugle call sounded in the distance.

"I suppose we'd better go back," I said. "The instant replay of the battle is about to begin."

"I don't know," Michael said, glancing down at his red-stained uniform. "I think maybe I've had enough battle for one day. After all, I'm already a casualty."

"Won't the *Gatinois chasseurs* be upset if you're AWOL?"

"I doubt it. They're pretty mellow," he

said. "And anyway, although this weekend has been fun, maybe I should rethink this whole reenacting hobby thing."

I uttered a silent prayer of thanks.

"All the guns — too much technology, not enough swordplay," he went on. "I think I'll see if I can find a group that does something a little earlier — Renaissance maybe, or the Middle Ages."

I canceled the prayer, and contemplated the even longer list of anachronisms that would probably be outlawed in a reenactment of the Middle Ages.

"How about the Roman Empire," I suggested. "Do they reenact that? Plenty of swordplay; you'd look nice in one of those bare-legged gladiator costumes, and they were really big on bathing in the Roman Empire."

"I'll give it a thought," Michael said. "Meanwhile, speaking of bathing, why don't we find someplace where we can get out of these filthy clothes and into the proverbial something more comfortable . . . like Mom's hot tub?"

"Attention!" squawked Mrs. Waterston's amplified voice from the battlefield. "Everyone take your places! We're going to start all over again. Please take your places. Will the audience stop milling around the field and sit down? We're going to start the battle again in a few minutes."

"I don't know," I said. "Are you sure your mother doesn't need us?"

"All you British troops!" Mrs. Waterston continued. "At least look as if you're trying to win! And I don't want to hear anyone yelling 'banzai!' or 'Geronimo!' this time. Please try to stay in period. Now, if you're all ready, let's take it from the top. . . ."

"Are you kidding?" Michael said. "She won't miss us for hours."

The employees of Thorndike Press hope you have enjoyed this Large Print book. All our Large Print titles are designed for easy reading, and all our books are made to last. Other Thorndike Press Large Print books are available at your library, through selected bookstores, or directly from the publishers.

For more information about titles, please call:

(800) 223-1244
(800) 223-6121

To share your comments, please write:

Publisher
Thorndike Press
295 Kennedy Memorial Drive
Waterville, ME 04901